# HE SHOULD HAVE NEVER LEFT THE GIRL.

He should have stayed with her, stolen her if need be. But she had remembered nothing, not even who he was, and she had been frightened of him when he visited her in the hospital room. He had left her there, certain there was no danger for a while.

Now rocks shifted from places where they had balanced for thousands of years, and chasms between boulders deepened slowly. The borders were stretching, thinning, and when they opened, the wendigo would once again come through into this world. Charlie had felt the changes from hundreds of miles away. She must feel them too, wherever she was. Enough power lived in her for that, even if she denied it. *It was time for Darcy Jacobi to finish her training.*

# THE
# WENDIGO BORDER

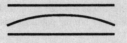

## Catherine Montrose

A TOM DOHERTY ASSOCIATES BOOK
NEW YORK

THE WENDIGO BORDER

Cover art by Jim Thiesen

A Tor Book
Published by Tom Doherty Associates, Inc.
175 Fifth Avenue
New York, NY 10010

Tor® is a registered trademark of Tom Doherty Associates, Inc.

ISBN: 0-812-52432-2

First edition: October 1995

Printed in the United States of America

0  9  8  7  6  5  4  3  2  1

To my brother John Peyton Cooke

# Author's Note

This is an imaginative fantasy. Although the historical material in this book derives from extensive research, no human or mythological characters are intended to represent actual personalities, legends, religion, or experience of the Native American people. The same goes for the residents of Laramie, Wyoming, and vicinity. The only character in this book based on an actual being is Cinnamon the horse, who was mine when I was twelve years old.

# CHAPTER ONE

S lick and dark in the rain, the highway reflected the shine of headlights from long semi trucks that skidded past and kicked up splashing waves. The man walking east on the shoulder of the road pulled the collar of his long coat tighter around his neck and turned his head away when the monster trucks passed him. The bottom of his coat slapped heavily against his knees, above laced moccasin boots that were caked with mud. The brim of his black felt hat sagged down over his eyes, and the four owl feathers in the band clung together like dripping weeds.

A bolt of jagged lightning seared a branch of a pine tree on the hilltop ridge beside the highway. The wind blew a smell of burnt needles and sap, until the hissing rain put out the fire. More lightning reached across dense black clouds. In the flashes of illumination the man seemed to walk in strange unconnected steps, one moment picking his way through loose gravel by a rancher's gate, an instant later fifteen feet further up the slope and pausing to look at the night sky, letting the rain run down his face.

The sky had been clear at sunset. He had climbed down from a pickup bed to the roadside and watched his last ride of the evening turn off toward Elk Mountain. In the four hours since then, the storm had gathered over the Laramie valley. Ten more miles to walk before he would reach the city and take shelter. Until then thunder voices rolled over him and lightning danced; in warning or in outrage or in greeting, he did not know. It was six years since he had last been here. The land would remember him, if the people did not.

Some psychologists have compared the brain's storage of memory to a cluttered attic, where artifacts from last month and ten years ago lie piled together in random order to be stumbled over by the wandering mind. Other researchers have put forth an experimental model of associational strings, a way of sorting memories by common aspects that tie them together. Most of us are familiar with the phenomenon of associations: a smell of baking cookies, for example, reminds Andrea of her mother, and calls forward a memory of a moment in the kitchen when Andrea was eleven and her mother received bad news over the phone. Today, that smell of cookies may remind Andrea instantly of her aunt's funeral. The theory of associational strings provides a useful model for . . .

A sudden thunderclap shook the ranch house, and Darcy looked up from the textbook, startled. Through the blowing curtains of her open bedroom window she saw a band of lightning slash over the hills. Stark line and shadow lit the horse barns and the corral fence across the ranch yard. She pushed back her chair and hurried over to the window. The wind angled into her face, carrying icy rain. The rain pounded the gravel driveway and poured noisily from roof gutters into rattling pipes. From the stable below she could hear the sounds of frightened horses: high, shrill cries and thudding kicks against stall slats. Darcy pulled the window shut.

It was late in the year for thunderstorms. Usually by mid-October the Wyoming weather would be poised for winter, with a few dry snow flurries, early morning frost, wind in the afternoons. Darcy felt the next boom of thunder cracking over the house. The psychology textbook's chapter on memory hadn't been that engrossing. She should have noticed the storm's approach. If it stayed directly over them for long, she would have to go down to the stables with Alice and try to quiet the horses.

Lightning arced down, and Darcy thought she could smell it, like burning metal. It flashed in a violent rainbow, and she could see the dark outlines of the Vedauwoo hills a few miles from the western edge of the ranch. The rain brought a picture to her mind that was like a memory: a brown-haired girl of thirteen with a broken leg, crying beside an overturned car, with the massive boulder hills of Vedauwoo crowding around her, indifferent. The picture came from what people had told her. She did not remember the accident or the night that had followed, or even the first few days she had spent in the Laramie hospital.

An associational string could lead to an empty place. Thunder and lightning reminded her of something she could not remember even after seven years. Her mother had wandered away from the crashed car, perhaps disoriented from a concussion, to fall to her death in a crevice of high rocks. They had found Sarah Jacobi three days later. They had not told Darcy until a week after that. Laura Ghormley, her best friend, had died in the first roll of the car. She did not remember the accident, but she remembered the guilt she had felt, as if it must have been her fault. She remembered the grief that had made her a sullen zombie in school the next fall.

Even with the window closed, Darcy felt threatened by the storm. The glass rattled, the curtains rippled, as if the wind were trying to drive its way inside. To go down to the stables would mean walking out under the hungry lightning. The electricity in the air made Darcy feel light-headed and full of unfocused energy, like a battery giving off sparks. Her muscles contracted as if ready to spring every time thunder cannoned around the house. A little ashamed—she was twenty years old!—Darcy turned off her desk lamp, closed her textbook, and went looking for company.

"Alice? Are you down there?" The narrow upstairs hallway was dark, but the stairway was lit with a warm glow from the first floor. Darcy shut her bedroom door behind her and padded down the steep wooden stairs, her thick socks muffling her footsteps. "Alice?"

"I'm here." The living room was hazy with smoke. Lamps cast circles of light on the dark-paneled walls and the red leather chairs. Alice Kennan knelt in front of the fireplace with an iron poker, scattering a smoldering mass of paper and twigs into the grate. "I didn't close the damper in time, and the rain came down the chimney."

Darcy selected a long-handled shovel from the stand of fire tools and reached in past Alice to scoop up some ashes from beneath the grate and throw them on the last smoky flames. "Where's Ed?"

"In the basement starting up the furnace. It will be a cold night." Alice stood and wiped her soot-grimed hands on her jeans. She had long legs and short black hair, and from the back, people often mistook her for a teenager. Her face, though, tanned and dry with fine wrinkle patterns around her eyes and mouth, looked every year of fifty-three. She had been a friend of Darcy's mother. This spring, summer, and fall, Darcy had worked for Alice and her husband at the ranch. When the winter hit, she would move back to a dorm room in Laramie to avoid the commute over the icy mountain highway.

A lightning flash showed through the heavy drapes on the front windows, and thunder rattled Alice's show horse trophies in their glass case. Darcy leaned over the couch and pulled back an edge of the drapes. The yard was awash with rain. The big floodlight that lit the stables and driveway had gone out. "Do you want me to go check on the mares?" she asked worriedly.

"They should be all right." Alice's voice was low. "I blanketed them tonight and turned on their heater, just to spite the Denver weatherman. You never know in October."

"They're frightened by the storm. I could hear them from upstairs." Darcy let the drape fall back and sat down on the couch.

"We'll give it a few minutes to pass. They're safer in the barns than we'd be crossing the yard." The older woman settled into one of the deep chairs and put her slippered feet up on the stone rim of the hearth. She picked up a magazine.

Ed Kennan had left one of his scrapbooks open on the couch. Darcy glanced at a few pages. Articles and pictures from supermarket tabloids, UFO digests, and newsletters were carefully taped down, with comments written in the margins. "Same old crapola," was scrawled on one; "Fairy tales!!!" on another; "Man knows something—write him" on a third.

Ten years older than his wife, Ed Kennan could not handle the heavy work of the ranch anymore. He had time to pursue his obsession. A notorious Laramie eccentric, Ed was convinced he was in continuing contact with a group of aliens. He allowed the space travelers to land on his ranch, and in return they helped him with their superior technology. Among other things, they had told him where to dig for artesian water, and that he should run for governor as a write-in candidate. He had found the water, but lost in the primary this spring. Wyoming people weren't ready for a governor with friends from other worlds.

Darcy had been five or six years old when she had asked her father if Ed's stories were truths or lies. Gilbert Jacobi had cocked his head thoughtfully and said, "Don't think of him as a liar, honey. It's all true to him. But if you or I waited out on those hills all night for weeks we'd never see a light in the sky besides the stars or hear any voice but our own. Understand?" She was grateful to her father for not telling her that Ed was crazy. UFOs were a harmless little madness, like some men's mania for model trains.

"Nothing from the furnace yet," Alice said with a frown, reaching a hand down beside her chair to feel in front of a vent. "Do you suppose Ed's having trouble getting it lit?"

"I'll go see." The storm made Darcy restless. She left Alice sitting before the doused fire and went into the kitchen, where a door opened on the basement stairs. The dangling chain of a lit bulb trailed over Darcy's hair as she descended. She heard a soft clattering noise from the unfinished room. Boxes of books and toys blocked her view; left behind by Julie Kennan, who lived in a tiny condominium in Denver. The furnace was like a sea creature in the middle of the floor, with ducts rising up like tentacles. No flames showed in the little window, and the pilot light was out. The clattering noise was not coming from the furnace.

"Ed? Mr. Kennan?" Darcy called loudly. The old rancher's hearing had faded recently, and Alice had not yet talked him into getting a hearing aid. There was no answer. Darcy peered around boxes and into dark corners, until she finally saw him at the end of the long, dimly lit room.

Lean and stooped in baggy jeans and a sweater, the old man crouched on the cement floor by the wall. Plaster chips rose around him like a blacksmith's sparks as he used a chisel to break the wall away from around a stud. As Darcy watched, he put the chisel down and picked up a wrapped object about the size of a small hammer. He wedged whatever it was behind the stud and looked around suspiciously. His pale blue eyes caught the light from the overhead bulb; he had the look of a gnome hiding treasure in a dim recessed cave.

Darcy stepped back into the shadows and called again, knocking on the metal door of the furnace. "Hey, Ed! You down here?"

This time he heard her, and answered. "Sure, honey. I was just looking for some tools." Darcy watched him pull one of Julie's boxes in front of the hole he had made.

She went back to the foot of the stairs, feeling like an intruder. Ed needed his mysteries. She hoped that whatever he had hidden in the wall would not be missed in the day-to-day work of the ranch.

"Here we are." Ed hurried around the furnace, holding out a long match-holder Darcy had seen in his back pocket earlier. "Won't take a moment now for the pilot. Tell Alice I'll be right up, honey."

"Okay." Darcy trotted back up the stairs to the kitchen. Clicks and pops from the basement indicated that Ed was getting the furnace lit now. She wished she could guess what had delayed him, what he had hidden and why. Maybe his aliens had told him to do it.

"Any trouble?" Alice asked from her chair. The rain was falling heavier now, but as Darcy listened she heard no more thunder.

"He was looking for some tools. How's the storm?"

"Moving off. I don't think there will be any need to go out, Darcy. You can go back to your studying."

The oppressive heaviness of the air had passed. "I'll do that. Dr. Ghormley may lecture on past lives or something tomorrow, but this chapter on memory will be on the midterm."

"Good night, dear."

"Good night." She climbed the stairs again to her bedroom, Julie's old room, and pulled her chair up close to the desk to resume her reading. The rain outside the window was no longer threatening. The curtains were still. She had to get to bed soon, and she had fifteen pages to go. Where was she? Associational strings ... the smell of cookies baking ... here:

Bits of memory lie encoded in brain cells, switched on and off by the passing of the neural current ...

Corner shadows receded from his vision. The heavy shapes of guest bed and dresser, the ruffled lace of curtains, drifted away into a place he could not follow. The low attic ceiling seemed to rise into a smoky night. Patterns of light, points of flame ... Richard Ghormley drew the patterns over and over in his mind, fingering them in the palm of his hand. Three interlocked pentagrams, set with flickering candles at each chalked point. Clear wax dripped onto the bare wooden floor.

He could feel a gathering, a thickening of the air around him. It was getting hot. The candle flames rose higher. He felt the intensity of his concentration burning through him into the patterns. Something was happening. A shudder gripped him.

"Do you feel it, Paul? Something's coming."

Beside him at the edge of the chalked circle, the young man leaned forward. "Quiet now. Don't allow distractions."

No. Paul was right. He must remain in control, though he was afraid. "Ahhh ..." He breathed out slowly, allowing himself only this sigh of wonder.

The candles began to go out, one by one, in sequence, starting with the first pentagram. He had drawn that one three days ago, chanting from a Kabbalistic manuscript and laying herbs in bunches around the room. The second pattern began to disappear, the flickering fires damped as if by an invisible breath. That pentagram he had drawn in strokes as fine as his Shinto master could teach him; he had dropped round, smooth pebbles in random patterns around the herbs. The third pattern—the third had happened quickly, tonight, after the candles had been lighted for the first two. He and Paul had drawn the third at the same time, beginning from a single point and going in opposition, lighting and placing candles on the precise measured points. When it was complete, Ghormley had felt its power. He had never come close to this achievement before. He had longed for mastery, had pursued it all his life.

"Command him to appear as the last candle fails," Paul said.

Ghormley felt the heat of the demon's closeness, as surely as he felt the pulse leaping in his neck amid the tight, corded muscles there. The name. He must speak the thing's name, bind it within the darkened circle, bind it to his will. God, all the times he had read ancient summonings, all the trance states, all the hallucinatory voices and sounds he had experienced, none of it had been like this. This time he had reached beyond his dull reality. Paul had shown him how.

He peered down at the hand-lettered wooden block in his grasp, and forced air into his straining lungs to speak the word there. The demon's name was a melodious word, not harsh or strange to the tongue. It was easy to pronounce. Ghormley said it fiercely and held up the wooden plaque like a shield before his eyes, unable to take another breath.

Dusky fire gathered in the center of the dark room. Heat emanated from the intelligence that formed there, a wavering, twisting form. A soul in agony . . . Ghormley felt his tongue dry out and refuse to move into the ritual phrase. He was supposed to remind the demon that it was here at his bidding and must do his will. He couldn't say it. Fear was drowning him.

"It will escape. Tell it to be still. Give it commands."

Paul's handsome face, an outline in the dark, was not frightened. Scornful?

Ghormley stammered, "Begone . . . I . . . don't know how to keep you here . . ." His memory helped him now with a dismissive phrase in Latin. He said it breathlessly and felt the heaviness lift from the room. Paul sighed and sat back on his heels. Ghormley's field of vision widened once again to take in the bedroom furniture that had been his daughter's. The yellow ruffles on the curtains—Laura had loved that dormer window with its high view of the backyard.

Nothing lurked within the circle of candles now. There were no cloven feet trapped in the lines of the pentagrams, no demon spirit held by the conjuror's raw courage and power. Yet Ghormley felt elated, not disappointed at all. "The next time I'll be better prepared for it. It was real. It was really here! God!"

"I thought you believed in the spirit world," Paul Delacache said mildly, getting up from his knees and brushing chalk dust off his loose black trousers.

"I do—I did—but believing and actually seeing, feeling the presence of something like that . . ." Ghormley laughed. "There's a great distance between them. I've crossed that distance tonight. Another time, I'll be better prepared."

The power and assurance were draining from him. His soft, middle-aged belly protruded again beneath his gray corduroy jacket. He was falling back into himself, becoming only Dr. Richard Ghormley, professor of psychology, again. He smiled ruefully and stood up beside the scowling younger man. "Don't blame me, Paul. I succeeded tonight, beyond anything I've ever done before. You're the cause of it, the catalyst. You've helped me see power in myself—well, that I've always wished I had."

Paul shook his head. "I came here to be your student, Richard." He spoke with a slight foreign accent Ghormley had yet to place.

Filled with new exuberance, Ghormley patted Paul on the back. "You may lack in years of knowledge. You haven't taken all the paths of the Society yet. But you have vision! More natural gifts than anyone I've known before. Fate has brought us together, Paul. I'm sure of it."

Paul Delacache bowed to him, apprentice to master, and a smile lightened his narrow face. "So I believe also, Richard." He reached out with one foot to topple three of the dripping candles, then bent down and picked one up to put in his pocket.

"Come have a drink. I'll clean this up in the morning."

"I have to be going. See you in class." Paul put his hands in his trouser pockets and turned to go down the attic stairs.

Richard Ghormley stood quietly for a moment, smelling for a hint of sulphur or brimstone in the attic room, but the only scents here were the usual ones: old dust and the memory of his daughter's perfume.

On the edge of sleep, Darcy tangled up her bedclothes as she twisted back and forth. Her eyes kept drifting open, and her gaze moved restlessly around her room. In the filtered light of the ranch yard, Julie Kennan's 4-H ribbons seemed to flutter from the shelf where they were pinned, and her plastic horse models cast many-legged shadows. Half-fallen on the floor, the ruffled quilt on the brass bed and been Julie's, bought at an auction two years before. There were few traces of Darcy in the room. Her books piled on the floor and the desk, a picture of her mother and father from ten years ago, and a closet stuffed with clothes, boxes, and suitcases, everything she had wanted from her old house in Laramie.

This was not her room, and with the house sold, Laramie was not her town anymore. Her father had moved to Denver, where a master carpenter could find more steady work. Darcy felt unconnected to anything anymore, drifting, without an anchor except for the mountains, the land itself. They kept her here.

Pulling the quilt over her again, Darcy curled up on her other side. Hanging on the bedpost where she could touch it when she wanted was her good-luck charm. It was a silly thing to keep, like a baby's blanket or a stuffed toy, but she was not ready to give it up. A fringed leather bag with a thong to tie around her neck, it contained a few feathers, odd-shaped pebbles, an ancient arrowhead, and a dried bit of fur that might have been half an animal's ear. The beading was faded on the white leather, and some of the fringe was gone. It looked very old. She didn't remember where she had gotten it. She must have bought it somewhere, or had it given to her. It looked like an Indian medicine bag, something a warrior would carry into battle for luck, but it was probably just a replica. She might have picked it up on a trip she took to the Black Hills with her Girl Scout troop when she was ten years old.

She lifted the medicine bag off its post and held it in one hand, closing her eyes. It warmed her palm as if alive, and brought strange pictures to her mind, animals with deep human eyes and campfires in the woods. The final image she saw before she slipped into a dream was a man walking in the rain, in the storm, his face shadowed beneath a black hat brim. Gleaming dark eyes guarded behind broad cheekbones; a thin, high-arched nose, skin the color of reddish clay; a sleek, predatory face. He tried to say something, but she could not understand his language. Then he drifted away.

Two hours after midnight, Charlie Edgewalker lay awake on top of the blankets in the Motel 6 bed. Though rain angled in through the screens of the open windows and the air was chill, he wore only an old pair of cut-off jeans. His lean, muscled body was seamed with scars, some scarcely healed, some so long past that they were no more than fine white lines against his red-brown skin. Like the distress rings of old trees, the scars bore witness to bad years. Quiet years left no marks.

He should never have left the girl alone these past seven quiet years. He should have stayed with her, stolen her if need be. But she had remembered nothing, not even who he was, and she had been frightened of him when he visited her in the hospital room. He had left her, certain there was no danger for a while.

Now rocks shifted from places where they had balanced for thousands of years, and chasms between boulders deepened slowly. The borders were stretching, thinning, and when they opened, the wendigo would once again come through into this world. Charlie had felt the changes from hundreds of miles away. She must feel them too, wherever she was. Enough power lived in her for that, even if she denied it. It was time for Darcy Jacobi to finish her training.

Charlie lifted one hand up before his face and stared at it, seeing his body on the bed softly outlined by the light coming from the parking lot. He chanted an old song he had learned from his first teacher, letting himself fall into a waking trance, seeking the road of spirits.

The bed fell away beneath him as his breathing slowed, and the sounds of rain and the highway outside the motel faded and blurred and vanished. Stillness held him suspended. Darcy's spirit, too, quested along this road, though she did not know it. He let his mind seek her, and saw her clearly for a moment.

She looked like a ten-year-old child, terrified and lost as she had been when he had first met her. Light brown hair tangled with pine needles and twigs, pale green and gold eyes like aspen leaves, the sharp scent of power around her betraying her to be a daughter of the mountain spirits. Charlie had chosen then to save her, to give her protection and teach her what she should know. If he had not intervened, the wendigo would surely have killed her before she lived much longer.

She faded away from him even as he reached out to touch her mind. He could not hold her. If the power was still there, it was as unformed now as it had been when she was ten years old. Charlie let himself feel the cool rain on his skin back at the motel room. He might have to begin again with Darcy somehow, with the first old stories he had told her that night in the forest. He hoped she would listen.

# CHAPTER
# TWO

An icy wind blew through the sleeves of Darcy's sweater, and she shivered on her horse's back as they climbed the hill. A thick gray cloudbank hid the sunrise, like a glacier lit from within by some subterranean light. The clouds were brooding, waiting for the day, gathering themselves for snow if the sun proved weak enough. It was past time for the first snowfall of the year. Darcy wished she had brought a hat and scarf this morning. The wind was fierce in the high pasture.

Her horse's hooves etched sharp prints in the frozen mud of the road. She rode Cinnamon behind the herd, where he urged the fifty horses on without much prompting, nipping in the sleepy animals who would have been content to graze on the dry grass along the path. Ahead of them, Alice Kennan drove her yellow Chevy pickup through the open gate into the pasture on the hilltop. The herd was mixed, the Kennans' Arabians and purebred quarter horses along with an assortment of riding horses Alice boarded for people from Laramie and Cheyenne. The younger horses crowded through behind the pickup, while the others bunched together and awaited their turn to pass. One bay gelding grew bored of the routine and trotted down the slope toward some grass clumps in a ditch. Darcy loped Cinnamon around the herd to cut him off, and her horse nudged the bigger animal back toward the others.

Grass in the pasture bent and rippled in the wind as if small creatures were running from sagebrush to sagebrush. Darcy leaned from Cinnamon's back to close the gate behind the last horse. The pickup was parked between the water tank and the hayrack, and the herd had begun to mill around like children waiting for the ice cream truck. The horses could have munched on hay all night in their stalls, but they were always eager for breakfast.

Alice climbed out of the cab in a parka and gloves and began to fork hay into the rack from the opened bales in the pickup bed. It was quiet now, except for the swish of falling hay and the horses' soft breathing and jostling of one another. Darcy dismounted and unhooked Cinnamon's halter rope, letting him join the crowd. She got a hoe from the pickup and pushed her way through the horses to the water tank. A crust of ice had formed overnight. She began to chip at it with the hoe, feeling a warmth in her shoulders as her muscles began to waken.

On mornings like these she felt she belonged here: out on the hill with the long gray sky overhead, with mountains in the distance and no houses around for twenty miles, with a cold wind to remind her she was alive, with real work to do for animals that depended on her for food and water. She had worked part-time jobs in Laramie before, selling things to people who didn't really need them, taking money that went into the cash register and was carried away nightly to the bank. She had no connection to those people; they didn't need her, and she didn't know them.

She was a part of this, the land and the sky. Alice understood how she felt. They rarely talked when they were out working in the mornings. Darcy felt her ears growing numb, and she worked faster, breaking up the ice layer into floating pieces. Her hoe bumped against something solid at one edge of the water tank.

A mottled gray and white form bobbed in the water. Darcy hooked her hoe over it and pulled it toward her. It was a dead hawk, a young bird with thick feathers and strong claws. She put the hoe down and picked up the soft weight in her gloved hands. It was stiff, frozen. "Look, Alice. Lightning struck it, maybe." She imagined the blaze of fire, a bird falling out of the sky like Icarus into the water. Two horses nosed curiously over her shoulder at the dripping shape she held.

Alice vaulted down from the pickup bed and came to look. "Probably was perched on the side of the tank. It's metal, the most likely thing to be hit up here." She touched the icy feathers gently. "Don't tell Ed about it. He told me to look for signs up here. Says his aliens landed somewhere around here last night."

Darcy pictured the hawk circling, looking for a place to land in the storm, when the whirling lights and poisoned exhaust of a flying saucer descended in front of it and sent it spinning to the earth. "I'd bury it, but the ground is frozen."

"Take it and drop it out past the fence where the horses won't be bothered. Poor thing." Alice looked at Darcy with a hint of laughter. "And if you see spaceship tracks, I don't want to know."

They rode back to the ranch house ten minutes later in the cab of the pickup, down the muddy road into the yard, through ice-rimmed puddles, past the barns and the riding arena. Alice parked the truck in the driveway between a long horse trailer and Darcy's green Subaru station wagon, and they jumped out and hurried to the house, as eager as the horses for their breakfast.

The peeling blue paint on the house looked brighter, but no amount of rain could improve the weathered white trim on the porch and doorway. They climbed the steps of the porch, stamped the mud off their boots, and went inside. The living room was too warm, with fireplace and heater both going. The kitchen was quiet. Darcy didn't see Ed anywhere. Coffee simmered in the percolator, and a muffin pan half-filled with blueberry batter sat on the kitchen table. A cool draft came from the back door of the kitchen, open into the yard.

"Ed?" Alice pulled off her parka and threw it on a chair. "We're back. The oven is hot enough. I'll put the muffins in." She opened the oven door and shoved the pan inside. Alice moved quickly in the kitchen, always looking a little out of place. She did not have the patience for recipes. If she could not find an ingredient, she would substitute, and her measurements were hardly precise. Her husband was more careful. He did most of the cooking now that he couldn't help with the outside ranch work.

Darcy took orange juice from the refrigerator, poured herself a glass, and sat at the table. "I'm starved. How long for muffins?" At home she had always just had cereal, but Ed Kennan had spoiled her with big breakfasts after the first morning chores.

"Eight minutes. Think you can wait?" Alice smiled.

She would be sorry to move into the dorms for the winter. She had loved living with the Kennans these past few months, but the twenty-mile commute to Laramie was too dangerous on icy roads. The Kennans were her godparents, though she had never spent much time with them before. Her father used to drive her here after school so she could ride her horse for an hour or two while he sat by the fire and talked with Ed. Alice had let her help with the kids' riding classes sometimes, but she had never been close to her or Ed before; she had thought of them as only her parents' friends.

Alice pulled the back door shut and disappeared into the

hallway that led to her bedroom. Darcy heard her calling for her husband, and the clatter of Alice's boot heels on the hardwood floor of the dining room. "Ed? Come on to breakfast," Alice's voice shouted up the stairs to the second floor. Darcy pushed her chair back and went to the basement door on impulse. She peered into the darkness.

"Ed? Are you down there?" Surely he wouldn't be without the light. Darcy flicked on the bulb and went down there herself. Nothing but boxes, dust, and the clicking and humming of the old furnace. She hurried back upstairs and closed the door, with an odd empty feeling in her stomach that was not hunger. She was now certain that Ed was not in the house.

Alice's worried voice preceded her into the kitchen. "Darcy, will you go out to the broodmares' barn and check Farah's stall? Maybe Ed went down to the trailer."

An old house trailer a mile from the main ranch buildings served as Ed's study, where he kept most of his files and books, but he never went there when the weather looked bad. His fifteen-year-old Arabian mare was too delicate for the cold, and his own arthritis usually kept him near the fire and the heater on days like this. Darcy borrowed Alice's parka and hurried out the door and across the yard. She checked the barn where the quiet mares stood in their stalls; Farah was missing. Her saddle and bridle were gone from the tack room.

"He took Farah." She jogged back into the kitchen to the smell of nearly done muffins. "He must have felt good this morning."

Looking older than she usually did, Alice sat at the table sipping scalding coffee, licking burned lips absently. "I tried calling the trailer. He didn't answer. He might have gone somewhere else. He might have gone looking for his aliens."

"Maybe he had the vacuum cleaner running." Darcy peered into the oven window. "We need to clean the place up for the new wrangler." Alice was hiring a man named Charlie Stone to help with the ranch work and the Arabian breeding program. He was supposed to arrive in a couple of weeks, and he was going to live in the trailer.

Darcy hoped nothing strange had happened. One evening she and Alice had been calling Ed for an hour before they found him standing as stiff as a statue around the side of one of the barns, staring off into the night sky with unblinking eyes. It had taken a good shaking to bring him back to earth. Alice had wanted to drive him to the hospital that time, but Ed had talked her out of it. His aliens had been communicating with him, that was all.

"I'll drive down to the trailer and look for him." Darcy opened the oven and scooped two hot blueberry muffins from the pan onto a paper plate. "Don't worry, Alice. I'm sure he's around somewhere."

A Jeep trail overgrown with weeds rattled under Darcy's Subaru as the car rumbled in four-wheel drive over the rise. The trailer was set among pine trees in a hollow, half a mile from the main ranch road. Down the slope, a swift-running stream was crowded with willow bushes and the thin trunks of aspens that had lost most of their fall color. Faded green paint peeling, the trailer looked like a Buck Rogers spaceship sagging on concrete blocks, with a rounded front end and tail fins giving it a vaguely aerodynamic look that no modern mobile home could match.

Ed and Alice Kennan had lived there for a few years right after they were married, before Ed's parents retired and moved to Florida, leaving them the main house. From here, Darcy couldn't see Farah tied to the porch railing. Maybe Ed had picketed her in the woods where she could graze. She drove carefully down the hill on the bumpy road, stopped by the porch, and got out to climb the three wooden steps to the trailer door. It was unlocked.

The place was dusty, but it did not look bad. The overhead light worked. The kitchen had a stove, a sink, and a refrigerator, and the bedroom down the hall held an iron bedstead. A desk and two chairs stood in the den, covered with papers and scrapbooks, cardboard files bulging with clippings, magazines with old, lurid covers. "Ed?" There was no answer. Darcy went down the hall and opened the door of the tiny bathroom. No one was here.

Driving back to the ranch house, Darcy stopped her car at the top of the rise on the Jeep trail. She had a clear view of the back of Vedauwoo Park, shadowed by the glowering storm clouds that still hid the sun. Past the ranch boundary, dark pine trees climbed the slopes of the boulder hills. In the valleys along streambeds and beaver ponds were clumps of golden aspens, some of them holding their leaves late in the season. The low places held the life of the park: rabbits and foxes, antelope, hordes of picnic-loving chipmunks. On the heights, when the summer rock climbers and shouting children were gone, nothing remained but the bleak, bare, granite boulders hunched in eroded piles against the wind.

The name Vedauwoo meant "earth-born spirits" in Arapaho. A woman at the University of Wyoming had given the park that name at the turn of the century, but the Indians must have called it something like that. There were local legends about bottomless caves and rocks that moved quietly from place to place at night. Ed Kennan had his own theories about Vedauwoo. He had collected stories of alien abductions there, and he was sure his own alien friends came and went from the park. That was where he might have gone, Darcy decided. She would have to follow him on horseback.

Back at the house, she made Alice promise to stay at home in case Ed returned. She hoped she could find him quickly. He was too old and frail to be out for long in the cold. Especially if he was in one of his dazed trances, communicating with aliens and not paying attention to the real world. She had to find him quickly, get him back home, so she could stop worrying about him and get on with her day. Her psychology class was at one o'clock this afternoon, and at four she was teaching an advanced dressage class to five rich teenage girls with fancy horses.

Armed with sandwiches, a canteen of water, a warm jacket, hat, gloves, and scarf, Darcy went back up to the high pasture and saddled Cinnamon to ride after Ed Kennan. Cinnamon had cost her only fifty dollars three years before, because his owner had been tired of him and let him go wild in a pasture for two years, then discovered he couldn't sell him for what he was worth. He was half Morgan and half Welsh pony, a short, stocky roan with a stubborn streak. He could work all day and still have the energy to gallop for fun in the evening. Now he was eager for a ride. Darcy trotted him out of the pasture and down the hill, then let him stretch out into a lope across the prairie toward Vedauwoo.

The wind was biting now that she was up high and moving fast. She turned up the collar of her blanket-lined jeans jacket and squinted her eyes against the cold. Cinnamon ran a jagged path around clumps of sagebrush, leaning into the reins, his hooves kicking up pebbles and chunks of frozen mud. Darcy was afraid that Ed Kennan would be hard to find. One old man on a white horse in a ranch that was a series of hills, ridges, canyons, and hollows; it was nearly impossible. She did not really care about missing her classes, but she wanted Ed and his old mare home before snow began to fall.

Faintly through the wind in her ears, Darcy heard a coyote howling. Sagebrush and stunted pine and juniper trees covered the rolling plateau land. At eight thousand feet elevation, nothing grew very tall. She would see Ed moving if he was on the heights, but if he was in one of the canyon draws or downslope on the other side of a hill, she might never find him. Darcy shivered, hugging the saddle tightly with her knees. She hoped Ed felt strong this morning. If he grew tired and stopped, fell asleep outdoors somewhere, he might easily freeze to death. Farah might run into trouble too. The pampered mare would not be capable of a long trek.

"We'll find him," Darcy muttered to her horse, whose ears pricked back at the sound. "If he's even still out here. If I were Farah I'd have headed back to the corral by now." But Farah was no dude-ranch horse, indifferent to her rider's whims. She would do what Ed Kennan asked her, even if she thought he was asking something foolish.

Another mile, and they passed the border between the ranch and the Medicine Bow National Forest, the back edge of Vedauwoo Park. Darcy had to ride for ten minutes down the barbed-wire fence line before she found one of the line gates. She had wire cutters in her saddlebags, but Alice wouldn't thank her for breaking the fence and forcing the new wrangler to ride out to repair it. The gate was narrow. She dismounted to open it. Cinnamon shied a little but let her head him through.

The coyote howled again, very close, loud enough to make both Darcy and her horse jump a little. "Don't be afraid," she said as she stood with the horse for a moment, her hand on his nose. "A coyote's a little thing. You and I are too big to be in any danger." But an old, tired horse, maybe injured from a fall in a gopher hole, could be bait enough for a hungry coyote. Darcy could imagine dozens of dangers out here for Ed Kennan. The old fool. She was angrier and more worried every minute.

Cinnamon nudged at her hand and blew through his nostrils. Darcy took a moment to get her gloves out and put them on, then mounted again and rode straight into Vedauwoo. The granite rocks began to appear around them in piled outcroppings of three or four boulders, taller than the horse's head. The ground was soft and wet between the sheltering rocks, and Darcy rode through quickly. At the back of the park was a high ridge where climbers and hikers rarely ventured. You could get a good view of the surrounding formations from the top, and the slope at one side was gentle enough for a horse to climb.

Another howl, drawn out and mournful, like a ghost in the quiet ravine. Darcy guided her horse around broken rocks and the spiky arms of scrub pine trees, listening nervously for a growl or a bark. The coyote must be close. She was not afraid of it, but she was afraid of what Cinnamon might do if he saw it. He had bolted and thrown her before, leaving her with her breath knocked out in gullies and nests of sagebrush. He usually turned around and came back to see what was the matter, but he might not if he was frightened by a coyote.

She rode up the end of the ravine, crouched in her stirrups, looking from side to side like a soldier behind enemy lines. Wind tossed her hair as she reached the ridgetop and settled back into her saddle. Cinnamon walked carefully toward the edge, where sheer rock formed a wall like ancient ramparts. Faded green and brown hills rolled away from her toward the distant snowcapped peaks of the Colorado Rockies. She could see a curve of the interstate highway where huge trucks lumbered toward the summit on their way to Laramie. Nearer to the ridgetop, the massive piles of Vedauwoo hills shadowed the land as she looked through valleys and at the edges of forests. She saw no man on horseback.

"Ed Kennan!" she shouted. Echoes chased around the valleys before the last sounds returned to her. "Ed! Do you hear me?"

She saw motion in the sky near her and watched a speck grow clearer. Skimming the bottom of the low clouds with its white-striped wings, a prairie falcon rode the edge of the wind above her. It seemed utterly alone in the icy gray sweep of the sky. Darcy felt for a strange, shifting moment that if she wanted she could step out of herself and join it up there, feel the rush of wind beneath wings. She felt dizzy, as if she were spinning in flight, and thought of the dead hawk this morning, falling out of the sky.

Cinnamon shifted uneasily beneath her and snorted. His ears lay back against his skull and he turned suddenly, tossing his head and pulling at the reins. Brought back to earth, Darcy stared. The coyote was smaller than she would have imagined. It paced from side to side, watching her, only a dozen yards away. Dirty brown fur, thin and scarred, ribs she could count, a ragged silhouette against the jumbled rocks of the ridgetop. Eyes sharp and questioning, wild. One ear half-gone, torn in some old battle. Darcy felt her pulse beating in her throat, fast and hard. She held the reins tightly and felt her horse trembling through the bit. Cinnamon stamped one forefoot.

The coyote had recently rolled in dry grass that clung in shreds to its fur. It did not move when the horse took a threatening step forward. Darcy shivered. Tiny snowflakes had begun to fall, almost invisible in the gray morning. Darcy felt them on her face and saw them melt on her horse's red hide. She had to get out of these hills before the storm struck, and she had to find Ed Kennan.

The coyote's narrow, doglike face seemed to laugh. A whining growl sounded in its throat. Its slanting eyes stared. Darcy wondered suddenly if it might be rabid. Real fear made her breathing shallow and fast, and lines of sweat slid down inside her shirt.

She shouted at the coyote, "Go on! Get!"

It trotted back a few paces and its ears twitched forward. Its tattered fur lay flat again, and it was no longer growling. The snow was falling heavier. Darcy saw a gleam of laughter in its eyes. Cinnamon, incredibly, had begun to relax. His ears were rising in curiosity, and this time when he stepped forward he leaned his head down in a friendly gesture. The scrawny coyote barked softly and turned, running a few paces toward a rock outcropping at one end of the ridge. It looked back at them, crouched on its front paws in an apparent invitation to play, and ran a few paces more.

Darcy had to laugh. The coyote wanted them to follow it. It was as plain as the rescue scene in an old Lassie movie. She watched the strange animal enter an opening in the rocks, where two huge boulders angled together to form a rough cave. Maybe Ed was in there, injured, and the coyote was leading her to him. The coyote's face peered out again, and it whined. Then it turned with a flick of its ragged tail and disappeared into the darkness. "This is silly," Darcy said to her horse as she dismounted. "Stay where you are, okay?" She left his reins dangling on the ground and hoped he would decide to obey.

She could not believe she was going after the coyote. A wild animal, that might turn and attack her inside the cave . . . yet somehow she did not expect that to happen. This was one of the strangest things she had ever done, and it felt like something she remembered, or maybe something she had dreamed.

Small rocks had once been piled before the opening, but they were scattered on the ground as if someone had disturbed them. Darcy picked up one of the rocks and saw scratched on it surface the shape of a wheel with six spokes. Another rock was streaked with a line of faded red paint. She felt a sharp sensation as if her senses were coming into focus. This was not ordinary. Coyotes did not act this way, and boulder caves in Vedauwoo did not have barricades of decorated rocks. An image of her good-luck charm, her Indian medicine bag, came into her mind and stayed there with an urgency that made her wish she had brought it along.

She took her gloves off and tucked them into her belt, to have a better feel for the rocks as she climbed down. The rock with the wheel etching felt smooth and cool in her bare fist. She put it down with the others and crouched under the pointed archway formed by the underside of the boulders. A step inside took her down the slanted surface of an angled rock, with the weight of tons of boulders over her head. The opening admitted little light. She lowered her body onto hands and feet and bottom, and crept crab-fashion down the slope into the dark, narrow cave. The granite rock was gritty against her palms.

She had explored many of the small rock-crevice caves in Vedauwoo Park, and the closeness did not bother her. Distantly, she thought that she should be looking for Ed Kennan, but it seemed less important than following the coyote. A blank wall met her at the bottom, and she stood on a thin band of dirt, the ground of the ridgetop. Her boots sank into the mud. She felt blindly toward either side of the harsh rock faces and found an opening at the bottom on the left, just big enough to crawl through on hands and knees. The way was level now.

She listened for a sound that might come from the coyote ahead of her, but it was silent inside the mass of boulders. The air was fresh through the small opening she felt. She shrugged slightly, against a small voice that told her this was a foolish thing to do, and she bent down and crawled through the mud into the mouth of rock.

Shards of mica glittered on the stone floor of the larger cave room she entered now. Light must filter through cracks, but Darcy could not see where. Her eyes adjusted to the dimness, just enough to find the outline of the slab of stone eight feet from her, and the bones of the buried man who lay there. Darcy got quickly to her feet, breathing fast, forgetting to reach a hand above her to check the height of the rock ceiling. She felt it press the top of her hair as she stood very still in the deep grave. Almost as much as she had wanted to find this place, she wanted to be somewhere else. She had never been so close to a dead body before.

The skeleton's arms were crossed. The bone fingers curved around two long objects that rested against the rib cage. Darcy listened to her heart thudding as she stepped forward, against the advice of her quivering legs. The buried man held weapons: a staff so old the wood was nearly rotted away, and a long stone knife that gleamed as if freshly chipped. Bits of leather clothing remained under the bones, and a woven band still circled one wrist. The slab on which he rested had been painted in stripes, but Darcy could not tell the color in the near darkness.

The coyote had led her here, deep within the boulders, but it was gone now. The only way out was back up at the arched cave opening. The coyote would have had to climb out past her while she came down the ledge of rock. Darcy shook her head and backed away from the skeleton, feeling like an intruder in a place where a man had rested in quiet for many years, armed against some enemy.

Alice could tell her if there were any stories of an Indian chief buried up here . . . no. Darcy would not tell Alice or anyone about this place. The dead man was here for a reason. She would not disturb his vigil. Awkward, wanting to show respect to the warrior, she bowed, then turned and crouched down again to crawl through the short passage. The sloped boulder was harder to climb than it had been to descend. She slipped once and fell to the bottom again, scraping her hands as she clutched at the rough stone. One knee of her jeans was torn.

When she reached the top she saw Cinnamon standing in front of the cave mouth, his tail turned into the wind that lashed snow in the beginning of a blizzard. The sharpening cold made her cough. She paused to pile the marked stones up against the opening again, trying to make them look like a natural rock fall. Finally she was satisfied that no one who hiked past would notice the cave. Still the coyote had not reappeared. She felt light-headed, as if her mind had been far away. She put her gloves on again over her scraped hands. Cinnamon whinnied urgently, and she gathered up the reins and swung into the saddle.

The snow clung to her hair and blew into her eyes. She

turned around and opened the saddlebag to pull out her hat and scarf. This was awful. They couldn't stay out in it, couldn't keep searching for Ed Kennan. She would have to hope he had returned home on his own. The storm might not last long, but Darcy knew how quickly both she and her horse could tire out and lose their way. It wasn't just in frontier times that people froze out on the prairie.

As she tied her scarf around her neck, she made one last survey of the land around the ridgetop. This time she saw movement. Riding down a steep slope not far from her, Ed was slumped in the saddle. His white Arabian mare moved slowly, her head bobbing up and down. Darcy stopped herself from shouting to Ed; the image of the grave's guardian filled her mind, and she did not want to attract attention to the ridge. She would ride to meet him at the bottom of the ravine.

"Let's go," she said softly, and started down the ridge in the bleak whiteness of the thickening snow. Watchful that Cinnamon's hooves did not slip on wet rock, she did not look back up at the ridge until she was nearly at the bottom. Then she saw the coyote standing looking down at her, its fur flattened and wet, its torn ear flopping in one eye. It sat down when she saw it and howled up into the wind.

"Darcy? That you, girl?" Ed's voice was rough and tired. He had stopped Farah at a dry riverbed, gathering strength to clamber up one of the banks. Darcy loped her horse over to the old man and took Farah's reins. She led the mare up a gentle slope to the prairie level.

"Where did you go, Ed? I was worried."

The storm blew at their backs as she headed their horses toward home. "I couldn't find the place," Ed said angrily. "I was supposed to go back, but I couldn't find it. Rocks got to looking all alike. The blaze I left was gone. Something must have been trying to stop me, but I can't figure what."

"What place were you trying to find?" Darcy peered at him over her scarf.

"It was evidence. About my aliens. People will believe me one of these days if I find enough evidence. They want me to tell people, but it's hard when no one will believe me." He was near tears. Darcy hoped he was not going to be sick. Alice would be angry with them both.

"I'm sure your friends won't be disappointed. You tried. Maybe you should go sometime when you can be sure of the weather. And take somebody with you."

He looked at her with some suspicion. "I won't go again. Don't worry. I couldn't find the place, so I'll forget about it."

"If that's what you want." She wondered how far she should humor him. Alice never pretended to believe in the aliens. But Alice was convinced that Ed was really all right. One recurring hallucination was not enough to make someone crazy, was it? Darcy was not sure, but it worried her. What would the aliens ask next?

A thought struck her as she rode: if she tried to tell anyone about the coyote, or the ancient tomb, they would think she was as crazy as Ed. Like the aliens, the coyote had come from someplace outside. No wild animal would have acted that way. Darcy rode quietly, wondering what she had followed, and what she had found.

# CHAPTER
# THREE

M aybe that's where past lives come from, Dr. Ghormley," said a dry-witted older student who sported a beard and ponytail. "Bits of genetic memory. But then you should remember your ancestors' lives, right?"

"I'd like to find a scientific justification for the past-life experiences I've uncovered through hypnosis. Unfortunately, the government won't fund that grant proposal." General chuckles, vaguely on his side. Dr. Ghormley returned to his lecture on memory storage, letting his eyes wander around the small auditorium where they stuck overflowing general education classes like Intro to Psychology. Complacent, incurious faces gazed at him. A few heads were inclined together, whispering. Half-asleep, his legs stretched over the seat in front of him, Paul Delacache lounged in the back row.

Ninety-five students in this class, here to fulfill college requirements. Most of them were at the University of Wyoming only by default; it was the only four-year school in the state.

Aside from Wyoming high school graduates, the school attracted athletes who wanted high-altitude training, foreign students looking for low tuition rates, and an array of people who needed mountains: skiers, rock climbers, geologists.

Dr. Ghormley attracted some students himself. His was an internationally recognized program, but on a very small scale, and not advertised in the admissions catalogue. The Esoteric Society kept a low profile. Ghormley dabbled publicly in hypnotic past-life regressions, UFO abductions, and other trivia. Serious, scholarly research in the occult would not have impressed the Board of Trustees. They looked at his good teaching evaluations and the grant money he brought into the psychology department, and overlooked the rest.

Students tended to like him. He liked them, or at least the idea they represented: new energy, new ways of looking at things. He continued to hopefully survey each incoming class, searching for light behind someone's eyes. The tentative psychic explorations he dared to make during classes sparked enthusiasm in only a few. One a year, one young mind interested in going beyond what it had been taught to believe, that was his usual quota. This year was exceptional. He had five interesting novices in this class alone, not to mention Paul, who had shown up on his doorstep with a backpack at the beginning of the fall semester.

"Next week we'll all take the DeVries Standard Psychology Profile test," Ghormley said when he had finished his memory lecture. "But before that I thought it might be interesting to cast your horoscopes." He weathered a few giggles and rolling eyes, and went on. "I'm not talking about the Sunday astrology column here. You'll be looking up precise planetary positions and even using some math. When you're done we'll compare the results to the profile test and attempt to eliminate random correlations. Take a look at the probability section in Chapter Ten before next Friday. Your analysis and comparison of the two methods will be your midterm."

He had found this a useful project in the past. Students tended to enjoy it, whether they were curious about astrology or they just wanted another funny story to tell about Dr. Ghormley's class. Ghormley had even discovered some hidden psychic potentials while looking through the rough student charts. One young man who had shown up that way was in Venezuela now, working with Eduardo Huiza on spirit travel.

"We'll break into small groups. A through G, go with Maryann, room 315. H through N with Paul in the graduate lounge. The rest of you move to the front here with me." The students began to shift, leaving the hall and climbing over rows toward him.

He watched Roxanne Hall and Darcy Jacobi hurry out together, laughing, behind Paul. Laramie kids, both had been friends of his daughter, Laura, before she died. Roxanne had come to one of his seminars while she was still in high school. Now a novice in the Esoteric Society, she was helping to pay her way through school this semester by taking curious students on guided peyote excursions in Dr. Ghormley's back parlor.

Ghormley had once been interested in Darcy. She and his daughter had had a few psychic experiences at the age of thirteen, but whatever spark was in Darcy must have gone after the hormones settled. Now she was one of the ordinary ones. Ghormley got out his mimeographed stacks of condensed ephemera tables and passed out blank natal charts. He had fifteen minutes of class left to teach before he could go back to his office.

"Horoscopes." Darcy grumbled to her friend Roxanne as they walked toward the graduate lounge. "I can't believe we're taking class time for this." She didn't want to come in today. After her ride through the snow she had been tired enough to sleep for the afternoon, but Alice had asked her to pick up the new wrangler after class. Charlie Stone had come into Laramie yesterday, two weeks early, and we was waiting at the Motel 6.

They walked down a hallway that always made her think of a submarine: low ceilings, battleship-gray walls decorated only by recessed track lighting. Roxanne's hiking boots clumped loudly on the tile floor, and her tie-dyed cotton dress swung against legs clad in thermal underwear. It was a carefully plotted ensemble, intended to mean that Roxanne was into sixties nostalgia and the environment. Two years ago it had been torn lace camisoles and leather skirts, in her punk phase.

"You can learn a lot from your horoscope if you do it right." Roxanne peered seriously from under her heavy blond bangs. "The only trouble is interpretation. Even an accurate chart can prompt different readings from different astrologers. A certain level of psychic insight is necessary."

"Come on, Roxy, listen to yourself. That's grocery store tabloid philosophy. You might as well be in one of Ed's UFO digests. 'I Married a Scorpio from Centaurus 7.' " She smiled.

"A lot of people believe in astrology. It's totally mainstream. Keep an open mind," Roxanne said loftily. "You never know. You could find out the true meaning of your life."

The graduate assistant who was leading their section looked up when the two young women entered the lounge. A direct gaze and then a smile, a little delayed, as if he had decided to smile after seeing something about them. Darcy couldn't believe she hadn't noticed him before. He had a wild, handsome face like a Greek painting, a Dionysus, with thick black hair that waved over his eyes. The eyes were a deep forest green, almost black. An image of what he might look like naked flashed in Darcy's mind, and she flushed, embarrassed at the thought. He looked around the room again, leaving her, and she settled onto one of the couches feeling oddly disturbed.

Roxanne scribbled something in her notebook, held it over an inch. *He's something, isn't he? Ghormley's discovery, transfer from Canada. Paul Delacache. Doesn't have a girlfriend.*

Darcy wondered where Roxanne had met him. This was silly—she never reacted this way to men. Not wanting to touch them so much that she could almost feel curved muscles under her hands already. She leafed absently through her notes from the lecture, hoping he wouldn't notice her wide-eyed admiration. The old upholstery of the student lounge couch was poking at one of her legs. She shifted to try to get comfortable and saw his eyes on her again.

He passed out instructions then. The rustling of mimeographed pages filled the room. Darcy spread the blank chart out on her notebook and began to fill out the box in the upper corner: exact date, time, and place of birth. One young man asked how precise the place of birth had to be: he was born on his parents' yacht, somewhere in the Caribbean. Paul Delacache told him to look up a latitude and longitude and get it as close as he could. His voice was low and strangely accented. Roxanne had said he was from Canada; it didn't sound like Canadian-English or French-Canadian. Stop thinking about him, Darcy told herself.

"That isn't right," Roxanne said, frowning at Darcy's paper. "You weren't born in Laramie. Your mom told me the story once. On a hike in the mountains, wasn't it?"

"Laramie is the nearest town. On my birth certificate it says Laramie." Darcy began to erase the word. "It was at Vedauwoo, in one of the rock caves up there. Mom wasn't expecting me for another two weeks." Her father had driven them to the Kennan ranch as soon as Sarah Jacobi could walk down the mountain. Ed and Alice had put Darcy's mom to bed and talked her exhausted husband out of sending for an ambulance; mother and baby were both fine, and they didn't need the hospital. It was a favorite birthday story. Darcy had been horribly embarrassed by it as a child.

"Vedauwoo?" His voice. Paul had overheard. "You said you were born at Vedauwoo?"

"That's the rock-climbing park, over toward Cheyenne, right?" said a freshman from the East Coast.

"Does it matter for this?" Darcy asked sheepishly. "I could just put Laramie to make it easier."

"No," Paul said. "It matters." His look was intense and interested. Darcy had to let her eyes fall again to the papers in her lap. If she had felt his gaze before, it had been nothing like this. He might be seeing her thoughts.

"A few degrees difference east or west could change your ascendant planet." Roxanne glanced through the tables in her handout sheets. "You might get the totally wrong reading."

"Vedauwoo," Darcy said as she wrote it in. She glanced at Paul. He was still staring. "Do I need to put which mountain? Milepost on the scenic trail?" He didn't notice her sarcasm.

"It won't make a difference for your chart," he said. "But on the mountain is different than in the valley. According to some systems of belief . . ." He paused, seemed to continue differently than he had intended. "There are Native American legends about mountains and mountain births. Some specific to the Vedauwoo area, I believe. That might be something to investigate for your midterm paper. See what the local legends have to say about mountains and the mountain-born. It may or may not coincide with your astrological chart or your DeVries profile."

"Maybe I will." Darcy dared to smile at him. He wasn't anything strange, just an excitable graduate student, fascinated by his field of study, and better looking than any teaching assistant she'd ever met before.

He turned away from her now and explained some of the instructions to the group. Darcy worked with the others, until she had a rough beginning of her natal chart, with her sun sign, her ascendant, and a couple of aspects. It was like a complicated game, or a children's secret club, with its own made-up symbols and meanings. She could not believe anyone would take it seriously. Roxanne did, but next year Roxanne might believe in Tibetan meditation or fundamentalist Christianity.

The class period over, Darcy stuffed her half-completed astrology project into her purse and got up to walk out with Roxanne. Paul Delacache stood up and leaned toward her with a hand out to stop her. "You're a skeptic, I can see that," he said rapidly, his odd foreign accent more strongly marked now. "I'd like to talk to you a little more about this. How about coffee in the Student Union? Or do you have another class?"

"I have to meet somebody in town," Darcy said, feeling a dreamlike sense of disbelief. He was asking her out. "Then I have to go teach a class at the ranch where I work. I won't be back in Laramie until tomorrow noon." She didn't know how to react, what to say.

"That's great," Paul said. "When's your last Friday class? There's a party tomorrow night, and I didn't know if I was going, but if you want we could go together."

Go with him to a party? He didn't even know her name.

"You'll enjoy it," he said. "We could go to dinner first."

"Sure. I mean, I'd like to go. I . . . my last class is over at four. Do you want to meet somewhere?" She hoped she could think of something to say to him by then. She hoped he would stop bothering her so much. Standing this close to him was like being on a cliff's edge, about to fall.

"Dr. Ghormley's lab is where I work. Room 17, the basement of White Hall. I'm off work at four-thirty. Can you come there?" He smiled at her confused nod. "Good. You don't have to worry. I'll get you home as early as you like."

"I'll see you then. I have to go now." Darcy slung her

purse over her shoulder and edged around Paul to Roxanne. "Thanks for asking me." He bowed slightly to her and turned back to the stack of papers on his chair. She walked quickly out of the graduate lounge and hurried around the corner with her awestruck friend.

"How did you do it?" Roxanne demanded. "Amy Martin made a play for him with torpedoes loaded, and she didn't get three words. You haven't even talked to him, girl."

"I didn't do anything. I'm a skeptic. Maybe he wants to convert me to spiritualism."

"Destiny," Roxanne said mysteriously. "Karma. Fate. Call it what you will. Did I not warn you, unbeliever?"

No romantic illusions, Darcy told herself, listening to Roxanne chatter as they headed toward the parking lot. No one who looked like Paul could be very interested in an ordinary person like her. He might be some kind of religious fanatic. She wouldn't be surprised, his eyes were so intense. She wondered what it would feel like to sit beside him in a car, to hold his hand, to kiss him. She couldn't imagine it.

She started toward the highway, driving in a soft-edged daze as if wrapped in cotton wool, before she remembered she had to pick up the new wrangler. The motel was on the other side of town, at the other end of the interstate loop. She turned the car around, still aware of the tangy smell of Paul's presence near her, the undefinably different feeling she had experienced standing beside him. His face was already fixed in her memory, as if he had been appearing on magazine covers. She saw the deep green of his eyes in the trees that lined the old streets headed downtown.

Preoccupied, she passed the library, the courthouse, a row of bars. The streets were busy now, after three o'clock on a school day. Grand Avenue was backed up a few blocks. She avoided it with an automatic swerve, heading down First

Street between the railroad tracks and the oldest run-down shops.

At a red light, two boys with jacked-up pickups revved in front of her, daring each other to race at the green. They settled for roaring starts and a few miles an hour above the speed limit. Darcy had dated boys like that, ranch kids and would-be cowboys, the ones who would never escape from Laramie. Her first sex had been in the back of a pickup under a gun rack, looking up at the stars on top of one of the Sherman hills. Maybe that was all that fascinated her about Paul Delacache: he was different from Laramie boys. She couldn't imagine him wearing a tractor-brand farmer hat or two-stepping in the Cowboy Bar. That lingering scent of his presence was probably just the old allure of city lights.

Why had she stayed in Laramie? It was a recurring question. She had had her chance a year ago when her father moved to Denver. Her excuse then had been that she didn't want to change schools and pay out-of-state tuition. But that reason no longer convinced her. There was something about this place that was holding onto her, something she didn't want to leave. The few times she had gone on vacations she had been nervous and uncomfortable the whole time, like a Snowy Range lake trout forced to swim in some eastern aquarium where the water wasn't cold enough.

The red lights stopped her more frequently now as she approached the interstate, passing motels and fast-food restaurants and gas stations. The Motel 6 parking lot was right beside the off-ramp. It would be like sleeping through a series of small earthquakes, to stay there with the big trucks passing through the night. The parking lot was nearly empty now; too early for anyone to pull in off the freeway. There were no cars near the motel office, but a man was standing on the porch, his face shaded by a black hat with feathers in the brim. Darcy pulled her car in beside the office, noticing the big dog that stood next to the man, its nose pushing at his hand. For a long moment she was sure it was a coyote, the same ragged-eared coyote that had led her into the tomb in the rocks this morning. She saw a glint of mischievous eyes, but then the animal shook itself and she could tell that it was only a gray and white Border collie with pricked-up ears.

She hadn't known that Charlie Stone was a Native American. He lifted his head as she got out of her Subaru, and she saw the braids hanging down beside his dark, broad-boned face. She felt immediately nervous and unsure of herself. Should she say something—So, what tribe are you from?—or would that be impolite? She decided to ignore his hat and his tall moccasin boots, his defiantly long hair, his flat, challenging gaze. He was young, maybe four or five years older than her, and that made her nervous too. She had expected some old hand, weathered and wrinkled, stubborn, with years of experience.

"Hello, I'm Darcy Jacobi, from the Kennan ranch. You're Mr. Stone?" She stepped up onto the porch and looked for his bags. There weren't any. Just a heavy oiled raincoat folded over the railing.

"Charlie," he said. They shook hands. He was a short, stocky man, only an inch or two taller than Darcy in his flat-soled boots, with shoulders as wide as a wrestler's. He took up the whole porch, though, in a sense Darcy couldn't explain. She felt like an intruder standing in front of him. There was an edge to him, a quiet intensity, that reminded her of the Vietnam veterans she knew; he was too young to have been in the war, but he had the same feeling about him. He might be on alert, waiting for the next bomb to hit or a sniper to spring out from ambush. Stop it, Darcy told herself. Your imagination is out of control today.

"There's room in back for your dog." She went back to her car and opened the passenger door. "I thought he was a coyote at first. Funny thing. I saw one up in the hills today and it stayed with me, I guess."

"He's a motel dog." Charlie got in and threw his coat in the back. The dog whined in its throat, but stayed on the porch.

Darcy drove them out onto the highway to loop around Laramie and up toward the summit. Her passenger's presence filled Darcy's car like smoke from a brush fire, but he only sat and looked quietly out the window. His profile beneath his hat brim was like a painting, or an old coin, red-brown with eyes that squinted slightly as if focused far away on the hilltops.

"Did you come in on the bus or the train?" Darcy said after five miles, the words forced out of her like squeezed toothpaste.

"Walked, mostly, and got some rides," Charlie said.

She had seen the caked mud on his soft boots, but hadn't made the connection. "I hope you weren't out in the storm last night. It was pretty scary where we were."

"I saw a tree struck by the lightning, but it only burned for a minute. I was more wet than scared." He turned toward her with a slight smile. It had a strange effect on her, a prickling at the back of her neck, a sense of déjà vu, dream or memory or both. She had seen him smile before. She knew what his laugh would sound like when he laughed. That was as far as the memory went, if it was a memory. Yet Darcy was certain she had never met Charlie Stone before today.

"Storms scare me," she said, looking steadily at the highway, pushing her gas pedal to the floor to urge the Subaru to climb toward the summit. She passed a truck at thirty miles per hour and pulled to the right to let an old Chrysler with a V-8 engine roar by her. "I was caught out in a snowstorm for an hour this morning. I thought it was going to be a blizzard. We were miles from the ranch house." She shivered, remembering the long ride home with Ed Kennan sleepy and cold on his stiff-legged mare.

"That was where you saw the coyote? Strange for one to be out in the middle of the day."

"It was a strange coyote. It almost seemed like it could talk to me if it wanted to . . ." She glanced at him in apology. "At least that's what I thought. When I was little I had an imaginary coyote for a friend."

The Subaru whined as it struggled up to the summit. Charlie was a profile again, gazing up at the stubborn pines on the top of the road-cut cliffs. They passed the bridge that led to a rest area and the Happy Jack road into the national forest.

"Look." Darcy nodded over her shoulder as she drove. "There's the Lincoln memorial. A sculptor from Laramie carved it. That's why they call this the Lincoln Highway. It always seemed silly to me, way out here. Lincoln never went further west than St. Louis."

The somber bust on a granite-block pedestal glared down at the road as if condemning the passing cars for some sinful behavior. At night it was lit by spotlights from below and looked more like a devil's face than Honest Abe. The jutting eyebrows stuck out like a natural rock formation; a much less serene Lincoln than the one at Mount Rushmore.

Darcy remembered the stone faces of Rushmore from her trip there as a Girl Scout, but more like a postcard picture than as any carved mountain she had actually seen. Once when she had been writing an autobiographical essay for school, she had tried to recall details and had been almost frightened at the collage of strung-together holes that were all she recalled of that trip. A moment of effort now produced an image of a campfire in deep woods, but that was impossible. The Girl Scouts had slept in a church basement.

"He always seemed so out of place here. Lincoln, I mean." The monument had vanished as they turned down the sloping road away from the highest point. "Like something transplanted. Even if he is made out of the same kind of granite as the Vedauwoo rocks."

"What was his name?" Charlie Stone asked, turning around now to look at her with his sharp eyes. "The coyote you had for a friend, when you were a child?"

Now she could see the dark humps of Vedauwoo among the yellow hills below them. "His name?" Darcy laughed self-consciously. "I just called him Coyote."

"He isn't a child's companion, not in my people's stories. More the kind of person parents would tell children to avoid."

"I don't remember much about my invisible Coyote. Just that I had him for a couple of years, and it worried my parents." She remembered her class today, and took the chance to ask him, "Do you know many of the old stories, the Indian legends? I'm supposed to try to find out about some of them. Are there any legends set around here? Especially around Vedauwoo. It's for a class I'm in."

Charlie's hand touched a place on his yellow flannel shirt, around his breastbone. Something bulged there, and Darcy thought of the medicine bag she kept on her bedpost. He seemed unconscious of the gesture, but he was quiet for a moment with his fingers lightly pressed against the fabric. "There is a legend," he said slowly. "I think you may have heard it before. One of the Coyote stories."

"I'd like to hear it sometime, if it wouldn't be much trouble." Talking about stories embarrassed her oddly. It seemed a childish thing to do. Investigating Indian legends wasn't her idea as much as it was Paul's. But it would be nice to have something to talk about with Paul tomorrow night.

"It is a long tale." He seemed nervous, and eager somehow, and Darcy felt uneasy again. Was she intruding, to ask about his people's stories? But he had brought it up with his talk of Coyote. "A matter of three or four nights. If you like we could begin tonight."

"After dinner? I'm sure Ed and Alice would enjoy it."

"No." He touched the place on his breast again and looked

down at his hand this time. He let it fall into his lap. "This is . . . a story that can only be told to one person. There must be no distractions." He glanced at her and smiled slightly again. "That's the tradition, anyway. I hope you don't mind."

"You could start now," she suggested. "We have eleven miles to go to the ranch." Her curiosity was growing.

"No. Tonight, alone, and somewhere outside. I'll find a place." He turned away from her completely now, seeming to draw inside himself. Darcy laughed at herself, silently. She was as impatient now as a six-year-old promised something new at bedtime. Bedtime was still hours away, and she would have to wait.

# CHAPTER FOUR

---

Under the pine trees it grew dark quickly. Old dead needles pricked at Charlie's jeans as he sat cross-legged, his back against the cold stone of a granite boulder. The morning snow had melted here, but the cold was thickening in the dusk. He leaned over to add more wood to the small campfire. Along with the smoke, steam rising from a cup of hot chocolate drifted over Darcy's face, reflecting the light, filtering over her laughter and talk. They sat at the top of the hill that led down to Charlie's trailer, with a clear view of the Vedauwoo rocks. The rocks were shadowed and silent and revealed nothing. What could the old tale mean to her, Charlie wondered, without the knowledge that the wendigo were real?

"Alice wants to start working the yearlings." Darcy had been talking about the Kennan horses, polite conversation with the new wrangler. She must assume that was his main interest. "You'll enjoy them. They're untrained but they've been gentled to be comfortable with people. I'll introduce you tomorrow morning."

She would need to be gentled too, he thought, to be comfortable with him again. She was quick to smile and her talk was quick, like a bird's chatter to distract a cat from a nest. He could see the nervousness in her shoulders and neck when she moved slightly to drink her hot chocolate. She was made nervous by his dark skin, by his Indian clothes, by the guilty, fearful emotion an Indian's presence sometimes aroused in white people. Maybe she was wondering if he was going to make a pass at her, and whether it would be polite to reject him or if it would make her seem racist.

He answered her. "It will be good to handle young horses again. My last job was with a couple of pampered old stallions. Aristocrats, set in their ways, and as wild as fighting dogs. To try to get them to learning something new . . ."

"Alice doesn't put up with anything like that from Amahl." The ranch's only resident stallion was a large-boned dapple Arabian with a beautiful head, the foundation of the Kennan herd to come; Charlie had been introduced to him and the broodmares earlier this evening. He had eaten a pleasant meal with his new employers, but he remembered little of what Ed or Alice had said.

Darcy picked up a long twig to poke at the fire. Charlie watched her face, pale in the firelight, shadowed under thick brown hair that had fallen forward around her cheeks. She had grown up since he had seen her last, frightened and dazed in her hospital bed, thirteen years old. Her features were sharper now, like a fox or coyote, with arched eyebrows and a long, thin nose. She would seem beautiful to some men and plain to others. Charlie found it hard to decide for himself. A younger, rounder face kept interposing.

When they had reached the ranch, she had given him a hurried tour before the students showed up for her class. Charlie had found himself watching from the railing of the arena, fascinated, while Darcy led her serious young charges through the mysteries of the hunt seat and jumping style. She rode like an old-time warrior, firm in her saddle, finely balanced, demanding obedience with the slightest cues to her spirited red pony. The students were eager to please her. She was doing well in this life, this ordinary, hardworking, quiet life she had escaped into. Charlie wished he could leave her there. He wished he could choose not to pull her back into the shadows with him. Leave her there in the sun, with her hair tossing as her pony sailed over fences that made the long-legged young hunters balk.

Her chatter had stopped and she seemed calmer now. Charlie settled comfortably against the smooth boulder and touched his medicine bag under his shirt. "Here is the story."

"One winter long ago, the people of the plains huddled together in their houses of earth and grass and listened to the howling of wind and wolves in the hills around them. They had little to eat. The birds were gone. The small animals slept under the earth, and the fish stayed in the deep, slow waters beneath the ice of rivers and ponds. Bears and wolves watched the trails for lone hunters. Like the people, deer and antelope sickened and starved. They ate pine branches and pawed through the snow for dry grasses.

"Coyote walked in the forest day after day. His tail hung low and sometimes dragged on the ground, brushing twigs and dead leaves across the snow. He was so hungry that he began to hunt close to the people, hoping to steal some morsel of food. One day he saw three brothers out fishing. They had cut a hole in the ice, and as he watched they drew five small fish out on a trapline. When they left, Coyote slid onto the river and made his way to the hole. It had already frozen over, and when he tried to dig it clear the cold hurt his paws. He sat on his cold tail on the ice and howled. He kept howling until a big gray wolf came to the riverbank and spoke to him.

" 'What has happened, little brother?' said the wolf, scratching its jaw with one hind leg.

" 'I am starving,' Coyote howled. 'There is nothing to eat. I would rather die than be this hungry all the time.'

" 'If you have the strength to run, I will show you a place where you can get plenty of food,' said the wolf, showing its teeth in a wolf smile.

"Coyote said that he could run all day if he had to. The wolf led him away over the hills, for a day and a night of running through the snow. It was clear that the wolf had eaten well, because it never stopped to hunt. It only drank a little from the fast-running mountain streams that had never frozen over, and then ran on. Coyote was faint with hunger by the time they reached the place where the wolf's friends lived.

"It was a deep valley surrounded by hills of great rocks, and the people lived there all alone. No other tribes were near them. Coyote could smell cooked meat, antelope and buffalo, and he went down into the valley eagerly at the heels of the wolf. He saw that the people had thrown bunches of green grass, green as summer, over the snow, and many animals were there eating the grass. As they passed the animals, the wolf got up on its hind legs and began to walk like a man. Soon it had changed itself into a painted shaman, and the man turned and beckoned to Coyote.

"Afraid, for he knew that this was great magic, Coyote followed the wolf man into the camp of the rock valley tribe. There he was allowed to join in a great feast. He ate so much that his belly was like a drum stretched tight under his fur. As he lay by the fire he heard the rock valley people telling stories of the new place they had found. There was a door in the rocks, where they could go through and gather green grass from a strange world. It was not a human place, and the people who gathered the grass there had changed. That was where the shaman had learned to turn himself into a wolf.

" 'You have such good fortune here,' Coyote said, feeling shy after his good meal. 'I wonder if you could help the people I know. They are starving on the plains.'

" 'Go and bring them here,' said the shaman with a wolf smile. 'We will give them a great feast, and then as much food as they can carry to take home with them.' The people around the fire also smiled and said that they would be happy to help Coyote's friends.

"So Coyote trotted back over the hills, moving slowly because he was so full of meat. When he reached his country again, he found the three brothers fishing once more in the icy stream. This time no fish had come to their lures, and they sat quietly and without much hope dangling lines into their holes.

"When they saw Coyote they were going to shoot him, but he hid behind a tree and called out to them. He told them what he had seen in the rock valley, and promised to lead them there, and all their people if they wished. The brothers argued among themselves until at last the youngest said, 'I will go with you. I think I am strong enough to make it over the hills.'

" 'We will go, we three,' said the oldest brother. 'But none of our people can walk that far. We will have to carry the food back for them.'

" 'If it is true that these people will help us,' said the middle brother. 'Who would share their food in this horrible winter? With a tribe they do not know?'

" 'You will see,' Coyote said eagerly. 'They are good people. And there are so many animals there that you might take ten antelope home with you and they would not be missed.' "

"So Coyote led the brothers along the path where the wolf had led him. They stopped to drink from icy streams, and climbed harsh hillsides in the bitter wind. It was three days before they reached the place where the rocks sheltered the valley people."

"The rock valley is Vedauwoo, isn't it?" Darcy asked. She sat with her arms around her knees, staring into the fire. "And the people there are evil, in the story." She was shivering.

"Yes." Charlie had been watching her, and he did not like the way she was reacting to his words. She looked troubled, half-frightened, glancing over toward the dark Vedauwoo hills and back behind her shoulder into the woods. Somewhere in her mind were memories of the first time she had heard this story, unpleasant memories. It wasn't hard for Charlie to go back. He needed only to let Darcy's face blur in the gloom, and remember her sitting that same way in front of his campfire, arms wrapped around herself, not speaking, scarcely thinking. She had been half-wild when he had found her, so terrified that she did not know her own name.

"But this time when Coyote walked down into the valley he saw only a few animals. The three hunters wondered if he had been lying about the herds of antelope and buffalo, and if he might have been lying about the rock valley people too. But they had come a long way to get food, and they were brave young men. They lashed their bows and arrows to their backs as a sign of peace and walked into the camp with open hands . . ."

Charlie did not know if the story was helping. The little girl had stopped crying, but she might just be exhausted. For all he knew she might not speak English. Plenty of foreign tourists came to Mount Rushmore in the summertime. Whenever he tried to sit beside her she would get up, hunched over and trembling, and move to the other side of the fire.

He did not know why she had gone off by herself into the forest. The lights of the park and the highway were miles away. She must have walked for hours before she was attacked. Charlie had heard her screaming, breaking the silence of five weeks of tracking and cornering the wendigo. He had come to the Black Hills on the trail of stories about dead hikers and a ranger who had gone mad and shot and killed his partner and himself in the deep woods. He had known the wendigo was out there; at last he had found it.

Nine or ten years old, the girl was scratched and battered from running headlong through juniper and thistle in the meadows, but when she was caught she fought the wendigo with all her strength. She was unhurt when Charlie rushed in to pull her away and finish his enemy himself.

"There was not as much food as there had been the night Coyote had feasted there. Yet no one went hungry, and the three brothers went to sleep well satisfied that the people of their tribe would survive with their new friends' help. Coyote curled up at the side of the youngest brother, sharing the warmth of his blanket. The fires of the camp went out and the night stars showed in a band of sky over the narrow valley."

The little girl looked up at this, but the trees were too thick over their heads to see the stars. Charlie looked with her, silent for a moment, hoping she would speak. She understood his words at least. Her hand went up to pull a few leaves from her tangled hair, but her face was still closed up and frightened.

"As the hunters and Coyote slept, they did not hear the wolf shaman and his friends talking together in a nearby tipi.

" 'The meat is sure to be stringy and tough,' said one. 'We will have to boil it in a stew for any flavor at all.'

" 'I will roast the hearts myself,' said the wolf man. 'They are brave young men, and they will give me strength.'

" 'My hunger is so great,' sighed another. 'Each time I go into the green world and come out again I need more food, more food. I have eaten enough for ten fat men this past moon, yet I am as lean as that skinny coyote.'

"But the sleeping hunters heard nothing, and so the oldest brother had no fear when one of the young women of the tribe crept to his blankets and asked if he would like to come with her to her tipi. He only thought that this was great hospitality, and he gathered his bow and arrows and blankets and went with her gladly. So the middle brother went with another woman when she came to him two hours later.

"A little before dawn the youngest brother awoke, feeling cold. He reached out and felt no one but the coyote lying beside him in the darkness. 'Coyote,' he whispered. 'Wake up. Where are my brothers?'

" 'They went off with pretty women,' Coyote said, laughing a little, still mostly asleep. 'Do not embarrass them. They should be back in their sleeping places soon, before the camp wakes up.' He rolled over and stretched his front legs out straight across his nose to sleep some more.

"The youngest brother stood up and rolled his blanket quickly. He tied it around his waist and took up his bow and arrows. 'Coyote, get up. Help me find my brothers.'

" 'They might wish to stay lost.' Coyote got his back feet under him and got up slowly, shaking one stiff leg. But he followed the boy as they peered into the nearest tipi. It was empty. The sleeping blankets were rolled on one side and the fire was out. The next tipi was also abandoned, and the next. Where were the people? Where could they have gone?"

Charlie looked expectantly at the child. He remembered himself when he had first heard this story, bouncing eagerly on his heels, answering the moment he heard a question: *to the otherworld, to the green world.* He had known what the people in the story were doing and what Coyote and the young hero would discover. But the little girl only watched the fire and clutched her scratched knees with her hands.

"They had gone through the door to the otherworld, the

green world," Charlie said quietly, letting his words rise with the smoke, perhaps unheard. "Coyote and the boy followed the tracks of the people. Some had human footprints and some the pawprints of large animals, wolves and bears and cougars. The tracks led to a deep cave in the boulders. The boy was frightened, but he was about to go inside when a man of the rock valley people came out.

"The man was carrying part of a joint of meat. It looked like an antelope's leg and it was half-eaten. He grinned at the boy and waved a hand toward the cave. 'Go on in and share in the feast.' He passed them and the boy started into the dark opening. But Coyote sat down on his tail and howled. The boy stopped to ask him what was the matter.

" 'I have a long nose. I can smell what a thing is and what it is not. That meat is not from an animal.' Coyote howled again in terror.

" 'My brothers?' said the boy. 'I will kill these murderers!' But Coyote caught his loincloth in his teeth and dragged him back.

" 'We cannot fight them. There are too many and they are sorcerors. Climb on my back, for we must run faster then any man now.'

"The boy was weeping, but he sat on Coyote's back and leaned down to hold onto his fur. Coyote sprang away into the darkness just as the wolf shaman came bounding out to find the last victim for his terrible feast.

"Coyote ran and ran with the wolf behind him, over the hills, across the streams, far away from the evil valley. Once the boy shot an arrow at the wolf, but the sorceror caught it between his teeth and grinned and ran on. But the further they got from the rock valley, the weaker the wolf's power was, until at last he could not run. Besides, he had not eaten much yet that morning, and he was terribly hungry. He turned around and hurried back to join in the feast in the cave with his people.

"Instead of returning to the plains where the boy lived with his tribe, Coyote went into the hills under the great mountains. The boy told the people what the rock valley tribe had done, and warriors quickly armed themselves and rode after Coyote. Thus they went from village to village, from tribe to tribe, until they reached the great stone circle where the Council of Elders had come together to meet and talk. They told all their story then. And the warriors and the Elders decided what must be done."

The girl's head was nodding and her eyes were blinking heavily. Charlie decided that was enough of the story for one telling. He wrapped the child in another blanket and picked her up in his arms to carry her into the rough pine-branch shelter he had built her. She did not struggle, but she was wary in his arms, like a wounded wild animal. She did not seem to fear him quite as much as she had before. He settled her into the blankets and stroked her hair softly.

"I'll take you home soon, little warrior," he said. "But I have to know who you are first, and where your home is. Sleep now. Maybe in the morning you'll remember."

"That's all for one night's fire," Charlie said, looking warily over at the Darcy who sat and watched the Vedauwoo hills. "If told any more you wouldn't remember it all."

"You remember it very well," she said. "It hardly seemed like your voice. More like someone out of the past. From a long time ago." Her voice was thoughtful.

Stirring the fire, Charlie knocked sparks from a blackened piece of wood. "I heard it many times when I was a child."

"It hardly seems like a children's story. Cannibalism, starvation, an evil otherworld that turns people bad." She smiled and shook her head. "It's likely to give me nightmares."

"No worse than some of your European fairy tales."

"Maybe not." She brushed pine needles from her legs as she stood up. "I need to get to my books for a couple of hours before bedtime. Morning comes early around here. I'll see you then.".

He looked up, trying to read her cheerful face in the shadows of the trees. Had he awakened any part of her? "Tomorrow night will you listen to the rest of the story?" he asked.

"Sure. I want to know what the warriors and the Elders are going to do . . ." Her smile faded for a moment. "Oh. I can't, Charlie. I'm going out tomorrow night. I won't be back until late."

"Saturday morning, then, after the animals are fed. Maybe we could ride out together. Show me the ranch boundaries, and I'll finish the story as we ride."

"Sure. That's great. Well, I'll see you in the morning."

"Good night."

She walked away down the hill toward her car. Charlie listened to the motor start, the door close, the vehicle shift gears as she drove away. The silence of the night drew quickly around him when the car noise was gone. Pines muffled sound, with no autumn-dry leaves to rustle in the cold wind. The soft splash and fall of the water in the narrow stream below him was all he could hear, and it seemed very far away.

He had stopped feeding the fire, and now he watched the flames die down until they only lapped small tongues around the charred wood. The cold numbed his hands and made his skin feel dull, his body hollow. "Maybe I failed with her already," he said softly to the shadows behind the trees. "I should have guarded her, kept her with me, from the beginning." He had slept in front of the shelter that night in the Black Hills, and wakened at dawn to find the child watching him with blank eyes. She had eaten when he fed her, but she still did not speak, nor appear to think.

He had attempted a healing ceremony, singing over her, but that had never been his path; he was a hunter, a killer, not one who could mend broken things. It was not until Coyote had come without being called that the girl's eyes began to brighten once more. Coyote in the body of a pup, prancing and begging her to play, with old eyes in a big-eared head. Charlie had only watched and wondered. Who was the child, what was she, that one of the animal guides would appear to her in daylight to try to charm her back to herself?

She had listened to the rest of the story that night with Coyote curled in her lap, his nose under the blankets. Charlie had felt very strange telling the tale with one of its heroes listening with perked puppy ears. When he put the girl to bed she had finally spoken, a few soft words only: "It wanted to hurt me. I was scared . . ."

"You were very brave," Charlie said. "Don't be afraid anymore. The wendigo is gone, I killed it, and Coyote is here with you. Tomorrow perhaps I will take you home."

The moon was rising over the hills, a half-crescent that looked like a frozen smile. Cold had stiffened Charlie's legs. He shook them out like Coyote in the story and kicked dirt and pine needles over the last gleams of fire. He felt as uncertain of his path as he had those three days ten years ago. How could he get nearer to the hidden memories in Darcy; how could he awaken her without doing great harm?

He walked down the hill, scuffing his boots in the loose dirt. The moon hovered over his shoulder, seeming to mock him. He paused to bow to it, a stiff, correct bow like they had taught him in the missionaries' school. "Grandfather," he said with sarcasm, not homage. "Surprised to see me here on yet another night? You should be used to it by now."

The refrigerator hummed to greet him when he entered the old trailer. The floor creaked, a slightly metallic sound, and the electric light made sharp-edged shadows around table and chairs. Charlie went to the room in back and took off his boots and jacket. He pulled the thong of his medicine bag over his head and hung the bag on the bedpost. His thin stone knife, hidden in an army-surplus sheath, went under the sheets close to his right hand. He lay down on the bed and stared up at the age-spotted blue paint on the ceiling. It did not matter how sorry he felt for the girl. He would not throw away a weapon he needed because it was too bright and pretty to be used in battle. He let himself drift, and kept her image in front of him; when she slept tonight, he would be waiting to guide her dreams.

# CHAPTER FIVE

inger joints burned and hands shook, scraped raw by rock, clutching and releasing, holding now half her weight, now all of it. She climbed on, aware that they were watching and waiting for her to fall. If the rock would only remain the solid, sheer mass she had begun to climb, if it would not stretch and grow toward the orange-domed sky even as she reached what should have been the top: a lip of rock only, with a ledge to crawl onto, to rest gasping for a beat, another beat, while below they gloated that she must soon fail. They did not chase her here, however. They waited. If she wanted a place safe from them she might live here on this ledge, climbing up or climbing down to hunt for food and to search for a way to escape. They would grow bored of watching her, but how long would that take—she was weakening day by day, more and more fragile in this hollow world, this unnatural, unearthly place.

Darcy surfaced from her dream for a cloudy moment, long enough to wonder who she was and what she was doing in a teenage boy's body in a strange landscape of cliffs and chasms and watchful deadly enemies. Then she returned, falling back into pain and exhaustion and gasping, pounding rhythm of breathing and heartbeat.

Bristled fur lifted against the palm of her hand; Coyote growled as they crouched together, hiding in a soft-sided sloping hole like a badger's den. They had found it just before the hunt burst out behind them, but the running wendigo had not seen them wriggle into the earth there; the heavy footfalls thudded overhead and knocked down sprays of earth and clods that covered her face and made her want to sneeze. Coyote's body was big and warm against hers and made her feel safe, safer than she did when she was alone. Sometimes Coyote left her for weeks, even months, and returned phantomlike in the midst of a battle when she was about to lose heart and let the madness take her.

Her lungs ached, a deeper ache each day she breathed the thin, hazy air; they were starving slowly, leaving her like a summer fish whose pond was inexorably drying, weakly flopping from puddle to puddle. The air did not bother Coyote, but then he was not real, not living flesh, even though she could feel his warmth and the weight of him next to her, even though she could stroke his fur and smell the oily, dusty animal smell of him. His torn left ear drooped over his eye, half-healed, the wound still slick with pus although the ear had been torn in a battle a hundred years before.

"Out of here," Coyote said in his whining, catlike voice. "They are doubling back, they'll find you if you stay. Quick, boy."

Her ribs still thudded with her thick, aching heart; her breath was fast and deep, a knifing pain with every lungful. "Can't run." But she pulled herself up to the crumbled opening of the animal den and saw the shimmer of power and malice that was the wendigo band in the distance, turning the air blue before them as they ran back this way again. "Coyote, how can I . . ." She looked back and saw that he had faded again.

Grinning at the bottom of the hole was his bleak fleshless skull, teeth sharp and parted as if to speak, no wise shifting eyes or matted ear, no other bones but the skull, and it was not even really here; she knew where it was, in the canyon where they had killed him, taunting them with its power. Angry, she kicked at the skull, watched it fall back into clods of dirt. No help there. She had to climb out and run again in the red dust. They were coming, she could hear their cries. She scrambled up and out and ran staggering like a drunk, all her muscles afire and the chant pounding in her head with her heavy, clumsy feet: How long, how long, how long . . .

Darcy waked with strange memories of the night, of dreams that must have been prompted by Charlie's Coyote legend. She still felt an ache in her lungs, but it was gone by the time she was dressed and outside for morning chores. It was pleasant to get the horses pastured and fed quickly, with Charlie to help, and they were back at the Kennans' for breakfast before the pink streaks of sunrise were gone from the cold October sky.

Ed was cheerful this morning, ready to tell Charlie about his aliens so the new wrangler could keep a watch out for them as he rode around the ranch. They had landed, Ed was pretty sure, and he needed to find them. "Burned circles in the grass, probably," Ed said. His mouth was rimmed with orange juice and Darcy found it funny to watch how quietly and respectfully Charlie listened, the way he nodded and did not smile at all.

"You'd think these aliens would talk to someone else sometime," Alice said, "or leave some physical evidence to convince people." She had told Darcy yesterday that she did not know if she wanted the aliens to be real or not. If they were real they were too frightening, and if they weren't then her husband was crazy.

"Physical evidence." Ed scowled, not angry at her. "You can fool people pretty well with pictures and fake footprints. Did you see a couple of weeks ago, a salmon's head on a dried-out monkey body—some wise guy stuck it together and sent a picture of it to that supermarket paper, and they were calling it scientific proof?"

"But if you had a photograph people might take you seriously." Charlie leaned thoughtfully on the table. "Why haven't you taken any pictures of your friends?"

"Never seen them." Ed shrugged. "Just voices, presences I feel. But I know who they are. Who else could they be? There's proof. There's the water I found on my ranch. They told me where to dig the well."

There was a lot of underground water in these arid hills, Darcy thought. He probably could have drawn lines on a map at random and drilled for water at the first intersection. But Charlie was nodding, sober, interested. He had seemed to mostly believe in the legend he told her last night; maybe UFOs were no problem for him. Darcy had left all that behind with Santa Claus.

"I haven't introduced you to all the horses yet," Darcy said, standing up and pulling her jacket on again. "Want to get started with the colts?"

"Sure." Charlie took his dishes to the sink and turned back to Ed. "I'll keep an eye out when I'm up in the hills, Mr. Kennan. Maybe later today I'll have time to do a little exploring."

"I don't know," Ed was muttering as they left the room. "It might scare them off to have people poking around . . ."

"Are you taking him seriously?" Darcy asked softly after closing the front door.

Charlie adjusted his hat so the crown shadowed his eyes.

"Things happen in these mountains. I don't know who has been talking to that old man."

"But little green men . . ."

"The Shoshone believed that a race of little men lived in the mountains. They were supposed to be the first inhabitants. They were like African Pygmies. Used to shoot people with poisoned arrows." He finally smiled. "Maybe they were from outer space too."

Darcy laughed and led him across the yard to the corral where the year-old colts pranced, waiting to be trained.

The dark-paneled living room was hazy with marijuana smoke, and Darcy sat uncomfortably on a straight-backed couch, blinking her eyes and waiting for Paul Delacache to come back from the kitchen with drinks. The party had been crowded already when they arrived at eight o'clock; mostly men and women in their thirties and forties with long, serious faces bracketed by straight shoulder-length hair. There were a few beards, a few black and Asian faces, a few students Darcy's age, but no one she knew. She felt as if she had come to visit an asylum for aimless sixties leftovers. New Age harp music meandered through the smoky air.

That afternoon at four she had met Paul in the lab where he worked. He was finishing up a hypnosis session with a volunteer freshman; Darcy had watched through a glass window as he brought the blond girl into a yawning awareness of the world again. The glass was one-way and Paul did not see her even when he looked straight at her. He seemed unreal there, silent and austere in his white lab coat. He still reminded her of a painting or a sculpture, too disturbingly handsome to be human.

They had gone to a Mexican food place out in West Laramie and then to a French cafe downtown for espresso and dessert. Darcy had spent four hours with him now and she did not think she knew any more about him. They had talked about books and movies. Paul had read a lot of contemporary fiction and had seen almost every movie that had come out in the past two years, indiscriminately, from slasher films to conversational sleepers to experimental art films. He knew all the theaters in Fort Collins and Denver. It seemed to go along with his psychological research: observing people, what they did, what they created, outside of any feeling for craft or style.

He hadn't told her much about the party. It was at Dr. Ghormley's house, which made Darcy uneasy from her first step inside. She hadn't been here since Laura died in the crash. Even before that, she and Laura had mostly met at Darcy's house. Dr. Ghormley's house was in the old, tree-filled part of Laramie. It was a Victorian with a maze of small dark rooms and heavy drapes and narrow stairways, and it had always made Darcy feel trapped, as if something was going to come out from behind a door and jump on her. Laura had been convinced the house was haunted by the ghost of the previous owner, an old woman who had died on the toilet upstairs.

In the room where she sat now, a fire was burning in the mahoghany fireplace, and candles flickered on tables. Shadows stretched out dimly from people sitting in groups on the Persian rug or standing by the burgundy drapes of the window. On the couch beside Darcy a woman was laying out tarot cards while two young men watched intently from the floor. The woman was an artificial blonde with olive skin and heavy silver jewelry, plump in her Gypsy skirt and low-cut red blouse. She wore perfume that reminded Darcy of the incense at a Catholic funeral she had attended last year.

"You'll meet her soon," she said in a teasing voice to one of the men. "But not here, on some journey. The Queen of Cups awaits her messenger."

"Nothing deeper than that, Ariadne?" the other man said, unimpressed.

"The cards are shallow tonight, dear. Or maybe the two of you. Thoughts too much on worldly matters, hmmm?"

Paul passed through the crowd in the narrow doorway and came to Darcy holding out a paper cup of red wine. "Is this okay? You said you didn't want beer." He looked for space on the couch and sank down gracefully to the rug in front of her. The tarot reader had made a small startled movement when he approached, and now she turned to him and smiled, making lines in her thick, pale makeup.

"Paul, dear, you didn't introduce your friend. Perhaps I could read for her?" She raised a penciled eyebrow at Darcy.

"Darcy Jacobi . . . Ariadne." Paul made a slight bow from where he sat. "Certainly, read for her. It might be interesting."

The plump woman shifted in the other direction on the couch so she faced Darcy with space between them for the cards. She had gathered them up from the previous reading, and now she handed them to Darcy to be shuffled. "Is there a question you want answered?"

Paul answered for her. "No specific question. A life reading, potentials and future possibilities. No dark strangers." He grinned at Darcy; that much would have been true. Two dark strangers, she thought, Paul and Charlie Stone. What would Charlie say about all this? That the Indians had a legend about pseudo-Gypsies with cards, and anything was possible?

Darcy sipped her wine, which was smoky, bitter stuff, not to her taste at all. The marijuana fumes were going to her head, she decided. The room had begun to close in on her, and Paul was looking slightly strange, his outline blurred, his eyes oddly shadowed as if darkening from green to black. She watched the cards placed deliberately one by one in a sort of crossed circle, and wondered if Ariadne was supposed to be reading her mind. She didn't feel any connection with the woman sitting across from her, her weight dimpling the firm couch cushion. Ariadne might not have been there at all.

Paul was certainly there, though. She was strongly aware of him, physically aware, as she had been the first time she saw him in the graduate lounge. Her eyes kept drifting to his face and glancing away again to the odd symbols of the tarot cards.

Ariadne was frowning, putting the last few cards down on top of each other in the center. "Secrets, hiding," she muttered. "The Popess guarding her mysteries. The Tower, the moon hidden ... the Lovers, but reversed. Strange. And so many power cards, if I didn't know I'd say I was reading you, dear Paul, not your girlfriend. She's had no training, I must assume. You should remedy that soon."

"What do you mean?" Darcy said almost sleepily, lulled by the nonsensical phrases the woman strung together.

"I mean that you are a wild psychic talent," Ariadne said sternly, her mascara-rimmed eyes fixed on Darcy. "Your energies are terribly strong, and totally uncontrolled. You could be a danger to yourself and to people who are close to you unless you get some training, some control. If you don't retreat into further denial. Nothing could be more dangerous than that."

"Psychic talent?" Darcy swallowed a sip of wine and could not suppress a giggle. "You mean I could read minds or bend spoons, that sort of thing?"

"You see?" Ariadne said with a dramatic look at Paul. "Denial, trivialization, and yet I read more power in her than in a dozen of our Society novices Dr. Ghormley has so carefully chosen. Why has she been so neglected?"

"Perhaps she has turned some of her power into defensive walls," Paul said. "She's closed to most of my awareness. But I began to wonder yesterday when I learned that she was born at Vedauwoo, in the rocks."

The woman's reaction was almost violent; she gasped and a hand went to her breast as if she had just learned that Darcy was a notorious axe murderer. "Then she could be a guardian?"

Paul shook his head, some sort of warning in his expression. "Leave it for now, Ariadne. We'll see. She's my guest at this party tonight, that's all." He reached out a hand and Darcy took it after a moment's hesitation. He helped her rise from the couch. "There's music and dancing in the backyard. Want to check it out?"

"Sure." Darcy walked with him, shaking off her bewilderment. "What was all that? Did you take what she was saying seriously?"

"Ariadne tends to the melodramatic. But she does have insight." He guided her through the honeycomb of rooms. "We can talk about it later if you like. But I'm bored with sitting around, aren't you?"


The backyard was small, like another room, with a high wooden fence and severe hedges around the sides. The night was cold, but the wind had been stopped by the fence, and Darcy felt warmed by the wine. She glanced up: the sky was clear with a few stars shining through the Laramie night. A portable compact disc player had been set up on a picnic table on the patio. The music was mostly drums, heavy syncopated beats, African or Caribbean, with wailing flutes and the tinny sound of a thumb piano or a muted xylophone. Couples were dancing in a rough circle, the women facing out and the men facing in, but the dancing looked like what Darcy was used to at the rock clubs in Denver.

Someone made room for them, and then she was moving to the music, feeling dizzy and strange, watching Paul. He danced in front of her but just far enough away that they did not touch. His bushy black hair swung around his forehead and ears, and his pine-green eyes kept flashing back to her even when he crouched or spun. He was a good dancer. Even his sharp movements with the syncopation were graceful, smooth, as if choreographed. Other people were watching him, Darcy realized. Some of them stopped dancing. Paul seemed absorbed into the music, becoming something else, dark and dangerous like the echo of voodoo in the throbbing of the drums.

Paul danced, leaping and twisting, watching her. The air was close and cold around her, as if she had thrown off her blankets while she was sleeping and could not move to retrieve them. Her vision narrowed until she could see nothing but Paul in a place that had somehow changed.

The drums had crushed the flute and xylophone, and the deep, insistent beat pounded with the footsteps of Paul's dancing on the earth. Darcy was in a forest somewhere with scented trees overhead. Moss shadows dappled the bodies of dancers who moaned and writhed together under the sagging branches, and Paul moved into the center, half in shadow, half in pale light, his head arched back like a proud young stag's. Drums rolled and pounded, and the naked dark bodies moved jerkily, as if animated by the sound and not by any conscious mind. Eyes showed vacant whites, mouths hung slack, drooling, people clapped and swayed or crawled like beasts on the ground. Paul was slick with sweat and hard with passion, reaching for her. Aroused and confused, Darcy shut her eyes suddenly and whispered, "Stop."

The music shifted back into the ethnic-rhythm compact disc playing in Dr. Ghormley's backyard. Darcy looked again. Paul's eyes were no longer focused on her; they were bloodshot and tired, the color of old moss hanging from trees. He was breathing hard, and as he stopped dancing he reached a hand up to tug at his sweater collar. He looked back at her with a sheepish smile. "I guess I'm not in great shape for this. Want to go back inside?"

"Sure." She took his hand and stumbled onto the cement of the patio and inside the kitchen door. Her heart was beating wildly and her head spun. Hallucination or imagination, that had been a scary, sexual vision. Had there been something in her wine? She wouldn't be surprised here at reunion night for ex-hippies. Her body felt unbalanced and tingly, an unpleasant, half-sick sensation.

"I'll get us something with ice in it." Paul opened the refrigerator. The kitchen was empty, odd at a crowded party like this. The beer keg sat lonely in its nest of ice. "Would you like a Coke or some orange juice?"

"Whatever's easy." She leaned against the counter and looked at the cork bulletin board covered with pictures of Laura Ghormley and her mother, who had divorced Dr. Ghormley the year after Laura's death. It was strange to look at Laura's round face, frozen in time at thirteen, while Darcy had grown older, had grown up. She felt tears starting behind her eyelids and blinked sleepily to keep them away.

A door opened from the formal dining room and a face peered out. Roxanne, the first Darcy had seen of her at the party. She looked very somber and serious in a black turtleneck and leggings, with a pentagram pendant between her breasts. "Hey, Darcy, Paul, come on in. They've started, but Dion insists we have to have you two."

Paul raised an eyebrow at Darcy and smiled slightly. "Shall we go in? We can have our drinks later."

"What is it?" She followed him, still disoriented.

"The séance. You have to be completely quiet except if Dion asks you to say something." Roxanne seemed more subdued than Darcy remembered her being before. She led them into the room, which had been hung with black draperies and cleared of its usual chandelier and china cabinet. The table was long, with both leaves inserted, and the polished oak surface reflected the dim light of two candles under red crystal globes. Darcy recognized the bright blond head and silver earrings of Ariadne in one of the high-backed chairs at the table. She did not know anyone else.

The man at the head of the table, whom she supposed was

Dion, had reddish, wiry hair and a long beard that brushed against his thin chest. His eyes were hooded and peaceful-looking, like some pictures of Jesus. He wore an ordinary button-front striped shirt and a tie that barely showed behind the beard. His hands were placed on the table with the fingers curved as if he were about to play the piano. He glanced up in silent greeting and inclined his head to two empty chairs at his right. Paul took the further one and left Darcy to sit beside Dion. She sat down with an uneasy feeling in her stomach. The wine, she thought, and wouldn't it be funny if she threw up in the middle of the hocus-pocus?

"Clear your mind of thoughts," Dion intoned in a soft, hollow voice. "Close your eyes and let the tension flow out your fingertips. Yes. Put your hands gently onto the table with mine. Yes."

It was her imagination that made the wooden surface seem to vibrate with energy. Darcy opened her eyes to slits and saw that everyone else looked peaceful and concentrated. She closed them again and tried to relax. There was nothing dangerous about this even if it was nonsense. She could hear Paul breathing slowly and deeply beside her. She could smell him, sweaty and musky like the forest in her hallucination outside. She remembered how he had looked dancing naked in her vision. She was not going to let him make love to her tonight, but soon . . . it would be unlike the sex she'd had before, the fumbling local boys not sure how far or how fast they were supposed to go. He would know what he was doing. And he was so beautiful . . .

"Open your minds," Dion's voice said, whispery and far away. "Open your defensive minds and welcome the outside. Welcome the other worlds that float beside our own and the spirits that travel within them, the spirits that can travel to us tonight. Some perhaps will hear voices long forgotten and feel the presence of loved ones. Perhaps some wise soul will descend here tonight to guide us in our endeavors. Open your minds to them. Welcome them here."

The séance went on, spooky but hardly convincing. Darcy forced herself to keep her eyes closed. Dion spoke in high voices, mothers and sisters long dead, in gruff tones of fathers, in guttural accents and horrible syntax as a patronizing spirit guide. Other voices spoke sometimes with questions, hesitant queries, and the spirits speaking through Dion gave vague replies. Darcy was getting bored, though the small hairs at the back of her neck rose each time a new voice manifested itself in Dion's well-trained throat.

After perhaps half an hour the spirits came slower, and after a long silence Dion suggested that they take hands. Darcy reached for Paul's hand and felt Dion's cover hers on the other side. Paul gripped her hand tightly, warm and alive. Dion's touch was lighter, but strangely, she did feel connected to the entire group seated at the table. She almost felt the circle of power that Dion now said they had formed.

"And now," the medium intoned, "we ask the spirits if there are any among them who still have not spoken, any messages that have not been received. O spirits of past and future, guide us, comfort us, be not silent to our great need . . ." He went on prayerfully and Darcy felt more and more foolish. But Paul kept hold of her hand as if it were important to listen.

"Can you hear me, spirits?" Dion asked louder. "Can you hear me? Will you answer?" His voice grew more intense. "One comes . . . different . . . I will speak for you, come, into me . . ."

And then Darcy's world spun and her breathing stopped, because the voice that came from Dion's throat now was unlike any of the spirit voices before. Slow and slurred, a woman's voice undeniably, sounding old and ragged and exhausted.

"Dar . . . cy?" A rasping breath, as if speaking was a great effort or an activity long forgotten. "Can you hear me? I . . . tried to get through . . . to tell you . . ." Dion's hand now gripped Darcy's like a vise, hurting her.

"Mom?" Impossible, she was dead, Darcy had seen her buried. She had died falling from the rain-slick rocks of Vedauwoo where she had wandered after the car crashed that night.

"Darcy . . ." the voice said desperately. "Can you hear me? I'm here . . . I don't know . . . where . . ."

"Where are you?" Darcy whispered, tears welling behind her closed eyes.

"Over here . . . across . . . don't know . . . Can you hear me? I'm alive. Alive. Help me."

A spasm went through Dion and his hand convulsed, then released Darcy's, and she opened her eyes to stare at him. He held his head in his hands, trying to stop shaking. The circle broken, the rest of the people at the table began to murmur to one another. Paul still held Darcy's hand though she tried to pull it away.

"Turn on a light," Roxanne said in a brittle voice. "Turn on all the lights. That was weird."

"You're Darcy, right?" Dion's voice was bewildered now, and he looked at her wide-eyed. "That was intense. I haven't felt anything that strong before. Your mother?"

Paul had finally let go of her hand. She crossed her arms and hugged them against her ribs, blinking back angry tears. "She died seven years ago. How did you know that? Who told you? Roxanne?"

"No, no one told me about you or your mom," Dion said, his face open, frank, as if he could not possibly lie to her. "I didn't know anything but your name, the girl Paul brought to the party tonight."

"It couldn't have been her," she whispered, trying to convince herself.

"She couldn't express herself very well. I got more than she said from the contact." Dion leaned toward her, speaking just for her. "She said you had to come and get her, or open the border so she could get back on her own. She's still alive, but she can't last much longer over there." He blinked slowly. "Does that make sense to you?"

"No. Over where? She's dead, I saw her buried. I saw her body. She's dead."

"It wasn't her body, I got that much too." Dion shook his head. "I don't claim to understand it. I can't interpret it for you, I'm just a medium. But she sounded . . . she felt . . . really desperate. If she's alive she needs help."

Darcy stood up, feeling really sick now. It had been her mother's voice, but how, from where? How could she be alive? "I don't know," she whispered. "Where . . . what kind of place could she be in? What . . . border does she need me to open? How?"

Paul put a protective arm around her. "I don't know the answers to your questions, but there's a way to find out. From what your mother's voice said, you already know the way to help her. It's just buried inside you somewhere. Like Ariadne said. Secrets, mysteries, the Popess hiding her power. You know where she is and you know how to help her."

"No. No, that's crazy." She pulled away from him and hurried out of the room, aware of people watching her with concerned faces. "Take me back to my car, all right? I want to go home."

Paul was right behind her, walking fast. "You know, somewhere inside you. It was your mother's voice. Dr. Ghormley can help you in his lab," he said softly, insistently. "Come there tomorrow afternoon. It's Saturday, no one will be around. I'll meet you there with Dr. Ghormley. Three o'clock tomorrow. He can hypnotize you and take you back to the time your mother died. Find out what you know, what really happened. How she can still be alive."

"But she can't be alive. She can't." She felt violated, sliced open, as if she had been raped. Her mother's voice . . . if it wasn't real, how had Dion imitated it so precisely? "Don't talk to me about it anymore. Just take me to my car, okay? I want to go home."

# CHAPTER
# SIX

Headlights tried to puncture the blackness, picking up the small, winking eyes of roadside reflectors. Darcy stared fiercely at what she could see of the highway, gripping the wheel with both hands, keeping her car on the road mostly from a kind of rhythmic memory of the curves. She drove this pass every day, but it was different late at night. The cliff edges of the hills where the highway builders had dynamited through the rock were outlined vaguely against the pale, distant stars. The ditches and slopes beyond the reflectors might be a thousand feet deep. She was reminded of the place she had dreamed of last night, where she had been running with Coyote. The mountains had seemed alive there, always changing, not to be trusted.

How could Sarah Jacobi be living anywhere seven years after her death? Darcy had seen her burial. She had insisted on getting out of the hospital for an afternoon. She had missed the funeral, but her father had told her about it. Her mother's casket had been open in the mortuary parlor. Darcy's father had described a bewildered, frozen expression on her mother's face, and hollows under her eyes that had not been hidden by the makeup. He said that he had touched the quiet face with one hand to make sure. Then he had turned away. Dr. Ghormley had been there too. His daughter's casket had been closed. Laura had died in the crash, pinned in the backseat where the car had landed after it rolled down the slope from the narrow Vedauwoo road. Ghormley would realize how ridiculous it was to say that Darcy's mother might be alive.

The crash had happened only a few miles from here, but far enough from the interstate highway that no one had found Darcy until morning. The staff psychiatrist at the hospital had told her that her memory loss was a natural, healthy defense mechanism. Her mind had made the judgment that it was better not to remember those hours of lying hurt in the rain. Paul had said that Dr. Ghormley could hypnotize her to pull those memories back up to the surface. Darcy could not decide if she should try it. The idea frightened her. Surely it was impossible that they would discover some buried clue about her mother being lost in an across-the-border otherworld.

She passed the lights of the summit and headed downslope toward the ranch turnoff. The night pressed in around her as if trying to crush her sturdy car. She still felt shaken and hurt by what had happened. If it was a trick—how could it be anything but a trick?—it was a terrible one, a cruel one, and Roxanne or someone should apologize for it. Vague messages from the dead were one thing, but a desperate plea for rescue was something different, not as harmless. She did not know if she would be able to sleep tonight.

She could have slept with Paul. He had asked her if she wanted to go back to his apartment, but she had refused. He had kissed her and she still felt the excitement of touching him, her hands meeting around his neck. After all that had happened this evening she was still infatuated with Paul, like a first crush. She had never been the kind who fell for rock stars, but she imagined this must be the feeling that had prompted her friends to tape posters up all over their bedroom walls. It was the way he looked, but also something else that drew her to him, a feeling she had when she was next to him. It scarcely mattered what he said, or what irrational superstitions he believed in.

An image of her mother drifted in and out of thoughts of Paul; the remembered face was changed, worn and lined, as weary as her voice had been. Her hands were outstretched as she drifted in a flattened shape like an exiled criminal in the Superman comics. What if it was true? It had been her mother's voice. Darcy had been sure of that as she listened to it, heartbroken at the sound. No. She flipped on the car radio to drown her thoughts. It was madness to believe any of it.

On a whim, she pulled her car up onto the slope that led to Charlie Stone's trailer. If he was awake, maybe he'd want to tell her the rest of that story. It could distract her, maybe help her sleep. But the lights were off in the darkened hollow and she wondered suddenly why she wanted to go to him for comfort. She hardly knew him. She backed down to the main road again and drove to the ranch house, dreading the peace and quiet she knew she would find there.

Watching himself listening to a story, Charlie had gone far back in his dream. He was six years old, silently impatient with the old man who sat across the fire from him. He did not want to know what arguments Coyote had used at the Elders Council or where the great Medicine Wheel was spread over the rim of a hill far to the north. He wanted to know what happened, what happened to the evil rock valley tribe and what happened to the boy hunter whose brothers had been killed. Still the old man went on about the sacred land of the wheel and the power of visions in that place.

His name was Owl Child and he was Cheyenne. Tomorrow

he would be sent with twenty other children to a white man's school in Nebraska, away from his parents and the Oklahoma Indian Territory where he had grown up. Tonight was the last of a series of nights with the old man, his father's uncle, a Dog Soldier who had lived long enough to value peace. The old man's name, Every Buffalo Robe, had been given to him after he raided a Crow camp and took enough robes to load two stolen pack horses. That was in Wyoming, when the Northern Cheyenne had hunted with their ancestors. Owl Child lived on the reservation and now must go to school. He feared he would never be a warrior; how, then, could he ever be a man?

"Great-Uncle," he said, wiggling his toes in the rug where he sat. Every Buffalo Robe paused and waited for his question. "But what did they do about the rock valley tribe? Did they kill them?"

"The council debated for five days." The old man seemed to laugh at him with his eyes. He did not answer the question. "At last they decided to go to the rock valley and see for themselves if the people there had become evil. So they rode away from the great Medicine Wheel, down the stone hills, into the prairies, stopping at different villages to gather warriors and wise men of all the people. For no one tribe must judge this matter, when an entire people must be punished." He went on as he had before, telling the story in the way he had learned it.

Rain lashed the sides of the dark tipi, and Owl Child thought of his mother stowing their blankets and goods in the rafters of their cabin for fear of flooding. The creek only a few paces from the cabin door had risen to half again its height today. Owl Child's father had never liked the small piece of land the government had told him was his. The ground was too low and the creek too wild, but he had been told he could not move. The tribal council could search for another family who might wish to trade homes, but that would not happen.

Owl Child's father was gone tonight, as the creek rose. He and his two older sons were in town breaking horses for Edwin Scott the stableman. Owl Child wondered if they would be paid this time or if they would come again with only drink in their bellies. His mother said that Oklahoma was no place for Northern Cheyenne anyway, it would not matter if they had a different piece of land. It was not their land, and would not listen to them.

Every Buffalo Robe did not live in a wooden cabin. His tipi was old, the buffalo hide patched with canvas and resewn many times, but he could move it to higher ground if the creek flooded. He had come to live with Owl Child's family for the past two weeks to tell the boy the stories he should know. "Strengthen him against the missionary tales," his mother had begged the old uncle. "He must not forget any of it, the way the others have. He will be a Guardian. He must not forget." And Every Buffalo Robe had treated Owl Child almost as if he were not a six-year-old boy, but a sober and thoughtful young man, as if he had been initiated already into a men's society.

"How do you think the Elders and the warriors, Coyote and the youngest brother, approached the rock valley tribe?" the old man asked now.

Owl Child said fiercely, "They galloped in with lances ready and shot their arrows and routed the camp!"

"No, that is not so. They called out in friendship and were invited to join in a feast. Coyote and the youngest brother hid in the rocks overlooking the camp, knowing they would be recognized again. Why did the Elders not attack, then, as you said?"

Owl Child felt water moving under him, under the canvas floor of the tipi. He stood up and stepped with one foot and the other. The ground squished away from his feet, unsteady as a muddy creek bank. "Because they wanted to know if it was true," he guessed. Every Buffalo Robe handed him his hat and threadbare blanket coat. "Maybe Coyote and the boy were lying. Who would trust Coyote anyway? And maybe because it was such a bad thing they said had happened. People eating other people. They had to make sure the tribe was really that evil."

The old man nodded, putting on his moccasin boots. "Come, we will have to fold the tipi and go up the hill. Your mother will be too busy to do it for us." It was woman's work, but Owl Child was used to that. He had no sisters and his mother was often alone here with him. He had learned to help her with food and washing and planting, though he was a boy and should have been left to boys' games.

"Will you tell me the rest of the story?" he asked now, going outside with his uncle to pull out the tipi poles. "This is the last night before I leave."

"If it means neither of us sleep before we put you on the train," the old man promised.

"Will any of the other children know this story?" He thought it might be a fun game to play. He would want to be Coyote.

"No. I would not know it if the old Guardian had not told me when our family was taken south. This is your own medicine story, child. Keep it as secret as if you had it from Coyote himself."

"Does my mother know it?"

"She knew enough to go to the proper place when you were born," the old man said. "But no, she was never told the story, not as I am telling it to you. You will tell it someday to another Guardian, but it will be a long time before you know enough to see who that will be. It is your own story, Owl Child. Yours to keep, true no matter what the missionaries say at school."

His own story. Owl Child felt a warmth inside him like

food in his stomach. He would keep it safe. Maybe that was his first test as a Guardian, to guard the story. He did not know what it meant to be a Guardian, but people had always told him he would know when the time came. It was too bad that you couldn't know everything at one time and not have to wait.

The rain ran into his eyes and he pulled his hat down. His mother called to him as she waded up the trail toward the Red Deer family's house a mile away. They lived on a stony hillside where nothing would grow, but at least they were above the water. "I will come there as soon as I finish help-ing my uncle," Owl Child told her. She waved to him that that was all right, and walked on. They trusted him, he thought importantly. His mother and Every Buffalo Robe trusted him to keep secrets and to help save things from floods. He promised himself he would remember that, no matter what happened at the white man's school.

Charlie was a long time returning from the dream. He al-most never went so far into his past. There were few good memories of those years, but perhaps there were things to be learned. He remembered how unsure he had been if it was right to tell Darcy the wendigo legends. She was a Guardian, that was true, but he did not know if she could be trusted with the secrets. He still did not know. Her life, her culture, were so different. What meaning did Indian tradition hold for her? Only as much as Charlie could convince her to accept.

A dull headache remained from last night's wine. Darcy walked through her morning chores without really waking up, shivering in the biting wind in the pasture. At breakfast she was so quiet that Alice asked if she was all right. Charlie Stone watched her without expression, but Darcy saw curios-ity in his eyes. She shrugged and smiled. "A little too much to drink."

Ed offered her a shot of tequila in her orange juice—"a

hair from the dog that bit you"—but she declined. She had a class of eight-year-olds to teach at ten o'clock this morning. She had to be alert for them. She had slept only a few hours, and she was trying her best not to think about the séance and the voice she had heard. She could not talk about it to Alice or Ed. Alice would be worried about her, and Ed would probably be excited about the possibility that her mother had been abducted by aliens. Maybe everything he believed in was true after all.

"Darcy and I are planning a ride around the ranch today," Charlie said as they were cleaning up the dishes. "Is there anything you want me to watch for, Mrs. Kennan? Besides fences that might need mending?"

"If you see any stray cattle you can push them back over to the government land," Alice said.

"Remember, burned circles in the grass. Or crumpled sagebrush bushes." Ed pointed a finger at Charlie. "Keep your eyes open, young man." He began to cough harshly, something that had begun after his ride in the snow Thursday morning.

"I will, sir."

"I'll pack you a lunch." Alice frowned at her husband. "Be careful of the weather. You never know this time of year."

Darcy had forgotten about the tour of the ranch she had promised Charlie. Hadn't he said he would tell her the rest of the Coyote story while they were out? That would be better than worrying about whether she would drive into Laramie to be hypnotized by Dr. Ghormley. "We'll be careful. Come on, Charlie. Help me get the horses ready for the little girls."

A few working ranch horses were kept with the Kennans' high-bred Arabians. Charlie chose a short-bodied pinto gelding with a sour face and powerful legs; it looked like a horse he could work with. He and Darcy rode out a little before noon, under a cold, pale blue sky with wind strong enough to unwrap the scarves they had tied around their necks. Charlie kept up the deception that he needed a guide. He let Darcy point out features of the hills and valleys, the creekbeds, the patches of pine and aspen forest. Actually he knew this land as well as he knew his own body. It was his birth place; he was its Guardian. It was his land far more than it was the Kennans'.

As they rode along a high ridge on the southern side of the ranch, he continued the story of Coyote and the wendigo. He told her the part he had heard in his dream, exactly as his great-uncle had told it to him. "So Coyote and the youngest brother hid in the rocks above the camp, knowing they would be recognized again.

"The Elders were indeed wise men, who knew how to listen, how to see evil when it was before them. They knew of doors into this otherworld in three places: in the rock hills, here; in the Black Hills to the north; and on the plateau where the ancient people had built the Medicine Wheel. Men of wisdom had gone through those doors from time to time, but they had found nothing beyond to their liking.

" 'Where did they get the food they eat tonight?' the youngest brother asked Coyote in the place where they were hidden. 'They had killed all the animals when they feasted on my brothers.'

"Coyote lay with his nose across his paws, feeling guilty. 'If it had not been for me your brothers would be alive. I led them here.'

" 'They deceived us all. It wasn't your fault.'

"The Elders were old men, shabbily dressed, and they complained of their hunger and the horrible winter they had to endure this season. Winters were never this harsh when they were boys, they said. The wolf shaman of the rock valley tribe lamented with them and marveled at their luck at reaching this haven of food and warmth. 'For we have found a place where grass is always green and the sun shines to warm our bones. I cannot keep you from it any longer. Come with me to see this paradise.'

"When the old men stood up and followed the tribespeople into the rock cave it was a signal to the warriors who were also waiting hidden in the rocks. They strung their bows and held their feathered lances ready. Coyote pushed his head under the youngest brother's hand and let him scratch his ears. 'I must go with them now. Stay here.' He ran down into the camp just as the Elders began to cry out against their attackers.

"The warriors thundered down into the camp like eagles, killing anyone in their path and knocking down the tipis and shelters of the enemy. The Elders made a circle in the middle of the rock cave and began to sing a song of power. The most evil of the tribespeople changed into wolves and bears and wolverines, their eyes glowing with the unearthly power of the otherworld.

"Coyote led the charge into these animal ranks, and the wolf shaman recognized him. 'The one who escaped us, who stole the boy!' he howled. 'Chase him down and tear him to pieces!' All the animals roared into pursuit of Coyote, who ran past the Elders and their singing, and ran all the way through the beckoning door in the rock and into the strange world beyond.

"With the worst of the evil sorcerors through the door, the Elders turned their song into a banishment. They cursed the rock valley tribe with a terrible curse that took away their humanity and made them creatures of the otherworld they had found so alluring. They cursed them with the name of wendigo, the demon wind-spirit of the north, that can never find rest or peace but must wail forever tormented through the air. As the warriors killed the last of the people who had been left behind, the Elders cursed their spirits to wander with no peace. They were not to be given honorable rest in the trees, but scattered through the valley for the animals they had so greedily slain to feast on their bones.

"And still Coyote ran through the green grass and over the strange undulating hills of the otherworld. The animal men who chased him suddenly realized that the door behind them had been closed. They were trapped in the world that had made them evil and insane. In their fury they ran to the other doors they knew, chasing Coyote all the way. They found them closed as well. At last poor Coyote was worn out, his strength fading in this place where his power had not been born. His enemies had a supernatural strength. They surrounded him and killed him on a mound at the back of a deep canyon. They tore him to pieces and pulled off his head and mocked it.

"In the human world was heard a chorus of howling, yelping, barking, as wolves, coyotes, even dogs stopped in the hunt, in play, in nursing their young, to mourn the fallen Coyote. The wendigo had performed a final act of such evil that the world itself cried out against them. For Coyote was no ordinary animal, but an Ancestor, the first and greatest of his kind, and he was not supposed to die.

"It was the task of three Guardians to watch the three doors into the otherworld, so that no one from the earth would try to go through them again, and none of the wendigo could return from their banishment. One at the Medicine Wheel, one in the Black Hills, and one in the rock valley itself, these men waited with sacred weapons in their hands and watched through long lifetimes. One of them was the youngest brother who had been out hunting one day and followed a coyote to this place. When the Guardians died, they were buried before the doors with their weapons still ready in their hands. Their spirits, more powerful than in life, still watch to see that the curse remains. And Coyote may roam both worlds in spirit, but his life was taken by the wendigo in that strange land. There are no true Coyote stories after this one."

In the telling of the story they had ridden down the ridge and along a creekbed under overhanging willow bushes. Now Charlie stopped his horse to let it drink from the icy water. A boulder outcropping of jumbled granite cast a wide shadow across the creek. The sun was high overhead, but far away, giving little warmth. Charlie felt colder than the autumn air around him, and old and weathered as the twisted pine trees that had forced their roots into cracks in the piled rocks. The tale was his medicine story, the Guardians' legend. To tell it was to bleed an old wound, leaving him drained. And the girl—what could it mean to her? She was no longer a child, quick to believe.

"What does it mean?" Darcy asked, echoing his thoughts. She was running her fingers through her red pony's mane, untangling the coarse hairs. "You told it so well, and I was really trying to understand it, but I don't. Don't most of those old myths try to explain some natural feature, like rain or winter or where the sun goes at night? There wasn't any of that in this story."

Charlie urged his pinto up the slope under the trees, and Darcy followed him, settling into a trot. They made a wide circle around a beaver pond, headed back toward the center of the ranch. "I heard the story first when I was six years old," he said when she had caught up to him. "I didn't wonder what it meant. It was a story of something that had happened, like the time my grandfather found himself between a mother bear and her den."

She was quiet for a moment, riding with the wind blowing back her brown hair. "I wonder what Paul would think," she said thoughtfully. "He'd probably read all kinds of psychological symbolism into it—doors, and animal transformations, and cannibalism."

"Paul is your friend, the man you went out with last

night?" Charlie tried to keep his voice polite, the conversation of new acquaintances. "I hope you won't tell it to him, or tell him about it." If he were still her teacher he could simply say that she was not to tell the story to anyone. He had gained her trust so easily when she was ten years old, by rescuing her from the wendigo. She had known then that the story was true and known it must be secret. "I know it's a strange request. But this is not an ordinary tale to be shared lightly with others."

She smiled, humoring him. "All right. I promise I won't tell anyone about it." He could see her wondering why, if it was such a special story, he had told it to her. They were strangers, had barely learned each other's names.

"You'll understand soon," he said, puzzling her even more, and then he gave up. They rode together in a bewildered silence, listening to the wind and the muffled rhythm of their horses' hooves, the occasional clink of metal against stone when a horseshoe hit a rock. Charlie wanted to reach over and shake her, slap her, hold her face inches from his own and shout, *Don't you remember me, don't you remember anything?*

If she remembered anything at all it would probably be the time he had come to the hospital to visit her; she had been terrified by his questions about wendigo and opening the borders and whether her medicine bag had been any protection. He had realized in a few moments how much she had lost, and when he had desperately tried to break through to her she had become hysterical and called for the nurse. He had left in fear of the police.

After a few minutes, Darcy pointed out a rock outcropping a few miles away as a place where she had found arrowheads. Not Indian ones, but older, Folsom points from the Stone Age inhabitants. They relaxed into talk about the ancient history of the area. Oceans and dinosaurs, mammoths, the evolution of horses that had been extinct by the time the Indians' ancestors arrived from the north. Maybe the horses had gone into the wendigo world through the beckoning door. Charlie wondered if that could be true; there were horses in that world—strange, predatory horses that hunted in family groups. The otherworld had a way of twisting life from this place, infecting it with violence, with madness.

Later when they rode along the western edge of the ranch, at the back of Vedauwoo Park, Charlie thought of guiding her up to the high ridge, taking her in and showing her the Guardian's tomb. There, lying still but not at rest, was the youngest brother of the legend. A powerful Guardian, but a vulnerable one, as Charlie had learned over the years. He could not do it, not yet. He could not trust Darcy with no past to anchor her. He did not know her.

"I didn't see any UFO evidence," she said cheerfully as they rode slowly through the late afternoon. "The closest thing really was your story. Ed would probably say that the rock valley people were aliens, and the door in the rock was the door to their spaceship. They weren't evil, just misunderstood. They kidnapped the boy's brothers to study them, and the ignorant natives drove them away." Charlie laughed with her, and their horses stepped more lightly across the prairie as they headed toward home.

# CHAPTER
# SEVEN

W arm at last, the soles of her stockinged feet hot on the fireplace hearth, Darcy lounged in one of the red leather chairs in the Kennans' living room after supper. The fire sparked with colors from treated pinecones Ed had added to make it festive. The hot buttered rum Darcy sipped made her body feel like a banked coal, solid and ordinary on the outside but full of glowing fire. The conversation in the room was distantly soothing. She was getting sleepy.

Dinner had been wonderful. She and Charlie had trudged in after bringing down the herd from the pasture, feeding the broodmares, and grooming their horses and cleaning their tack. Alice had greeted them at the door and led them into the kitchen, where the table was set for a welcome dinner for Charlie. They had eaten roasted chicken, cheese-fried potatoes, and a spinach salad, with chocolate cookies and the buttered rum for dessert.

"Ten years ago we were raising quarter horses, working

horses," Alice was saying. "But I had thought for a long time that Arabians might do well here. People have the wrong idea about them. They think Arabians are like thoroughbreds, delicate, needing to be pampered. Or that because they're desert horses they have to live in a warm climate."

"There are mountains in Iran and Iraq where it gets pretty cold," Charlie said. His voice was ordinary now, quiet and soft, not the intense, rich tones that he had used to tell the Coyote story this afternoon. He seemed to be a different person inside a house, Darcy thought.

"Exactly. So I brought in five mares. Farah was one of them, she's Ed's favorite. I had them bred and their foals took to the land here like natives." Alice was eager for approval for her scheme; it had taken her a long time to convince Ed it would be worth their money.

"You have what, twenty mares now, and the stallion?"

"Yes, the mares from the original five, and the stud imported from Turkey. Amahl fathered all the yearlings you'll be training. Fifteen of them, a good crop, I think. One more stud horse and I'll be satisfied with our breeding stock. That's something I'll want you to do, Charlie, go with me to the sales in Denver and look for another good stallion."

"Shouldn't bring the new boy in until spring, though," Ed said in the hoarse voice he had acquired in the past few days. The rum had settled his cough this evening. "It will be a rough winter this year, looks like."

"It looked like it Thursday when you went riding out in the snow," Alice reminded him, her voice sharpened with remembered worry.

"What were you looking for, Mr. Kennan?" Charlie asked. "The same thing you told me to watch out for today? Evidence of spaceship landings?"

Darcy turned in her chair to watch them. Ed sat on the couch with a lap robe over his thin legs, sipping his drink slowly. Charlie leaned forward in his chair, his face serious, interested, alive between his long braids. He was good-looking, Darcy thought, but not as handsome as Paul. The warmth from the rum was making her feel like a cat who wanted to be stroked. If Paul were here she wouldn't have said no this time.

"They called me out." Ed looked thoughtfully at Charlie. Darcy thought he was unsure about Charlie's interest; should he be flattered or suspicious?

"But you didn't see them, or anything of theirs?"

"Never seen them." The old man relaxed, laughing a little. "I thought once I had. I was sure I must have been abducted in a spaceship at least once, because they kept talking to me, and from what I read I thought that's what aliens do with people, abduct them."

Darcy had an upsetting image of her mother locked in a cage on an alien ship. She spoke up to distract herself. "From what I've read you wouldn't remember if you had been abducted."

Ed nodded soberly. "That's right. And I didn't remember it, but I was sure it must have happened. That was when I had myself hypnotized, Alice, do you recall? That Dr. Ghormley down at the university."

"I remember," his wife said patiently. "He counted you backward in time."

"You had Ghormley hypnotize you?" Darcy said, surprised.

"Poor man was disappointed. No trace of an abduction experience, he said. But he did write down all my stories about when they talked to me." Ed was pleased with the recollection. "He was jealous, I think. He'd give his right hand to talk to aliens. It's sad for people like that, who believe in it but never have the experience."

Charlie settled back in his chair and put his worn moccasin boots up on the pine-log coffee table. "What do they sound like when they talk to you? Like human voices, speaking English?"

"Yes. They've been studying us long enough to know our language." Ed went on eagerly. "They know so many wonderful things! When they decide that we're worthy to receive them, they're going to give the human race all their wisdom, all their technology. They can cure diseases, even old age, and stop war. They just have to know they can trust us."

Alice shook her head, tired of encouraging him. "Then why are they spending years hovering over an isolated Wyoming ranch talking to one old man? They should be talking to world leaders."

"No," Ed said impatiently. "No, I've figured that out. You can read it in all the stories, Alice. It's ordinary men and women, small-town people, who've seen them and spoken to them. The aliens are learning about humanity from the people. Honest, simple people who won't lie to them like politicians. If they decide that we're basically peaceful and worthwhile, then they'll make themselves known to the world."

Alice took another chocolate cookie from the tray by her chair. "I just wish they'd land in my front yard so I wouldn't have to keep taking your word for it, Ed."

"It's all part of their plan," he said with religious certainty. "It will all be clear in time."

"I'm curious, Mr. Kennan," Charlie said. "When did you first hear from your friends? How long ago?"

"A long time, years and years . . ." His eyes searched the ceiling beams for answers. "When was the first time, Alice? Oh, sure, that's it. Just a couple of days after Darcy was born, while her mother was still laid up in the house here. I rode up in the hills to pick up some things the Jacobis had left in the rocks there, when Sarah was having the baby. A camera, some binoculars, a backpack with their lunch in it, like that. I remember the aliens talked to me first when I was up there finding their things."

"So that was about twenty years ago," Alice said.

"They've spoken to him regularly ever since. I thought at the time he had probably fallen in the rocks and hit his head. But there wasn't any lump. I checked."

"That's strange," Darcy said. She hadn't heard this before. "That they talked to you right in the same place where I was born." It made her feel as if there was an odd connection between herself and Ed's aliens.

"There must be a story about your birth," Charlie said to Darcy. "I'd like to hear it sometime. If you were born in Vedauwoo on one of the hills, that would make you a daughter of the mountain spirits. With a sacred trust to guard the land." He smiled, but it did not reach his dark eyes. "According to my people's legends, anyway. Mountains are places of power to us."

Darcy smiled back at him, wondering why he seemed troubled. This was something she could tell Paul, at least. It wasn't part of the Coyote story she had promised to keep secret. Daughter of the mountain spirits—that sounded impressive. Which reminded her, she had homework to do this weekend. She had spent the whole day out of the house. "I need to go open some books. It's getting kind of late. Thanks for the dinner, Ed. Good night, Alice, Charlie."

"Yes, I suppose we all have things to do," Alice said. "Well, Charlie, we're glad you're with us. Let me know if there's anything else you need out at the trailer."

"I will. Thank you." He finished his drink and put on his hat to leave.

Darcy left them and went upstairs to work on an essay for her English class. Tomorrow, she thought, if Paul didn't call her, she would call him to apologize for not being at the lab this afternoon. She would have to explain to him that she thought hypnosis would be a waste of time. Her mother was dead, and there was nothing anyone could do to bring her back again.

* * *

Another dream, open-eyed, in the creaking darkness of the trailer while a strong wind blew through the hollow. Charlie felt something pulling him back. Maybe there was something he was supposed to notice this time, something he had over-looked or forgotten . . .

Owl Child lay on top of the wool blankets of his canvas cot, sore from a whipping he had gotten today for not wear-ing his hard new shoes. The moon shone through a window too high in the dormitory wall for him to see outside. "Coy-ote," he whispered, "what am I going to do?" He had begun to talk to Coyote in his mind, the way some of the older boys talked to the Jesus picture who watched them from a frame on the far wall.

All around him he heard the night breathing of strange boys: Kiowa, Comanche, Arapaho, Sioux. In the two weeks he had been at the missionary school he had learned to sign insults with his hands and speak a few words of English. Mr. Devereaux, the headmaster of the primary boys, had taken Owl Child's medicine bag tonight when he inspected the boys' beds. He had said in English, "It is a heathen amulet, the devil's work." Owl Child remembered the sounds of the words, and later he would find out what they meant from one of the older Cheyenne boys. Mr. Devereaux had looked at Owl Child's sad face and said, "You'll soon understand, Charlie."

His new English name was Charlie Gray Stone. Gray Stone was what his father's name meant in English, and he did not know what Charlie meant. He wondered if he was still a Guardian, with a white man's name. Would the Old Ones, the ancestors, recognize him anymore? He had to get the medicine bag back. His great-uncle had given it to him before he went with the other children to the train station. It was a small white beaded bag with fringe, and inside was powerful medicine, really too powerful for a child. Owl Child could not begin to use the power yet. He thought of the things in the bag; he did not understand them, but he knew how strong they were. An owl's feather, a speckled stone, a broken arrowhead, and a piece of dried fur that he imagined to be the part of Coyote's ear that was torn off in his final battle.

The headmaster's office was in another building of the school, and there were night guards on the walls to keep children from running away, or renegade parents from coming to rescue them. Owl Child slid carefully out of bed and took off his white nightgown so it would be harder to spot him, then went naked to the high window. Two empty water buckets stood by the wall; he knelt and stacked them, then climbed up carefully and reached for the window.

With a clattering crash, the buckets fell, and Owl Child hung by his fingers from the windowsill. He heard boys yelling and laughing. They could see him in the moonlight.

"Stop this noise! What has happened?" A teacher ran into the room.

*Come, little brother.* Furry rough hands grasped his wrists and Owl Child climbed up the side of the wall with his feet and squirmed out under the raised window. Coyote was there, bigger than Owl Child had imagined, as big as a wolf or a black bear. His torn ear flopped over one eye and he waited patiently while Owl Child climbed down and got on his back. Then he ran, as he had run with the youngest brother in the wendigo story. Owl Child clung to his fur, leaning forward, amazed and delighted and only a little frightened. He was not yet old enough to know that such a thing was impossible.

While the teachers were shouting and running with lanterns around the outside of the dormitory, Owl Child and Coyote were slinking through the shadows by the headmaster's office, under an open window. Lights flashed and passed, and when Coyote told him to, Owl Child climbed up and stood on the animal's back and pulled himself in through the window. His medicine bag was in a desk drawer along with two

beaded Sioux dance belts and a bear claw necklace. He left
the other things and took the bag, and climbed back out to his
friend.

*Hang it around my neck.* Owl Child carefully opened the
thong ties of the bag and reached around Coyote's neck, feeling bristly fur along the inside of his arms. With Coyote's
muzzle resting on his shoulder, he tied the thongs in a tight
knot. He hugged Coyote and stepped back to look. His medicine bag hung against the ruff at Coyote's throat, the fringe
dangling slightly between his front legs. *I'll keep it for you.
One day I will bring it back.* That was right, the headmaster
would miss it, and the teachers would find it again no matter
how carefully Owl Child hid it.

"Take me with you," the boy begged, throwing his arms
around Coyote's neck once more. "Take me home, please,
Coyote. I don't want to be here."

*There are things you must learn.* The big animal pulled
away from him, ears pricked, eyes bright. *But remember me.
Remember that you have power, even if it is hidden.* Then
Coyote turned and loped away. Owl Child followed him,
frightened of the teachers' lanterns, but Coyote was gone
when he rounded the corner of the classroom building.

The headmaster caught him when he tried to run toward
the walls, thinking he might escape and find Coyote again.
He got another bad beating, the lectures in English that he did
not understand, and for a week he had to do extra chores in
the evenings when the other boys were allowed to read or
play. But he did not forget what Coyote had said: he was Owl
Child, a boy with his own medicine and a strong spirit guide.
One day he would be a Guardian.

Charlie wakened to an old sorrow. The narrow bedroom of
his trailer seemed dim, distant, not as real as the past. He had
guessed, years afterward, the reason why Coyote had not rescued him from the missionary school.

He had never received any word from his parents, no dictated letters written by Indian agents like the other boys got, no new clothes, no visits. When he was ten he had demanded to write to them and had finally heard back from the Cheyenne tribal council in Oklahoma: his mother and father and two brothers were killed. They had taken the trail north with Dull Knife in 1878, soon after Charlie was sent to school. They had died at Fort Robinson in 1879, before they reached the lands of their ancestors. Charlie had been an orphan since he was seven, but he had not known it. Learning about his parents had set him on his own trail; he had begun then to hate the white men.

So many years ago, so far away in time . . . those had been the rapid years, the years of his childhood, when time had passed for him as it did for all men. He had left that behind when he was seventeen, when his hatred and bitterness had driven him to desperate action. That was when he had learned that the wendigo were worse enemies than any white man. That was when he had learned what it meant to be a Guardian and to fail in your duty.

"So you're certain she's the young Guardian," Dr. Ghormley said when Paul had finished his report to the Esoteric Society. "If that's true, we must either get her to join us or get rid of her. If she won't help us she's a danger to us." He let a slow gaze pass over the room, meeting sleepy eyes, nods, uncertain looks.

Paul stood in shadow by Ghormley's fireplace. The fire was barely glowing and the candles were dim. It was after midnight, and the leaders of the Society had been meeting since nine. Ghormley wasn't sure Paul had handled Darcy as well as he could have; she should have been at the lab at three, eager to plunge into lost memories.

"She is the Guardian, but she's unaware," Paul said. "I am sure I can make her an ally. She has no knowledge of the other side, after all."

"I would like to know who this older Guardian is, the one you say has worked to keep the borders closed over decades," said Ariadne from the couch. "Surely one of our contacts must have found out our enemy's name by now."

Ghormley shook his head. "Nothing yet. But I can't believe the girl has had no contact with her counterpart. Paul says she is ignorant, but she may be good at keeping her secrets. I want her in my lab. Maybe a name will come out of that."

Paul leaned against the mantel, his arms crossed. "She'll be there within two or three more days. I need more time to win her trust and spark her curiosity. And then there is the voice she heard. The voice we all heard, her mother speaking from the demon world. Even if I left her alone she'd come to us soon enough to find out more."

"I don't know what that voice was," said Dion, a troubled expression on his bearded face. He was leaning against the couch between Ariadne's legs. "It could just as well have been the voice of a demon pretending to be her mother. I still have my doubts about this proposed alliance. Demons make promises, we've all read the literature. Nowhere does it say they can be trusted."

"She was born at one of the borders, we know that for certain," said Ephron, a stout older man who wore a kaftan. "That means she should be capable of opening the door and going beyond. She can break the barrier that separates us from these great, wise beings. Dion, I thought you were beyond that old Christian propaganda. Demons are no more than intelligent life from another dimension. They've learned to use the mental abilities we are only beginning to pursue. They are not evil, they are not the legions of old Satanus. Put aside your prejudice, my friend."

The medium shook his head. "Propaganda is one thing. Folk tradition is something else. No legend or tale I've ever come across shows a demon providing any positive help to a human."

Ghormley wished he had more control over the Society; he was merely a senior member, not a leader with decision-making authority. If he had his way doubters like Dion would be out. "Power is what demons have always granted men," he said now, letting some scorn into his voice. "Men's foolish use of that power has led to the failures of the past. Wealth, gold, the philosophers' stone—we are not seeking such rewards."

"Knowledge," Paul said in a glowing, deep voice. His eyes sparkled with the firelight as he turned to them again. "Knowledge of this world and other worlds, knowledge we can use to help mankind."

"And power," said Ariadne, rising gracefully from the couch to stand with Paul. "The power that wise men have never had, to ensure that their wisdom is heard and obeyed."

"Are we to conquer the world, then?" Dion said in disgust.

"Not conquer," Paul answered. "Persuade. But they will listen to us this time."

"Are we agreed, then?" Ghormley asked impatiently. "We continue the work? Come, let me hear voices."

"Yes, of course," some said, and Dion grudgingly nodded. "The chance for knowledge of this kind . . ." he said quietly. "Yes, we continue, Richard."

"Good."

Little remained to be discussed. The circle knew its duties. Soon all had left except for Paul. Ghormley stood at his front door with the young man, watching the last car pull away from the street. "The girl may be what we need to break through," Ghormley said. "But we must be sure of her, Paul, do you understand me?"

"I'll speak to her tomorrow."

"There's no time to waste in a long courtship. She must choose the Society quickly."

Paul sat down on the porch steps, his long fingers inter-twined around his knees. "The mother may be a better lure than my flattery."

"Could it be true that the woman is alive in the demon world?" It seemed far-fetched to Ghormley, but then he reminded himself that the true existence of demons had never seemed real to him until a few nights ago.

"It is likely," Paul said. "Humans have been there before. She may be alive. She is almost certainly mad. But how to convince Darcy of it?"

"I've listened to the recording of the séance." Ghormley remembered something Dion had said: *It wasn't her body.* Darcy had said she had seen her mother buried. "I think we may attempt a little necromancy."

A slow, feral smile tightened Paul's face. "The cemetery tomorrow night? I bring Darcy there, and we open the Jacobi woman's grave?"

"Yes. I'll phone Detective Allen in the morning and make sure of the police. The caretaker of the cemetery will be Ariadne's task. But I tell you, Paul, we had better find what we need. If Sarah Jacobi's body is in her coffin we'll lose our chance with the girl."

"Until tomorrow night, my friend." Paul stepped off the porch and walked away into the darkness, avoiding the pool of light from the streetlamp. Ghormley shivered a little in the night air and hurried back inside. He hoped the Jacobi girl's talents would be worth the trouble.

# CHAPTER EIGHT

I've had some vivid dreams lately," Darcy told Charlie on Sunday afternoon as they led two of the sleek broodmares out of their barn side by side to be exercised. "I think your Coyote story might have suggested them. At least, Coyote was in them."

She cinched the practice pad around the Arabian mare's belly and bridled her. Charlie was doing the same with the other mare. They were a matched pair, both dapple gray. Darcy and Charlie had spent the morning working with the yearlings, but the afternoon had gone by slowly with cleaning the mares' barn and taking them out for rides two at a time.

"You should pay attention to your dreams." Charlie mounted his mare and urged her into a fast walk around the corral. "It's dangerous to ignore them, especially if they're strong enough for you to remember the next day."

"I don't remember that much about these. Except for Coyote, and some weird images." Darcy got her mare to trot and passed Charlie, blinking her eyes against the biting wind.

"The Iroquois were big dreamers," he said. "Every morning the family would sit down to breakfast and try to guess one another's dreams. If you dreamed about something, they thought it meant the soul desired it. A bowl of berries, a red dress, a beadwork belt. Sometimes it would be symbolic of something else. If you didn't get what you dreamed of, your soul would be unsatisfied. And if you dreamed you were going to do something, you had better do it, or it might happen to you in a way you don't want."

Darcy saw an image from her dream that she had not remembered in the morning. "I dreamed someone had stolen my medicine bag. It's a leather bag I got somewhere when I was a child. I thought it was magic." She leaned into a turn as her mare stretched into a lope. "I got it back in my dream, but I had to give it to Coyote for safekeeping. I tied it around his neck."

Charlie reached inside his jacket collar brought out a fringed bag, the size of his fist, nearly the twin of Darcy's. He showed it to her for a moment as she slowed her horse, then replaced it inside his shirt. "You have a medicine bag like this one?" he asked.

"Almost exactly like that." She felt embarrassed suddenly. Obviously Charlie still thought his was magic. She had made it sound like a childish thing; she thought it was childish, believing in an amulet's power. But if it was part of his religion she shouldn't say anything. "It has some strange things inside . . ."

He held up one hand. "No. Don't tell me the contents. That's personal, your own collected power. But you should pay attention to the dream. Your soul is telling you that the medicine bag is important. You need to keep it safe. Maybe you should start carrying it with you."

She couldn't keep from smiling. "I don't think so."

"Because you don't believe in it anymore?"

"I don't know if I ever really did. It was a kids' game. I

don't mean that you shouldn't take it seriously," she added quickly. "It's your culture, your heritage. But for me it was just a game."

"Coyote would say that life is a game." He started to gallop his mare in tight rings around the corral. The horse was eager for the movement, tossing her head and kicking up her heels, fighting the bit. Darcy leaned forward and joined them in a race until the horses were breathing hard and sweating in the cold October air.

Her dream might just as well mean that she should get a puppy, Darcy thought. Maybe it was Coyote she wanted and not the medicine bag. It was a strange idea, that souls expressed desires in dreams. Close to Freud, but more straightforward. She supposed that a dream about sex would simply mean she desired sex, not that she was neurotic. And the other part of it—if you dreamed of doing something, you should do it, or it might happen to you. She hoped that didn't mean she would have to climb a cliff somewhere. She did not want to meet the cliff she had climbed in her dream the other night, with some kind of strange enemy chasing her.

"Darcy!" Alice was calling her from the corral fence. The older woman leaned against the rails, smiling as the wind blew her short hair back from her thin face. "Your young man is on the phone."

"Paul?" She walked the mare over to where Alice stood. The dust raised in the corral by the running horses was settling slowly in the cold. "I'll come talk to him. I'll be back, Charlie." She dismounted. The mare stood by the fence, her pretty head up and her eyes lively from the exercise. Darcy climbed over and trotted back to the house with Alice.

Darcy met Paul at a trendy restaurant at seven, and he was charming throughout the meal, talking about his work with Dr. Ghormley in the hypnosis lab, describing some of the strange characters who came in to be regressed to remember their UFO experiences. At last he asked if she would reconsider being hypnotized; she told him what she had decided. Her mother was dead, she had to be, and there was no other point in remembering what had happened the night of the crash.

"There's a way to find out."

"What do you mean?"

"To find out if your mother is dead or alive." He did not have to speak quietly. The room was crowded and the background music blared from the speakers near their table. Darcy's head ached a little from the red wine she had let Paul order with their steaks. She had worked hard that day, and she felt pleasantly tired and full.

"She can't possibly be alive."

"But she spoke to you. We all heard it." He was so sympathetic, so concerned. She felt warmed by his eyes.

"It sounded like her voice," Darcy admitted.

"We need to know. If your mother is trapped on the other side, it's our duty to try to rescue her."

Her mother's voice had been in Darcy's dreams the night before. She had wakened that morning to the echo of the desperate words she had heard at the séance. *I'm alive.* Darcy felt herself moving backward, as if falling toward her childhood. She remembered when she had believed in magic, in Coyote, in her medicine bag—where had she gotten that?—in the power of wishes. It was wishful thinking to believe that her mother might be alive. Yet Paul was very serious.

She gulped down the last of her wine, feeling the tingle in her throat. "You keep saying we," she said. "You mean the people at the party?"

This time Paul did lower his voice, and leaned across the table. "The Esoteric Society. I belong to it. Dr. Ghormley is a member. Yes, they were the people at the party. We study the esoteric sciences, the lost arts, from all different cultures and traditions. We're the ones who can help you if your mother is in trouble."

"You said there was a way to know if she was alive."

"It won't prove for certain she's alive, but it will show us whether or not she died and was buried seven years ago." He leaned back in his chair again, looking at her intently with his green-black eyes. "You can still say no, Darcy, but we've already arranged it for tonight. We have the tools, the permission we need. We intend to exhume her coffin and see what's inside. I can almost promise you it won't be your mother's body."

"What? Exhume . . . no, you can't possibly . . . oh, no," Darcy heard herself say in a small, shocked voice. She felt stunned as if by a blow to the head. Her mother's coffin. She had seen it sitting by the open grave, and they had started to lower it in the ground while she and her father lingered by their car. She had gone to visit the grave every week for a while, then once a month, and now she only went on her mother's birthday. Her father paid for flowers to be placed there every Sunday. She still felt her mother's loss as if part of her body were gone, an arm or a leg or a vital organ, that could never be replaced.

Paul frowned. "You won't let us do it?"

"I . . . I can't . . . Do you really think she won't be there? But my father saw her body, a lot of people did. The rescue team, the coroner, the people who went to the funeral. She can't be alive." Darcy shook her head back and forth, back and forth. She made herself stop when she realized it, and sat still and frightened, looking at Paul.

"You won't have to look. We'll do it for you. If by some chance your mother is there, we'll bury her again quickly and respectfully. But if she isn't, you'll know. Don't you want to know, Darcy?"

It was like the dreams she had had the first few months after the accident. Her mother would come home after work as if nothing had happened. She would explain that she really wasn't dead, that she had just been gone for a while. Darcy had hated those dreams, hated waking up afterward and thinking for a moment that it was true.

"I want to know," she said after a long moment. "Yes. If you really think . . ."

"Trust me. Trust Dr. Ghormley and the Society. We know what we're doing." He reached across the table to take her hand. "Do you trust me, Darcy? You should. I only want to help you. I care about you. We all do."

"Why do you want to help me? You hardly know me." Yet she wanted to trust him, to believe what he was saying. He looked so intensely alive with the effort of convincing her. His eyes, his nearness, burned her.

His voice was almost hoarse. "I know enough. I feel the power in you. I know that I'm drawn to you, compelled by you. I want to show you everything I have seen, teach you everything I have learned. You can feel what's between us."

She could. This is crazy, a part of her shouted, but she nodded and held his hand tighter. "Yes. All right. I need to know about my mother. You said you were going to . . . to do it . . . tonight?"

"We're supposed to meet at Greenhill Cemetery at eleven. Most of the work will already be done." He was elated now, and he squeezed her hand and leaned further to kiss her softly on the lips. "You'll be glad you did this. You'll see, there's more in the world than you can imagine."

When they went out to his car it was only nine o'clock, and Darcy did not say anything when they drove the opposite direction from the cemetery. She guessed they were going to Paul's apartment, and she moved closer to him on the seat of his old Chevy sedan. She felt a kind of vertigo, a confused dizziness; she was horrified by the thought of opening her mother's grave, and excited by it, and amazed and half-frightened that Paul felt the same attraction to her that she did to him. No one had ever said that to her before: *I am drawn by you, compelled by you.* She had never wanted anyone to say it before.

They drove over a narrow railroad bridge into West Laramie, the poorer, more rural part of the town. Houses were small, wood or stucco, with patches of brown yards and old cars parked on the street and in driveways. Curtains were drawn, and the overhanging trees cast cold, reaching shadows in pools of streetlights. Most of the houses had been built by the railroad company in the early 1900s, when Laramie was a major shipping point along the interstate route. The people who lived in West Laramie were mostly Mexican-American, second- or third-generation, speaking Spanish among themselves and seen as aliens by the solidly white middle-class people of the town.

The rent was low on the west side, and students clustered in the small houses intermixed with poor families. Paul parked his car in front of a dark green box-house with flaking paint and a concrete step in front of the door. Three plastic beach chairs were arranged in a semi-circle in the weeds of the front yard. "Roommates?" Darcy asked a little nervously. She had been to a few houses like this: mini fraternities, where women always felt watched and judged, as symbols of the status of the young man who brought them there.

"Two other Society members. They're gone." He led her to the door, unlocked it, and turned on the inside light. The living room was piled with books and papers. There were no posters on the walls, no television set, no clues to the inhabitants' interests other than the books. Darcy glanced at a few. Dry textbooks mostly, though some of the titles sounded slightly occult. Paul did not offer her anything to drink or even start out with conversation on the couch; he led her back to one of the two small bedrooms and turned to kiss her without a word. She wrapped her arms around him, pressing his shoulder blades with her hands, and they moved slowly to the bed.

The way Paul made love was as insistent, as fanatic, as the way he talked, the way he danced. Yet it was graceful, gentle, and Darcy lost herself in the feelings of it much sooner than she ever had before. She was not embarrassed when her clothes were all on the floor; her body that had always seemed too angular, too muscular, pleased her tonight. Naked, Paul was the same as she had envisioned him that night at the party: supple, shadowy, proud, beautiful as a statue hidden in a secret chapel of a cathedral. His skin was cool to the touch, smooth as glass.

The time passed in measured cadences, like music, a succession of moods and feelings that cycled and changed and came back, and Darcy had never known before how deep and fierce her need for this could be. Paul never spoke, but the way he held her and stroked her and moved with her, she felt how strangely precious she was to him. She felt overwhelmed by him, lost with him in an unfamiliar place where she had been longing to go.

Was she in love with him? she asked herself when they finally lay still side by side in his narrow bed, hands intertwined. She did not know. This was what she had always imagined love was like. Her mother had told her once that she had fallen in love with her father at first sight, and he with her. Had they felt this blinding obsession, this wish to fuse yourself to another person, to join him to yourself like a second soul?

"It's time to go," Paul said finally, moving away from her. He started to put his clothes back on. Darcy hurried to the cell-like bathroom of the tiny house, used the toilet and washed her face, staring into a shaving mirror that distorted her eyes into wavy slits. She came out and dressed and followed Paul to the car, falling quickly out of her trance of pleasure into a sick feeling of dread. They drove without speaking toward the cemetery on the other side of the town.

Some of the graves in Greenhill dated from the 1870s, when Laramie was a frontier railroad town; the trees that shaded them, cottonwood and pine, had grown as tall as trees get at 7,500 feet elevation. The cemetery was well kept, mowed and groomed, but the tree shadows were sufficiently spidery and dark to be scary. Kids dared each other to meet in the cemetery at Halloween to look for ghosts. Darcy had never gone, even when she had believed her medicine bag protected her.

The dead had always terrified her. She thought of the skeleton she had seen in the rock cave. The dead were alien, unimaginably different from the living. When she had visited her mother's grave she had to make an effort not to imagine what the body looked like in its coffin. Now she would know. This was really crazy. She wondered if she might faint, or throw up. She felt off balance, like in a dream where you fall on your face with every step and can't figure out how to get back up.

The caretaker and his family lived in a house on the grounds, but the windows were dark tonight. Paul drove his car around to the back of the cemetery and through a narrow gate that had been propped open. Darcy had never visited her mother's grave from this direction, but she knew where it was. Toward the back, past the fancy memorial statues from the twenties and thirties, in a row of simple slab markers. Paul parked a hundred feet from the grave and they walked down the gravel path between markers to where half a dozen people were working over an open hole.

A low, monotonous chant was coming from a heavy man in a kaftan whom Darcy did not remember seeing at the party. Helping with the digging, in the shrouded light of a Coleman lantern at the bottom of the hole, were Dion the medium and

Dr. Ghormley. Two women Darcy did not know were kneeling at the bottom of the grave, probing with shovels.

"Darcy Jacobi," Paul said rather proudly, presenting her to the others. "You know Dion and Ariadne. This is Ephron"—he nodded to the stout man—"and Lucretia and Magdela. Have you almost reached it?" This was to Dr. Ghormley in the grave.

"A foot of dirt to go," said the woman who had been named as Magdela. She was forty years old, Darcy guessed, and she wore her hair in a teased flip from the sixties, which seemed incongruent with the eerie setting.

"I begin to believe what you said, Paul," said Dion, looking up at them. "I feel a sense of evil at my feet. Something not human is within."

"Keep digging, Dion," said the other woman, Lucretia. She looked too much like a stereotyped witch for it to be accidental. Her thick black hair was loose and tangled down her back, and she wore dark eye shadow that made her face skull-like.

It was cold out, but that wasn't why Darcy was shivering. Paul put an arm around her, not warming her. She had thought she would turn away and let them tell her what they saw. Instead, she found herself gazing fixedly at the bottom of the hole where the shovels dug more cautiously now. The dirt flung out on the opposite side had made a large mound. It was cold earth, almost frozen. They must have dug most of the hole with the cemetery's backhoe. Now they were clearing off the top of her mother's coffin, and Dion and the woman climbed out of the hole on a ladder someone had lowered. The varnished wood was pitted slightly with age, but it looked solid and heavy, an effective guard against the years and the weight of earth.

Dr. Ghormley looked up. His bearded face was lit from beneath, like the Lincoln memorial on the highway, and it looked mysterious, evil. Darcy nodded. "Go ahead." Paul held her tighter.

Ghormley cleared away the dirt from the latches on the coffin's side. His fingers gripped and released the metal springs and Darcy heard everyone around her holding their breath. The cemetery was hushed, the trees bending toward the earth to see what wonders the Esoteric Society would dig up from the ground. Darcy's eyes wandered to the toppled gravestone of her mother's grave, lying on its side near the mound of earth. "Sarah Jacobi, Beloved Wife and Mother."

Ghormley pushed open the lid of the coffin and swung the lantern over the decayed thing that lay on the padded silk. After the first moment of horror, Darcy knew with the rest of them that it was not her mother's body in the coffin. The head was swollen, misshapen, a skull only vaguely human with a ridge along the top like a dinosaur's; the arms and legs still covered with leathery flesh were long and bent oddly at the joints; the ribs curved sharply like a bent bow, as if protecting a larger and more protruding heart.

Whatever it was had been there for seven years. It was not Sarah Jacobi, beloved wife and mother. Darcy's legs felt like rubber and she sat down suddenly, dizzy. Paul let go of her hand and leaned forward over the rim of the hole.

"A demon?" Ephron said eagerly. "This is marvelous, Ghormley! Is there enough left of it to dissect?"

"Sweet Mother," said Magdela, "proof at last of alien life."

"We leave it here," said Paul. The others turned to look at him in surprise. "We don't need it. You'll see its living counterparts when we break through the barrier between the worlds."

"Yes." Ghormley closed the lid suddenly and latched it again. "I don't want to draw the attention of others like this, not yet . . ." The lantern light was faint, but Darcy thought he looked pale and shaken. "Let it stay here guarding its secret. Come, quickly, cover it up again."

He climbed out of the grave on the ladder and pulled it up behind him. The lantern was set on the ground near Darcy's knee and Dion and Ghormley started to throw dirt back into the deep hole. Dion kept shaking his head, pausing, looking down at the rapidly disappearing coffin.

"When does the caretaker get back?" Darcy asked, trying not to think about the pitiful dead creature in her mother's coffin.

"He'll be back tomorrow sometime. He thinks the cemetery is in good hands." Ephron laughed softly.

"He thinks we're the police," Lucretia said with a smile for Darcy. "A policeman friend of ours told him we needed to exhume your mother for a murder investigation. We gave him the night off to go to Denver and visit his parents. Took the whole family with him."

"So she might really be alive," Darcy said, overwhelmed by the thought. Her life had changed so much with her mother's death seven years ago. Her father had changed, had withdrawn into himself, becoming less of a parent than Alice and Ed Kennan were to Darcy. It was horrifying to think that her mother had been alive somewhere for seven years, unable to reach them.

"She must be," Dion said. "Across the border, like she said to me that night. I imagine the demon was killed by its own kind, and its shape transformed to look like your mother's body. You'll have to find a way to cross after her, girl. From what Paul says, you're the only one who can do it."

Ghormley leaned on his shovel and looked intently at Darcy. "Apparently you're supposed to already know how to cross. How to open the border. But Paul tells me you don't remember."

Darcy shook her head. "No. I've never even heard of anything like that. Crossings and borders ... I don't know. I don't remember what happened the night my mother ... the night the car crashed, but that was only about twelve hours, and I was alone."

"We must start with that night." Ghormley handed his shovel to the stout man. "Ephron, finish up here, please. Darcy, will you come with me and Paul to the lab tonight? We can take you back and see what you've lost. The secret must be there. Are you ready to remember it?"

Paul glanced at her and smiled warmly; she remembered the last hour they had shared in his bed and felt certain that she trusted him at last. Paul would not try to hurt her. Ghormley was an old friend, her friend Laura's father. She had nothing to fear from them. Now that she knew her mother might be alive, she would do anything they told her to help get her back.

# CHAPTER NINE

A t midnight on a Sunday even the campus library was closed. The wind blew stray leaves in eddies on the sidewalks, and the globe path lights that were supposed to protect lone female students made feeble attempts against the darkness. Darcy walked with Paul, past withered flower gardens and empty bike racks, as Dr. Ghormley hurried ahead of them to open the side door of White Hall and turn on the stairway lights that led down to the basement. The stairs and corridors of the building were sharp-edged and gray, less real than they were in the day, when students and professors walked there.

The lab seemed like a trap, ominously flickering as the fluorescent bulbs turned on, and Darcy felt uncertainly that she should not be there. Turn around, something told her, refuse to do this. As she walked forward with Paul she felt that she was stepping on balanced rocks, tipping them out of their resting places. She was probably a little drunk still, from the wine she had had with dinner. She trusted Paul, didn't she?

She had decided that she trusted him back at the graveyard, looking at the withered, alien face of the corpse that was not her mother.

"Don't be frightened," Dr. Ghormley said. He smiled at her from the windowed room ahead of them. Three chaise lounges waited side by side, all facing the same direction, like deck chairs on an old ocean liner. Ghormley had made an effort to avoid clinical details. The chairs were upholstered in comforting brown and gold tweed, with silk tassels on the pillows. The walls were hard and bare of any ornament, though, and when Darcy lay down in the nearest lounge she found herself looking at gray corners and darkened glass, not reassured at all.

"I've never done this," she said. "It isn't like in the movies, is it . . . I'll remember who I am and where I am, won't I?"

"You should be perfectly at ease," Ghormley said. "Paul will be right beside you, and I've done this hundreds of times. Consider me an experienced guide. You'll be traveling back into your past, just a little way, nothing so dramatic as birth experiences or past lives. Just a few years ago. Remember that you can stop the experience at any time, just by raising your hand where I can see it."

Darcy lifted her right hand and waved her fingers, unable to keep from giggling. "I feel silly," she admitted. "I'll try to take this seriously. Go ahead."

"Are you ready? Then lie back and relax."

Paul moved to the chair beside her and lay down, closing his eyes immediately and breathing deeply. Darcy also closed her eyes and tried to convince herself this was necessary.

Ghormley was telling her to concentrate on relaxing her muscles, starting with her toes. She worked her way up her body, imagining a gray blanket pulling up over her, warm and comforting. It was easy, very easy, to let go of a part of her self-awareness and feel the gentle fall into a trance state. She realized sleepily that she had done this many times before, but somehow differently. She was traveling in a deck chair this time, on an old-fashioned cruise ship, wrapped in warm flannel and staring off into the cold, choppy ocean. She felt the rock and sway of the ship, lulling her. Paul lounged beside her, wearing a fedora.

"She's under," she heard as if from another ship far off in the fog. "That was easier than I'd have thought." The voice was almost expressionless, low and monotone, pleasant to listen to. "Darcy. Raise your hand a little if you hear me."

She imagined reaching for a drink from a steward's tray. It seemed amusing in her foggy state to want another drink, but she took it and let her hand fall back onto the armrest.

"Good. Now I want you to answer my questions. Take your time, but remember I can't see anything you're experiencing unless you tell me about it. Do you know your name?"

"Darcy Jacobi. My father is Gilbert and my mother is Sarah. Was. Her maiden name was Orman." She envisioned an old lady fellow passenger, passionately interested in her life, with a soothing, deep voice. This was fun. She knew it was all her imagination, but it was so vivid, more concrete than a dream.

"Darcy, remember that I'm Dr. Ghormley, Richard if you like, and I'm going to be guiding you on a journey back a few years of your life. You can see things happen again, hear them, experience them just as you did before, but you cannot feel any physical pain. Do you understand?"

She nodded. "Just along for the ride," she said. Though her eyes were closed, she felt she could see further and clearer than before.

"Paul is with you too, but you can't see him or hear him. All right, Darcy. I want you to think about a day you remember from last year. It doesn't have to be anything special. Just an ordinary day. Go back there and tell me what you see."

Last year. She was nineteen. Darcy let herself float in her deck chair over the winter ocean, journeying. She found a day, and fell into it, a gentle fall that left her sitting on the railing of a front porch in the mountains. Roxanne's family cabin. Roxanne was next to her, stretching in her dance exercises on the planking of the porch, using the rail for a barre. "Look, Darcy, I don't think there's anything wrong with it. It isn't like a professor isn't human, is it? He's divorced, so there's nothing immoral about it anyway. I'd be getting a good grade even if I wasn't going out with him."

She went on with her argument, but Darcy heard a voice in her head saying, "That's enough, let's go further back. Now we're looking for something more important. Do you remember the accident? You were thirteen, the summer after eighth grade. Laura was with you, and your mom, and your car crashed in Vedauwoo. Let yourself drift back toward that night."

"I don't remember anything about that night," Darcy said, sure of that even in her floating deck chair. She felt the years going by as slowly as waves journeying across the ocean, from shore to shore. She found the right one: yes, she was lying in a hospital bed with her leg hanging from a high rack, distantly aware of grief. They had given her a lot of drugs. She told her guide that ruefully: "They give me a lot of drugs for the pain. That's probably why I don't remember. The days just float by. My leg hurts, though, under the drugs."

"She's in the hospital afterward," Paul's voice said. He was in another hospital bed beside her. She hadn't remembered being in a double room. "Take her further back."

"Wait," Darcy said. A man had come into her room and was arguing with the nurse. The woman said she didn't believe he was family, and the poor thing needed her rest, but finally she gave him five minutes and went out the door. The door shut. Darcy tried to focus her vision, but she couldn't get it to sharpen. She saw through the blur a dark man wearing a shirt and tie and gray slacks, his long black hair tied back in a clubbed ponytail. He looked like a teacher; was someone bringing her homework from school? She couldn't do it, she couldn't even think very well. "Go away," she said, starting to cry softly. She did that a lot, when she was awake.

"Who is it, Darcy?" asked the voice in her head. She watched the man come closer, and then she recognized him, from this morning.

"He isn't dressed right," she said, puzzled. "But it's Charlie. Charlie Stone from the ranch."

"Stay where you are," Paul's voice said gently, "don't lose the moment, Darcy. Forget what you know now. Who did you think the man was when he walked into your hospital room? Did you know him then?"

"I don't know him," she said decisively. He had started to talk to her. He had been worried, he said, but he hadn't dared to come earlier when her father was here. Was she all right? What had happened? Did she still have her medicine bag? It was the wendigo, wasn't it? He should never have let her leave the camp when he knew some of them were free. He hadn't thought they knew she existed.

She was frightened of him. He asked her things she didn't understand at all, and yet she thought she should know all those things, the wendigo, the medicine bag . . . oh, yes, she had the medicine bag. It's in my jacket pocket, she told him. How did you know about that? Who are you?

He was surprised, and angry, when he realized she did not know him. He came to the bed and took her by the shoulders, and she screamed, and the nurse came in and shouted at the man. He kept saying Darcy, you have to remember. Just think. You haven't lost all of it, you can't have. She was crying again, and she told him no, she didn't remember, if she was supposed to know him she didn't, and she wanted him to go away, he was frightening her. He looked very sad then,

and turned and left like a ghost, walking without sound.
When he stepped out into the hall, she could see that he was
wearing moccasins with his tailored slacks. The nurse followed him, still shouting, and shut the door behind them.

"You didn't know him?" the voice in her head said again.
She remembered that it was Dr. Ghormley, shipboard, and
Paul was sitting beside her on the deck.

"No. But I know him now, isn't that funny? He's Charlie
Stone. I picked him up from the Motel 6 on Thursday afternoon. He's been telling me a story, a legend really, about
Vedauwoo . . . oh, I forgot, I'm not supposed to tell anyone
about that." She was a little confused. What she remembered,
what she had forgotten, what she knew and what she wasn't
supposed to tell. It was an effort to think clearly. She thought
and said, "I wonder if I was just dreaming that scene in the
hospital. I didn't know Charlie when I was thirteen. I just met
him."

"Find out who he is," she heard Dr. Ghormley say to Paul.
"It could be important. Now, Darcy . . ." His voice relaxed
into the monotone sounds of the guide. "You have to trust
that the things you are seeing are truly memories. You've arrived just a few days after the accident. You need to leave the
hospital bed and go back. What happened in the morning of
the day the car crashed? You and Laura were at Girl Scout
camp on Pole Mountain, can you remember that?"

She nodded. It was a week-long camp for the older Scouts,
and she and Laura were junior counselors. But she hadn't
spent much time in the camp, really. She had been out in the
hills, and Laura had covered for her. No one was to know
where she had gone and what she was doing. She could not
remember what was so secret. She had walked around in the
hills. She did recall one long day, a night, and another day of
just sitting, alone, on top of a hill hidden between boulders,
waiting. For what? "I was learning something," she said
thoughtfully.

"What did you say? Darcy, remember we don't know anything unless you tell us," Dr. Ghormley's voice said. She felt the night fog closing around her and pulled her blanket closer.

"There are gaps in the images," Paul said, sounding irritated. "It looks like she went on a vision quest, but from what she sees now she was all alone, unsupervised, and nobody gave her the idea to do it."

"Darcy, you aren't remembering everything, are you aware of that?"

She nodded slowly. It was strange. She would be walking along through the sagebrush and turn to talk to someone, but there would be no one beside her, and she did not know what she was going to say. "Someone must have been with me. What's a vision quest?"

"Sitting alone on a mountaintop or in some holy place to receive power from the spirits," the guide voice said. "You must have known what you were doing then. Did you get any answers?"

"Coyote . . ." she said vaguely, and heard Paul's breath drawn sharply inward. "Yes. I saw Coyote."

"You saw a coyote," Ghormley repeated patiently.

"No. It was him, Coyote, out of the story. He couldn't really be there because he's dead, but he is my spirit guide. I have . . . in my medicine bag I have power from him." She didn't remember knowing this before. Everything was still wrong. She found herself sitting on a round log at the edge of the dirt parking lot where the parents were coming that evening to pick up the campers and the counselors. Laura sat beside her, kicking her feet in the dust. Her mother was late. Darcy had her medicine bag in her hands, and she was braiding and unbraiding the fringe at the bottom of it, until she grew afraid that the old leather would crack and fall apart.

"Who told you about Coyote and medicine power?" Ghormley said, sending her back into the fog where she floated in her chair. "Who was with you in the hills, Darcy?"

"Don't push her, she's getting there," Paul said. "Darcy, go back and think about the medicine bag. What is inside it? Do you know what's inside?"

Old medicine, very powerful, and she had to respect it and be careful of it. "Owl feathers, for death, for . . . for surviving death?" she answered in confusion. "A worked stone, a piece of flint worked by hand, because it's a part of the earth and people both . . . and Coyote's ear, a piece of it, back from across the border." She found herself laughing at an old joke that wasn't very good when she first made it. "Not everyone has the ear of their spirit guide in their pocket."

"Go on through the evening, Darcy," Ghormley's voice said with eagerness under the monotone. "Remember. What happened after your mother picked you and Laura up?"

She was holding the medicine bag and thinking so deeply she did not hear the car drive up until it was parked inches from her feet. "Hi, Mom, you're late," she said, and hurried into the car.


The rain had started almost the moment they left the camp-ground, as they drove alone up the narrow, twisting road out of the valley. The sunset was extinguished by the black clouds, and the road was dark and suddenly dangerous. The headlights seemed to stretch only a few inches in front of them. From the front seat, Darcy glanced out the window and saw a gaping ditch on the roadside right underneath them: "Mom!" she shouted, and her mother veered into the center of the rutted road.

"We're okay," Sarah Jacobi said, smiling, but keeping her eyes trained intently on the windshield between the flashing wipers. "I was helping Ed Kennan with the bread and it was evening before I knew it. I should have gotten here before the rain."

"Are we having dinner at the Kennans'?" Darcy asked. "Laura too?"

"Laura too. I called her father and he said it was all right for her to get home late." They had reached the fork in the road; one way led up to the interstate on-ramp, and the other angled back down into the pine-dark valleys toward Vedauwoo. "Not too late, though. Let's cut through the park."

She had already turned onto that road. Darcy sat back with a sigh, thinking that it was silly to be afraid of Vedauwoo just because she knew about the wendigo now. She would have to start spending a lot of time there if she was going to be a new Guardian. She wished she could have gone with Charlie to chase the wendigo who were free. And he had not taken the time to explain to her how they had broken through; she wanted to know that. He had come scratching at her tent late last night and whispered that he had to go, that some wendigo had gotten out. She wasn't to worry, and she should go on home and wait for him to contact her. Sometimes he treated her like she was still a ten-year-old kid.

"Charlie, and wendigo . . ." a distant voice said, confusing her. Another voice whispered, "Don't question her now, she'll lose it. Wait."

They drove slowly down the back road into Vedauwoo, rain sheeting the outside of the car, the wipers barely pushing it back and the defroster clearing only a small moon-shape at the bottom of the windshield. Darcy turned to look back at Laura, but her friend was off in a daydream.

Laura's face was reflected against the glass in the spooky light of the dashboard dials. After a week of camp, Laura's hair still fell in a smooth, side-parted blond curve, and she was wearing lipstick. Darcy's wavy hair was hopelessly tangled. She had given up trying to comb it two days ago, after her night out in the wind on the hilltop. It didn't look much worse than usual. Laura could read all the parts in Shakespeare plays in different voices, and she had spent the first half of the summer at the music festival in Aspen with her violin. She was a fierce friend, assuring Darcy that the junior-high boys who ignored them would be sighing at them and serenading them in high school. They were going to dress like artists and wear their hair up. They were going to be unique beauties.

The boulders loomed over them, dark, huge, stacked in twisted shapes that looked like surly old gods and demons. The Vedauwoo mountains were black shapes in the rain. On the steepest incline of the park road, Darcy's mother suddenly began to fight with the steering wheel.

"Oh, Jesus ... what's wrong, I can't ... hold on! Hold on!" The car flopped like a trout fighting the fisherman's line, back and forth across the curved road in the rushing furrows of rain, slipping on the grade and spinning toward the ditch.

"Mom!" Darcy screamed, reaching toward her. On her mother's shoulder crouched a wizened long-armed creature, grinning and showing its teeth. Its hands clutched at Sarah Jacobi's upper arms, fighting against her last control of the car. It leaned forward as Darcy stared at it, and took the wheel, wrenching it hard to the right. Darcy's mother didn't see the wendigo, must not feel its clawed feet on her shoulder. She had a bewildered, terrified look on her face.

The car spun all the way around once, then plunged over the low wooden barrier as if going over a waterfall. Darcy curled up in her seat, her head between her knees, her seat belt holding her as they flew for a long moment through the lashing rain, then hit on the front bumper and flipped.

The fall had seemed slow and timeless, but the crash was over in a moment. Darcy had closed her eyes when the car started to roll, and she hit her head on the dashboard as her body lurched forward, but the seat belt held her back. There was a shriek of rending metal and an awful scream from Laura, and the car was still. She was upside down.

"Get out fast, it might blow up," Darcy said in a shrill voice. She opened her eyes and saw the crushed car roof inches from her head. Her knees pressed against the floor above her, and the dashboard was in her lap. The door on her side had fallen open. She could just reach to unbuckle her seat belt, and she scrambled out the door on her back like an overturned turtle, turning onto her hands and knees on the muddy earth.

It was too dark to see much, but when she looked back inside the car she saw Laura's face still and darkened with thick blood, her body wedged impossibly between the roof and the backseat. The driver's seat was empty. Her mother must have been thrown clear. Maybe the latch of her seat belt had burst open.

"Mom!" she called into the freezing rain that swallowed all other sound. She started around the car, the soles of her tennis shoes slipping in the mud. She zipped her leather jacket up to her chin with fingers that were already numb. Her hat, gloves, and scarf were in the backseat in her backpack, with Laura.

"I'm okay, Darcy. I'm over here." Sarah Jacobi was sitting on the ground twenty feet from the car, rubbing one knee and squinting to see her. "Where's Laura?"

"Trapped inside. I don't know . . . I just looked, I didn't touch her, but I think she might be dead." All the stories Charlie had told her, with people dying, she had never pictured it like that, just a waxen, crushed silence, an emptiness in the eyes.

"Stay here, honey. I'll go see." Her mother stood up carefully and limped over to the flattened, twisted car. One wheel still spun in the rain. Darcy watched her creep back under the front seat of the driver's side and lean over to look.

A hard-skinned hand gripped Darcy's arm. She looked down and screamed. A wendigo peered up at her with yellow eyes, its wrinkled old man's face like a corpse's in the dark. She smelled a rank animal odor as she pulled backward and tried to get away from it. Another long-armed creature stopped her, grasping her around the waist. There were another twenty of them in the ditch where the car had rolled, and they gathered around her like a pack of wolves.

Her mother turned around when she heard her scream. She scrambled out of the wrecked car. Darcy struggled and kicked, but the wendigo lifted her up and carried her like a football hero on their shoulders, up the slope toward one of the boulder mountains. She was high in the freezing rain, gripped in a dozen places by clawed hands that scratched and pinched, so terrified that she did not know whether the crash was still happening and she was trapped in the plunging car.

"Darcy! Where are you?" Her mother was following, running, but Darcy knew that the wendigo's alien presence made her almost invisible. Only Guardians could see them. Her mother couldn't know what was happening. "Dear God, Darcy, come back . . ." Darcy could hear her cry out when she fell and picked herself up again.

"Here, I'm here!" Darcy shouted. The wendigo held her tighter. She closed her eyes against the jolting, feeling sick to her stomach. Her mother couldn't do anything to save her. Only border Guardians had the power to fight the wendigo. Charlie could save her if he was anywhere near. He had saved her before, when the wendigo attacked her in the Black Hills.

"Charlie!" she yelled into the wind. The rain seemed to devour her words. "Charlie, help me, oh, please, hurry!" She kept calling his name. The wendigo carried her between overhanging boulders onto the slippery rock face of the mountain. The granite was smooth, cracked in places, angled just steeply enough that Darcy and her friends used to dare each other to run up it until they couldn't go higher. The wendigo were more surefooted than Darcy, Laura, and Roxanne.

They dropped her once, trying to pass her up onto a rock ledge, and she rolled away and almost fell off into a wide cleft before they caught her again. She was lifted up, sobbing, and she saw where they were taking her. A balanced rock on a high outcropping gleamed and pulsed with a dark, alien power that made Darcy's bones ache as they climbed nearer.

"Charlie," she said, crying, "Coyote, anyone at all, please, please help me." She could hear her mother running, gasping and panting for breath, somewhere below them in the wind-blown trees.

At the top of the balanced rock was a hole, usually just a small, round crater the size of a birdbath. It had grown big enough for the wendigo to step through and vanish in a swirling emptiness. Darcy watched two of her captors disappear that way, like falling into a deep well filled with wind, or the center of a tornado. On the other side she was sure they would kill her. She screamed and struggled again, finding strength left in her frozen arms and legs. The wendigo held onto her and dragged her toward the expanding hole in the rock.

"Darcy . . ." Her mother was just below them, crying in fear. "Honey, come on down from there, it's all right."

Claws held her and cold, wet fur pressed against her. The wendigo moved to the edge of the yawning emptiness and Darcy felt her hair fly around her face in the tornado wind. She got a hand free and clutched at her medicine bag, crying for Charlie, for Coyote. When she had it in her hand she felt herself spinning around, pushed backward, jerked away from the wendigo. They could not hold onto her anymore.

One of them reached long arms and grasped the end of the medicine bag, though it howled in seeming pain when it had a firm hold. Darcy pulled back and the wendigo pulled forward, and the hole in the rock was getting smaller. The border was closing, she realized suddenly. Then the strap of the medicine bag broke, and she felt herself step out over empty space, as her mother climbed doggedly up onto the balancing rock.

"No! Darcy!" She saw her mother's anguished face and then Darcy fell backward off the boulder with the rain in her eyes. She landed with her legs crumpled up under her and rolled like an avalanche down the slope, breaking loose bits of gravel and uprooting bushes from their precarious hold on the sheer rock. She tried to hold her arms over her face as she rolled, but she couldn't keep them there. At last her momentum stopped in a crack of the granite and she lay there like a broken watch, still ticking . . . she could hear her heartbeat, loud in her ears, but the pain of her bruises and the slowly growing agony of her twisted right leg blocked out any other awareness.

"Mom . . ." she said weakly, then shouted, "Mom! I . . . I'm hurt, I think my leg's broken . . ." The mountain was spinning, rotating slowly in the heavy rain. She heard silence around her. She called again and again and got no answer. The wendigo were gone. No one climbed down to her from the slope of the boulder mountain.

It was her fault if the wendigo had hurt her mother. She had never told Sarah any of this, any of the unbelievable things Charlie had taught her. He hadn't taught her enough, though . . . she hadn't known how to fight when the wendigo took her. Only the medicine bag, remembered late, had done something. Her hand crept to her neck and felt the section of broken leather strap that still looped over her jacket collar. The medicine bag was gone. The wendigo had it in its hand when she fell.

The spinning had grown worse and her pain was like an animal with teeth, tearing through her, not staying in her leg as it should. She felt herself losing awareness, and her last thought was that Charlie Edgewalker had been nowhere near. He had abandoned her, he had not even tried to save her . . . he must have known she was in danger, and now . . . She spun away on a tide of pain, into the blackness, into the fog.

# CHAPTER TEN

ll right. Slowly now." Dr. Ghormley's voice counted her forward through the years. "When you feel ready, open your eyes."

Darcy listened to her pounding heartbeat and felt the past fall away again; then she was herself, lying in a chaise lounge in the laboratory with Paul beside her. She remembered what she had experienced while she was in the trance, but nothing more: if she really had known Charlie before, she did not remember anything about him. All she knew were the thoughts she had during the drive, the crash, the chase up the mountain.

She opened her eyes to dim light and Dr. Ghormley smiling at her, his forehead shiny with sweat. He looked tense and tired. Paul's breathing was shallow, and he did not open his eyes for a long moment. When he did, he turned toward her with a secret, shadowed expression, as if he were wearing a transparent mask. His eyes were almost black.

"I . . . don't know how much of that was real." Darcy sat

up and put her feet on the floor, feeling stifled by the processed air of the basement room. She tried to breathe deeply, but when Dr. Ghormley took her hand to help her to her feet she was shaking.

"I saw it happening," Paul said. "It was real."

"It was not a dream, Darcy." Ghormley led her into a comfortable office on the other side of the one-way glass and settled her on a couch, then collapsed into an overstuffed chair. Paul sat down by Darcy.

"How could you have seen it?" She had accepted that easily during the trance. Now it seemed impossible that Paul could experience her memories with her.

"You could learn to do it." Ghormley leaned forward and looked at her with the intent focus she had come to dislike. "If you have the power Paul senses in you. You could be trained to use your power for many things."

"I remembered being unconscious on the mountain, and my medicine bag was gone. But when the park ranger found me the next morning I know I was beside the car in the ditch. And I had the medicine bag. The strap was broken, but that's all."

"I wish you had remembered more," Paul said, still seeming distant, strange. "You were kidnapped by the demons and escaped, that's clear. Your mother must have gone through the border when it closed. But you didn't see how to get through and get her back."

It was hard to think clearly. Darcy tried to work it out, speaking slowly. She still felt suffocated by the air around her. "They aren't demons," she said, feeling her way. "They are wendigo. They must be the same ones in the legend Charlie told me, the ancient tribe that was cursed. But I can't believe they're real. How can any of it be real?"

"All peoples have different names for the demons," said Ghormley, the lecturing professor again. "But I have no doubt that these are the same demons that have given men knowledge and power over the centuries. We must break through to them." He turned away from them, frowning.

Paul took Darcy's hand and looked at her. His eyes were back to normal now, and eager as a hunter's. "You must think of everything you know. This legend you speak of. This man Charlie Stone who seems to mean something to you. The memories we've raised of the crash and the creatures you saw. Something must fit together to help us."

"Let's go outside," Darcy said, giving in to her dislike of the basement rooms. "I'll try to think."

They walked out of the office into the chill night on campus. Ghormley followed them, pacing slowly. Paul kept his hand in hers, warm and encouraging. Darcy thought of her mother, a vivid picture of her face, a glimpse Darcy had when she fell off the boulder. If she was alive . . .

"I'll do anything to help you, if you help me find her," she said, certain of that much.

Ghormley moved decisively to walk beside her. His voice was brisk. "I think we'll trust you, Darcy. We already know something of this demon world." She watched his face; he was more excited than he had ever been in class. "There are borders between our world and the demon one. A few people are born near the borders, with a power to affect them, to help keep them closed or break them open. I've heard those people called Guardians. You must be a Guardian, but you haven't been trained in the tradition. Unless that training is something you still can't remember."

"If this Charlie is a Guardian . . ." Paul began.

"I think he must be," Darcy said. "I wish I remembered more. He's not much older than I am . . . but he looked the same when I saw him in my memory, in the hospital. I don't understand that."

"He'll try to keep us from opening the border if he's in the old tradition." Ghormley spoke to Paul as if Darcy were not there. "He might be turned, but that would take time I don't want to spare. We'll have to consider him an adversary. Darcy, do you have any strong friendship for this man?"

"I hardly know him." But she looked at him worriedly. "You wouldn't try to hurt him . . ."

"If we move fast enough he won't know until the border is open," Paul said.

She nodded. It fit with her memory and with the legend of the wendigo. Guardians . . . there was a dead Guardian in the legend. A man who was buried near the border, who kept watch in spirit. She felt it over in her mind, like a tongue feeling a loose tooth.

"I think . . . I might have something," she said. The bones of the warrior in the buried cave where the coyote had led her. Could that have been the Guardian from the story? And the coyote, then . . . She had promised Charlie to keep the legend a secret. She had thought when she left the buried warrior that she would keep the location secret. But this was important. This was her mother's life.

Darcy took a deep breath and told them about her ride on Thursday morning and the cave she found. "It seems straight out of the legend . . . I don't know. It could just be an ordinary burial. But the coyote makes me think . . ."

"Yes." Paul's dark eyes glowed. "The binding can be loosened at the grave of the Guardian. And with Darcy at the border itself, surely we can open the way."

"We can't do any more tonight." Ghormley led them across a patch of lawn, a shortcut to the parking lot. Their feet crunched in leaves, and the dry smell began to clear Darcy's head.

"When should I come back into town?" she asked.

Paul shook his head. "Your friend Stone might sense something. It's too dangerous for you to go back to the ranch."

Ghormley agreed. "She can sleep in my daughter's room tonight."

She would have to call Alice and tell her she was spending

the night with Roxanne. "All right. There's another thing. His name in my memory was different. Charlie Edgewalker. I don't know if that means anything."

"More likely to be his true name," Paul said. "Richard, I wonder if we dare leave him alone tomorrow. Perhaps we'd better get him out of the way."

"I'll consider it." Ghormley looked at Paul as if warning him. "We must all rest and think about what we're going to do. But tomorrow night Darcy will lead us to the Guardian's grave, and we will open the door."

"And rescue my mother," Darcy said, reminding him. "That's why we're doing this."

"It's a worthy cause, but not our only purpose. I'll explain it to you tomorrow." Ghormley was smiling now. "I can hardly believe it. We're going to do it. And it should work . . . Paul, will it work, to use the grave? What if it isn't the Guardian spirit?"

"It is. It has to be." Paul let go of Darcy's hand. "I'll tell the others myself. I don't trust a phone call, not with this. We must be quiet tonight and tomorrow. Not speak about it even among ourselves. Darcy, you're wonderful, you've helped us more than I would have dreamed." He leaned over to kiss her and then turned and jogged away down a dark sidewalk.

"The Esoteric Society will owe you a great debt," Ghormley said rather pompously. "Finally, finally . . ." He turned his elation inward and walked quietly with her to the parking lot. Darcy stayed with him, as tired as if she hadn't slept for days, uncertain if she was doing the right thing or if she and all the Esoteric Society were completely mad.

Shallow, restless images had kept Charlie from deep sleep last night. He had wakened at dawn out of a dream of eating rice and beans over his stove. He had meant to go back into early memories again, but had gone no further than his kitchen. Disappointed in the night, he put his real breakfast on a plate and went out to eat it on the front step of his trailer.

He had broiled cheese and oregano on a tortilla, fried an egg, and wrapped them together. He ate as he watched the pink ball of the sun rise behind the pine trees in his hollow, over hills that soon had the morning texture of boulders and grass, light and shadow. Color slowly bled back into the world. He stood and faced the sun, but the warmth did not reach far inside him.

More and more he felt cold, detached, scarcely a part of this world at all. It could be seen in the way he had worked with Darcy since he had returned: cautious, quiet, waiting and watching instead of acting forcefully. He was the Guardian of this land. He should still feel a kinship to it, if he was akin to anything anymore, but that was fading.

Once he had been part of the world, full of dreams for his people, for the land. He could remember things he had done, but not how it had felt; not how it had felt to fight, to make love, to believe he could change the world. It seemed now as if he had always been half-dead inside.

Enough. He set his plate down for the squirrels to clean, and set his hat firmly on his head for his usual mile-and-a-half run to the horse barns. He had chores to do if he wanted to keep this convenient job. After the horses were moved and fed, he might take Darcy up to the Guardian's grave. The time had passed for caution. If she did not believe him or did not understand the importance of what he told her, he would show her something stronger; the border itself, perhaps.

Alice Kennan told Charlie that Darcy had stayed overnight at a friend's house and wouldn't be home at all today. And later, Alice was bringing a group of ladies, 4-H mothers, out to see the horses. She offered Charlie the afternoon off; he took up her offer with relief. He had never been comfortable in that kind of social situation. A few times in the past he had been trapped. "Ladies" in groups seemed unable to avoid asking him silly questions about Indians. There was also the chance that one or two 4-H mothers might remember having seen him around Laramie about seven years before, or even before that, unchanging, and that could be dangerous.

Even Ed Kennan seemed a little suspicious of him now. Last night the old man had asked him personal questions for the first time: what tribe was he from, where else had he worked, what made him want to work at their ranch? Charlie answered as truthfully as he could. He had references from three years' work on a ranch in western Colorado. But if Ed thought to check with the Northern Cheyenne tribe council in Montana, he would find no record in the registry of Charles Stone. The name of Charlie Gray Stone might turn up in a computer somewhere, but he was supposed to have died in 1890.

As he worked alone, thinking about Darcy, Charlie found himself drawn more and more into memories of his early life. Especially his first encounter with the wendigo, and his great failure. He needed the passion of his youth, his old fire, to win Darcy back as his apprentice. He could go back. In a vision trance, not in faded memories; experience it again, try to understand it, try to bring his young self up from the depths of his cold spirit.

Late in the morning he made himself some sandwiches and saddled the pinto to ride up into the hills. He had not named the horse, he realized as he rode it out of the corral. It was a tool, like a car, a means of transportation. That was not right. It was not how he should feel. It was another example of his detachment from the world and the land; his alienation from himself.

Layered clouds, thick and white, drifted low over the dry, yellow prairie and touched the tips of pines on the hilltops. The air was cold and damp, and the clouds seemed heavy, but as yet there was no snow. What had fallen a few days ago was already gone except for a few patches in sheltered places. The horse walked briskly, head carried high, ears forward. It was connected to the land, Charlie thought, alive and eagerly involved with what it saw, what it felt. It probably had a name for him by now.

When he was far enough away from the buildings of the Kennan ranch he began to chant quietly, letting the song fall into the rhythm of his horse's walk. *Coyote my brother, walk with me now, Coyote my brother, my brother Coyote, walk with me now . . .*

Over and over, quieting his own distracted thoughts, narrowing the world down to a simple place, calming his mind and sharpening his awareness of other things besides sky, sagebrush, trees, the horse. Slowly, with effort, the chant forced him to become the Edgewalker again. He knew the borderlands like no other man. Knew their feel, the taste of the air around them, the shadows that moved within them. The shadow that now paced with his horse, not quite solid, not made of fur and bone, but alive with wild, clever intelligence. Coyote trotted beside them, and Charlie told him what he sought: the connection, the passion he had lost.

They rode to a barren ravine where rocks had formed a dry cave, like the Guardian's burial place but not so hidden. With the horse picketed outside, Coyote sitting quietly by him, his back against stone and his legs crossed on the earth, Charlie let his spirit wander into trance and seeking. Himself he sought, himself young and full of life and anger. Memories drifted past like windblown clouds. He chose one and called it forward and Coyote's guidance helped him to forget himself, to lose his awareness as he fell into a boy's thoughts and emotions, so alien to him now that he hardly recognized them. Here it began, his rebellion, his crime. Watch and remember, his conscious self whispered, and then was gone.

\* \* \*

Before he stepped down from the freight car, Charlie shouldered his bag of books and clothes, all he owned, and squinted into the sunlight that slanted across the crowded platform. Dust hung in the air from the rattling of wagons and horses down the dirt streets of Rapid City. Most of the passengers had already gotten off. Charlies watched them: a pretty girl who had smiled at him on the train, and her mother, who had scowled and hurried her away whispering; they were bargaining with a liveryman for the price of taking their trunks to their hotel. A bearded man who had spat on the floor at Charlie's feet seeming by accident as he passed; he was greeted by friends, a woman and two young men, and he was as charming a gentleman as you could hope to see.

No one looked in Charlie's direction. He did not see the man who had written to say he would meet him, a tame Sioux doctor named John Surrey, held up to Charlie as an ideal by the headmaster at the school he had just left. At sixteen, Charlie was finished with what the boarding school had to teach him. The headmaster had tried to talk him into going on to college in the East like Dr. Surrey. He didn't want to go East. It would be more of what he had to face on the train. He would be surrounded by white people who saw past his short haircut and cheap cloth suit to classify him as a tame Indian, harmless probably but best avoided. He hated them anyway. He had hated them all ever since he learned they had killed his mother and father.

John Surrey had written him his first letter two months ago, on behalf of a Sioux medicine man named Angry Dog. The medicine man reminded Charlie that he was a Guardian and said it was time to begin his training in the old ways. Charlie smiled a little in memory, seeing the headmaster's red face and waving hands during the five-hour lecture he had given Charlie on religion and his duty to better his race. The man had intercepted and read the letter, of course.

To get away he had to promise them he would think about

it, and that he would talk to this John Surrey, who had done everything they wanted. The headmaster had even written Surrey back to suggest he take Charlie as an assistant at the Cheyenne River reservation. This Charlie would not do. He had a place already, in the cabin of Angry Dog, and his real education was about to begin.

"Move on, boy," grumbled a baggage handler. Charlie jumped down to the platform and moved through the crowd, fighting back fear at the feeling of so many whites so close to him. He was used to the teachers at the school, but except for them he had spent his last ten years with boys like himself. The white women especially scared him. They were so soft-looking, wrapped up in skirts and hats and shawls, glancing aside at him out of blue and green eyes, as pale and dangerous as ghosts.

Down at the edge of the station platform, sitting on a rough-coated horse and holding the reins of another, Charlie saw a young dark-skinned man dressed much the same as he was. John Surrey wore a braid down his back, though, not the short schoolboy cut Charlie had expected. The horses were thin and bony, big-eyed, wearing shabby saddles with old blankets to pad their fence-rail backs. Surrey signed a greeting, a slight movement of his hand away from his reins. The boys at school had used the Plains sign language to talk to one another without the teachers knowing.

"You're Charlie Gray Stone? I'm John Surrey," the man said when Charlie reached his side. "Tie your bag on back of your saddle and we'll go." Surrey had old pockmarks on his face. He must have lived through one of the white man's diseases when he was a child. Aside from the marks, he was handsome, much taller than Charlie, with a high-bridged, thin nose that showed his tribe. The Cheyenne had broader faces.

"Thank you for meeting me." Charlie did not meet the young man's eyes, feeling suddenly shy. He tied rawhide strings around his book bag and mounted the horse, awkward as a child; he had not ridden a horse since he was six years old. The school couldn't afford to keep a stable. He was eager to learn again, remembering the freedom he had felt once when his father told him he was big enough to ride by himself. The horse seemed much smaller, naturally, than horses had when he was six. It rolled an eye warily at him, and he petted its neck as if it were a cat. Its body felt strong and warm between his legs.

Five cowboys galloped by, too fast for this busy street, and one of them threw something that bounced off John Surrey's shoulder; an apple core, Charlie saw when it landed in the dust. Surrey said something to his horse in Lakota and it began to walk into the street. Charlie's followed without guidance from him.

"You just let them throw things at you?" he demanded of Surrey's back.

"I'm a doctor, not a warrior," the young man said. "And better so; if we started a fight those boys would be happy to kill us. They're sorry to have missed all the best Indian fighting."

"I am sorry too," Charlie muttered to his horse's ears. How was he to become a man if he could not fight? It was his right in the old way to avenge his parents' death on the tribe that killed them. But he knew that if he killed any whites he would be caught and hanged. The Plains were too civilized in 1890; he had been born much too late. At the end of things.

"Your Mr. McInerny said you might be interested in working for me," Surrey said as he turned his horse down a side street. "There's a lot to be done. I could use a helper who could look something up in my books if need be. Not many of us Hunkpapa have been to school yet, and most of the educated Cheyenne are working as policemen."

"You rode all this way for nothing if you thought you were getting an assistant," Charlie said, no longer trying to be polite. "I'm already apprenticed."

"To Angry Dog, sight unseen?" Surrey laughed softly. "I know that. He told me not to try to tempt you away from the path you must follow. Sanctimonious old buzzard. You're welcome to try his path, Charlie. I wonder if you'll be able to learn much, though. Angry Dog doesn't speak any English, and you don't know Lakota."

"He promised to teach me. I'll learn what I need to know." But the problem with language had not occurred to Charlie before. He felt almost as small as he had when he had first been sent to the white man's school.

"My offer stands," Surrey said irritably. "I meant it when I said I could use you. Wait until you get to the reservation. You'll see that what the people need is another doctor, not another religious fool."

Low black clouds cast gloomy shadows over the hills, though the sky was clear above the wagon road. Charlie's spirits rose as he grew accustomed to the brisk rhythm of the horse's walking, and he sat up straighter and breathed the pine-scented air. It was late in August, and the grass was dry, burnt-looking from drought. They passed streams that were beds of cracked mud. The Black Hills were dark with thick stands of trees, interrupted by outcroppings of high granite rock faces, cracked and worn by the weather. The hills were sacred ground to the Sioux, and the Cheyenne had migrated through them many generations ago and remembered their power.

"What do you call this horse?" Charlie said, breaking silence after long hours on the wagon road.

"He's called Mouse," Surrey said. "You know the children's story, Jumping Mouse who goes off to see the sacred mountains. It's a good name. The horse can go all day, always wanting to see what's ahead." He liked to talk, this John Surrey. He seemed eager to be friendly again.

"Mouse." Charlie barely remembered the story. The mouse

turned into an eagle at the end, he thought. There was a buffalo in it. His mother had told it to him once or twice.

"Mine is Star, for the mark on his forehead. I got him from the last station agent at Pine Ridge when he left. He's a quarter horse, though you couldn't tell by looking at him. There hasn't been much feed for them this year."

"Whose horse is Mouse?" They were bony animals, but not weak. Charlie thought that he would like to groom Mouse, and plait his mane, and find him extra food. He liked the horse's big eyes and the way he tossed his head when he wanted to go faster.

Surrey looked back at him. "Angry Dog traded for him, and named him, a couple of months ago. He's yours. I told the old man that you weren't riding from the school, you were coming in on the train. He said that a boy should have a horse."

Charlie felt a glowing inside himself, like a small newborn flame. No one had given him anything since he was a little boy. His books, his clothes, he had to work for at the school. He had no parents to send him gifts. He thought he remembered that to give a young man a horse was to promise to stand as his father; Angry Dog was adopting him, or at least making a pledge to look out for him.

"Teach me some Lakota," he said now to Surrey. "Enough that I may thank him when I meet him."

The doctor reined in his horse to ride beside Charlie and Mouse, and they began his first lesson in the Sioux language. There was so much he would need to learn. So much he would have to forget from the last ten years of his life.

In the late afternoon they passed a small train of five wagons, settlers headed for the newly opened land that had been carved out of the reservations. The men on the wagon seats moved rifles into their laps and looked at him and Surrey half in fear, half in scorn; women walking in the road dust clustered together like startled chickens. Charlie would have liked to be wearing war paint, or have a few scalps dangling from his bridle.

They trotted past the travelers. Surrey waved, but no one spoke. Soon they were alone again in a section of the road that cut through pine forest. Rotted logs had fallen across the path in places, and Charlie enjoyed the thought that the wagons would have to stop and the men would have to clear the road.

Charlie felt as if he were being watched—watched and judged—as he rode between the shadowed trees. He wished he had been allowed to grow his hair long like Surrey's. He wished he was not wearing a brown cloth suit with buttons and a starched shirt with a collar. His horse should not have a saddle with stirrups; though that would make it harder for him to ride. How could the land judge him as he was?

Neither he nor Surrey was a man, in the old sense. Neither of them would ever be a man. They had not stolen horses, had never counted coups or hunted buffalo, or trailed a wounded Crow after a raid; they would never kill an enemy and bring his scalp home to hang on the lodgepole so everyone would see how brave they were. All they could do, either of them, was what they had been taught by white men. Charlie's father and uncle would have been ashamed of him, if they had lived to see him at sixteen years. He hoped that Angry Dog would not be too disappointed in the Guardian he had pledged to teach.

# CHAPTER
# ELEVEN

T he world was made of heat and cold—heat and cold, bone-deep weariness, and a longing for sleep. The sweat lodge by the riverbank became the world for three nights and days, as the boy sat naked and nameless beside the heated stones or ran, chased by old men, to the river, where he leaped in and swam until they called him out again. They had taken his name the first morning, the medicine man and the two old Cheyenne helpers who interpreted for him. They gave him dried roots to chew while he crouched by the white-hot stones in the sweat lodge, until his head seemed as light as the steam that rose when the old men doused the stones with water from the river.

They told him stories and made him tell them back again, and whipped him with green branches when he forgot any part. They taught him songs in the Sioux language he did not understand; he had to sing them standing on one leg or up on the balls of his feet until his calves cramped up and he fell to the earth. Whenever his eyes closed and he began to drift desperately into sleep they yelled at him in two languages and hit him with branches or drove him up onto his feet and out the door of the hide-covered lodge, down the short path to the river, where the icy water sucked all thoughts of rest from his exhausted body.

The old men took turns going out and resting when they needed to, but it seemed that the medicine man was always in the lodge with him. Dark eyes beneath heavy brows pinned him sharply in place, holding him beside the aching heat of the stones. Often the medicine man chanted over him, dancing around him even over the hot river rocks, shaking a bone rattle or drawing symbols on the boy's sweat-slick body with an owl feather.

Early in the third day after the longest night yet, he was sure he saw Coyote dancing in the medicine man's place, and felt rough fur pressed against him, and a small heavy bundle placed in his hands; his mind wandered afterward in strange visions of monsters and creatures he had never seen, and he saw his parents' ghosts speaking sober words of warning from their places of rest, but he could not understand what they said. He did not come back to himself until he was half drowning in the river and the medicine man had waded in up to his waist to catch him under the arms and drag him back toward the shore.

"It was Coyote," he said hoarsely, his head barely above water. He struggled out of the medicine man's grasp. "He gave it back to me, my medicine bag. Where is it?"

The medicine man only smiled at him, and he remembered that the man could not understand Cheyenne. He felt as clean and cold as snow as they walked together out of the river, and the two old men came forward to wrap them both in old buffalo hides. The stones inside the sweat lodge hissed as they walked past, and he realized that the fire had been allowed to go out. It must be over, then. He hardly remembered anything that had gone before the heat and cold of the lodge and the river. His mouth and tongue were dry, and his stomach hurt, as shriveled and empty as a dry seedpod. They walked toward the cabin, on a rise overlooking the sweat lodge, the river, and a pasture where four horses were grazing on dry autumn grass.

"My ... my name," he murmured to the old man who walked with him, holding the buffalo robe around him. "I don't ..."

"Chah-lee," the medicine man said with a quiet lilt to his voice. He added another long word that the boy could not catch.

"Charlie," said the old man beside him, then added in Cheyenne, "and Edgewalker. It is your manhood name, your Guardian name."

"You've been purified, cleansed of the white man's stink that was on you. The white man's food is gone from your body now, and the clothes you came with were burned." The second old Cheyenne opened the cabin door for them and lit a lamp. The single room had no windows, only a smoke hole in the middle of the roof above the firepit. Two sleeping pallets had been unrolled on the men's side. A clutter of pots, baskets, and bundles wrapped in hides lay against the other three walls.

Charlie began to remember himself as the medicine man took his hand and led him to one of the pallets. His medicine bag, worn and familiar, lay there on a pillow of suede. He knelt down and picked it up, looking back at the medicine man for an explanation; how could it have come here? He remembered his dream when he was a boy, how Coyote had taken it; he had thought that the headmaster must still have it in a drawer of his desk. Maybe McInerny had sent it here before him as a goodwill gesture to a graduating student.

"Sleep now," said one of the Cheyenne. He put a blanket around his shoulders and he and his companion left the cabin. Charlie heard them calling their horses and riding away.

He lay down full length on the pallet, still holding the medicine bag in both hands. The medicine man, who must be Angry Dog, pulled a buffalo robe over him, and then lay down beside him on the second pallet. That was right, the man must be as tired as he was. Charlie wanted to ask questions, but his eyelids dropped as if weighted and he felt himself sinking toward the earth into sleep. Besides, he remembered before he slept, Angry Dog would not be able to answer him in any language he could understand.

When Charlie woke late in the morning of the next day, Angry Dog was waiting. He was an impressive-looking man, probably forty-five years old, showing muscles that must have been powerful when he was young. His hair was tied with rawhide straps, braided in four braids that reached his waist. He wore a headband with three owl feathers. He dressed in the old style, not even using trader blankets as most Indians had before the reservations. He wore a breechclout of soft fawn leather, fringed buckskin leggings, a shirt of beaded doeskin, and a buffalo robe fashioned into a cape that tied around his neck.

Charlie put on the garments he found beside his pallet. Leggings and breechclout felt strange, harsh against his skin that was used to cloth. The moccasins were soft on his feet after the hard white men's shoes, but would offer little protection against stones and branches in the forest. For a shirt he had only a fringed vest. He knew he was supposed to get used to the cold. It was part of his training to ignore it. The September weather might be comfortable sometimes, but mostly he would have to keep moving, keep working, to stay warm.

The Sioux language was his curriculum, along with wood-gathering and cleaning up after horses and cooking and sweeping the cabin. He soon fell into a routine: Angry Dog would sit on a log or a rock and shout Lakota words at him, while Charlie worked. It was a change from the white man's school, and it was easy to concentrate on the one thing his mind had to learn. The rest he could do while thinking about the language.

After a few days he was allowed to ride Mouse; then he spent most of his mornings in the meadows with the horse. Mouse was as impatient with him as Angry Dog, making no allowance for inexperience. Charlie often fell or was thrown, but learned to keep his seat when Mouse was running, turning quickly, even leaping through the air over a log or a stream. He was covered with bruises, but his body grew harder as days and weeks passed. He had no thoughts to spare for anything else. The valley floor became his world, and his tasks occupied his mind so that he never missed books or conversation. He had all his childhood to make up for, a childhood spent learning how not to be Indian.

After Charlie learned enough Lakota words to ask for them, Angry Dog gave him a bow and three arrows, and he did his best to learn to shoot, running to retrieve the arrows wherever they fell. One morning an arrow landed in the river. He waded in and felt around with his feet, but it must have been carried away by the current. Angry Dog whipped him with green branches, more to shame him than hurt him, and spent the rest of the day showing Charlie how to search for the right wood, how to peel and cut it, fletch it with feathers, and fix a steel arrowhead to the shaft. The arrowhead was one concession to the white men's skills. Charlie was grateful he was not forced to chip one out of flint. On one cold November morning, he brought down a small buck with one of his precious arrows, and Angry Dog showed him how to skin it and tan the hide, and allowed him to make himself a rough buckskin shirt to replace his vest.

The Lakota language came slowly, and it was long weeks before he could answer Angry Dog's questions in a child's simple words. But by the time the winter was howling in the pine valley, he could speak well enough to learn what Angry Dog would teach. He had been nowhere but Angry Dog's valley and had spoken to no one but the medicine man for months. Someone brought them food, flour, and beef from Angry Dog's reservation ration, but whoever it was left the supplies in a rock niche by the river three miles from the cabin.

Once Angry Dog could speak to him, the two hiked every day onto a ridgetop where wind-worn rocks marked a border between this world and the world of the wendigo. There was a grave deep within the rocks where the Guardian lay buried, holding his sacred weapons. When Charlie had been chewing on the trance-roots, he felt a strong pull from the border, a chain binding him to it. He learned the chants and the paths onto the vision road, and he learned how to open the border, how to sense when it was opening of its own accord, the strange mind-twisting effect of the wendigo's presence.

He quested alone on the ridgetop twice after days of fasting. Angry Dog waited in the valley while Charlie sang himself hoarse and sought a vision of his spirit guide. In a Sioux tribe he would have gone on his vision quests at the age of fourteen or so; he came to it late. Maybe that was why Coyote did not come to him either time, though he had always thought of Coyote as his guardian animal. He saw many birds and one young antelope buck, but none spoke to him.

He could not practice the wendigo magic he had learned. Angry Dog had told him that a Guardian might live his life from birth to old age without ever seeing a wendigo. He knew who the wendigo were; the old tale was true. They were an ancient tribe who had fallen into cannibalism and sorcery and had been banished by the wise men of many other tribes.

The border where he had been born was west and south near the new city of Laramie, Wyoming. He would be expected to go there once his training was complete. There was no reservation in southeastern Wyoming; he would find no one of his own tribe, but Angry Dog told him that a Guardian must learn to be alone. One day Charlie would have to find a wife and have children, born in the border rocks, to carry out the trust through the years. So the medicine man said, though he never spoke of a family of his own.

Angry Dog lived entirely in the past, the mythic past, and he believed in all the Dakota gods and legends as well as the Guardian lore that few men knew. Charlie was impatient with his teacher sometimes. When the boy wanted to talk about the white men and the wars, the massacre of his parents, Angry Dog would tell him to be silent or send him off on some strenuous errand to a hilltop for one or two herbs. The two of them lived cut off from the world, knowing nothing of what was happening on the reservation or outside it. They knew their rations were small, not enough meat to feed man and boy for the month it was supposed to last, but there was game enough in their valley to keep them well fed. Mouse and the other horse, Eagle, stayed bony and their winter coats grew in patches; Angry Dog said it was because the summer had been too dry.

After two months of seeing no one, not even speaking of the world outside, Charlie was stunned to see blue-coat soldiers riding into the valley one late afternoon. He was alone on the ridgetop near the border, repainting the small stones that marked the Guardian's grave. From the height, the soldiers looked like small clay figures moving through a child's snowy landscape. Angry Dog was in the cabin making a bitter medicine that he left sometimes in the rock niche in exchange for the ration meat. The horses pawed for snow-covered grass in their pasture, the smoke rose in a thin line from the roof, and the soldiers, thirty of them, rode down the hillside path in three-abreast formation, armed with rifles. The winter sunlight made the insignia on their hats glitter like jewels. The man in front had a saber at his belt.

Charlie dropped his paint stick and the stone he had been daubing with iron ocher. He ran headlong down the side of the ridge, sliding in gravel, bruising the bare skin of his legs. He was wearing only his breechclout and moccasin boots, with his medicine bag tied around his neck. He and Angry Dog had been fasting for two days to prepare for a vigil at the gravesite this evening. They were going to try to speak with the Guardian's spirit, bound there by his ancient vow.

Pine branches whipped against him, harder than Angry Dog hit when he punished him. Charlie lost sight of the cabin for most of his descent through the trees. He gasped for breath as he ran and slid over pine needles and rocks, falling and getting up again, his empty stomach cramped with the effort. Angry Dog did not speak English. He would not be able to talk with the soldiers, whatever they wanted. What if the soldiers grew angry with him, hurt him ... perhaps killed him ... The wars were supposed to be over, but Charlie was sure the soldiers hated Indians as much as he hated them. There might be men in that company who had helped kill his parents years ago. He had no weapons. His bow and arrows were in the cabin.

He reached the bottom of the hill and sprinted across the horse pasture, seeing Mouse and Eagle already caught and bridled by soldiers. They could not take his horse. . . . Two bearded white men saw him and trained their rifles on him, and Charlie slowed his pace. Suddenly, as jarring as a blow to his face, he realized how easily he could die. He was almost naked and the bullets would slam through him like cannon shot, and the last Guardian would be Angry Dog until they killed him too. Then would the borders open and the wendigo come through?

"Hands up! Get over here!" shouted a nervous-looking

young man, blond with a thin mustache. Others turned to look.

Charlie raised his hands and walked slowly toward the soldiers, feeling light-headed with fear and shame. What kind of warrior was he to be so frightened by a few men with guns? His uncle had been a Dog Soldier who thrust a lance through his sash in battle to hold his ground until he died or the enemy was defeated. Charlie was ashamed to learn how afraid he was to die.

Now he could see Angry Dog under the eaves of the cabin, talking quietly with an Indian dressed in soldier's clothes. The leader of the soldiers, a brown-bearded man in his forties wearing lieutenant's insignia, stood there looking frustrated and fingering the hilt of his sword. Charlie hated him in that moment. He had destroyed the peace of the valley. This was a sacred place, not for ignorant people.

The blond soldier who had called to Charlie was taller than the Indian youth by a head, and he looked down at him with ugly fear and contempt on his face. "Lieutenant!" he shouted, still pointing his gun.

"For God's sakes, Williams, put the gun down. I'm having enough trouble as it is," said the officer irritably.

Williams lowered the barrel far enough to prod Charlie in the stomach with it. "Move." He walked behind Charlie over to the cabin porch. Charlie kept his hands in the air, his face as still as a stone carving; he could not bear for these men to know his fear.

"Boy, tell them we cannot leave here," Angry Dog said, his voice a deep growl that suited his name. "I can hardly understand this fool of a Cheyenne scout."

"You have to leave," said the Indian soldier, a stocky man of thirty or so who reminded Charlie painfully of his father. He spoke Lakota nearly as badly as Charlie did.

Charlie turned to the lieutenant and said in English, "The land is his." It was strange to think in that language again.

"The tribe gave it to him when they parceled out the reservation. Why do you say we must leave?" He put his hands down as he spoke.

With a mild look of surprise on his face, the officer said, "It isn't part of the reservation anymore, and that stubborn fool knows it. It's ceded land. The Sioux Act of 1889. The tribe agreed to it, a majority of adult males like the law says. There are settlers coming in, and with all the trouble, I'm supposed to get every Indian back onto the reservation land, that's all. Now tell him that." He folded his arms and nodded once, as if there could be no argument.

"He says that land was given up by the tribe last year. Something called the Sioux Act," Charlie repeated to Angry Dog. He wondered what trouble the lieutenant meant.

"I did not sign that act. You know we cannot leave, Edgewalker." The name Angry Dog had given him was traditional for Guardians, meaning the border they walked between this world and the otherworld. Charlie had not grown used to it yet, and did not feel worthy of it, especially now.

"He says he didn't sign the act." Charlie glared at the white officer. "You don't understand. We can't leave here. This is sacred land. Angry Dog is a holy man. The settlers can't come here." He hated them all, hated their smell of wet wool and old sweat, hated their pale eyes and the way they looked at him.

"Sir? He must be one of those witch doctors," said a soldier who had just come out of the cabin. He held a totem fetish in his hand, a hoop with fur and eagle feathers and rabbit tails that Angry Dog was making for a chief of the Hunkpapa. "There's bones and heathen amulets all over. That's against the law, isn't it, sir?"

"And they've been hunting game," said the lieutenant. "Any Ghost shirts or the like?" The soldier shook his head. Ghost shirts? Hunting? Charlie began to think he was dreaming. He had had dreams enough of white murderers. Now the officer stepped forward and grasped Angry Dog's arm. "Come along, you. No more arguments. I should probably arrest you for practicing that superstitious nonsense. Come quietly and I'll just take you to the agency. They'll find you someplace else to live."

Angry Dog struggled with the man and cried out. Without any thought at all, as blindly as in a dream, Charlie leaped for the lieutenant's back. He tried to pull the man away from his teacher. But something hit him on the top of his head and he fell to his knees, retching with pain. Then he felt a heavy boot kick him in the back. He felt the sharp pain distantly as he fell full length on the packed earth, swimming into blackness. No! He fought unconsciousness, wanting to help his teacher, his adopted father . . . the blackness was too strong and it overcame him.

Roughness against his face, a jolting rhythm that matched the pounding in his head. He opened his eyes, but everything was blurred and doubled and he shut them quickly again. He had to vomit but only a thin trickle stained his lips; his stomach was empty from fasting. He wiped his face on the harshness of Mouse's mane and tried to sit up. His hands were tied behind his back. They felt hot. His feet were tied to a rope that passed beneath the horse's belly. His head hurt. He could scarcely think past the ache. His back hurt too, a pain that spread around his right side.

"Young hothead," a voice hissed in Cheyenne. A hand gripped his shoulder and pulled him upright. Charlie opened his eyes again and tried to see through the dizziness; the Indian soldier, the scout, was riding beside him. His horse crowded against Charlie's leg. "Here, drink." A canteen was pressed to Charlie's lips. He swallowed a little water while more ran down his chin onto his bare chest. He was cold.

"What happened?" he whispered, closing his eyes again.

The men and horses spinning and blurring around him upset his head.

"You attacked Lieutenant Ambrose and got hit with a rifle butt. You have a bloody knot on your head and a swollen ugly place where Williams kicked you after you let go of Ambrose. You're a fool."

"Why do you work for them?" Charlie asked bitterly. "Against your own kind . . . You can see what they think of us . . ."

The Cheyenne sighed. "Your teacher is worried about you. They have him riding up near the front."

"Tell him I'm all right," Charlie muttered. He forced himself to open his eyes and look around. They were riding down a dry wash he did not recognize. The hills around them were lower than the ridgetops and granite mountains near the border valley. "They didn't hurt him?"

"No. He put some kind of ancient curse on the lieutenant but other than that he came quietly. He isn't in trouble. But you are."

"They shouldn't have . . . taken him from there." It was hard to put words together. His head pounded, feeling as big and hollow as a cauldron. "It's dangerous."

"Dangerous for you, anyway. It's a good thing you didn't have a knife, and you didn't hurt Ambrose any. You might not get sent to prison for it. No, don't try to talk anymore. Rest. Sleep if you can. You won't fall off. We'll be at the agency by nightfall." He rode ahead.

Charlie couldn't sleep, but he fell into a trancelike daze of anger and hatred. What right had the soldiers to invade the valley, order them away, lay hands on Angry Dog? The land was sacred, nothing to do with their kind. No Indian would live there except a Guardian; the power was malevolent, not for men's use. So he had been taught. They would have to go back somehow. Sneak back, hide out on the ridgetop. They could not leave the grave unprotected, the border unwatched.

He was amused by a thought: what if the wendigo had come out while the white men were there? They were Indian; they would hate the whites, monsters that they were. It would have been something to see.

The Indian agency at Cheyenne River was a bleak cluster of clapboard buildings with low roofs. An American flag danced in the wind on top of a pole. Army troops loitered in front of A-frame tents, and soldiers walked patrols in front of the biggest buildings. Charlie gave up trying to count them, still blinking away dizziness. The sun was setting. What was the army doing on the reservation? He had thought there were no soldiers closer than Fort Bennett, past the boundary line.

A sentry saluted the column, and called, "Trouble, Lieutenant Ambrose?"

"Nothing serious. Brought in a few wild ones." The officer laughed.

The column dismounted. Williams strolled over to untie Charlie's feet and pull him off Mouse's back. His legs were unreliable, Charlie discovered. He fell down when Williams tried to force him to walk, and the soldier called to a companion, who helped half carry, half drag Charlie into the main building of the agency. Angry Dog was there ahead of him, speaking gravely to a Sioux chief who was with the agent. A harassed-looking white man, the agent listened to Lieutenant Ambrose's brief report, and waved his hand in weary approval when Ambrose said they would take the boy to the stockade. Williams and the other soldier turned around with Charlie, and he managed to stumble between them until they reached a small locked building with a single guard.

The door was unlocked and Charlie was flung inside a dark, windowless room. A drunken man sang a hunting chant softly in one corner. Charlie found a dirty pallet on the earth floor and lay down on it, grateful to be still and able to close his eyes again. His head hurt so much he wondered if it might burst. His hands were still bound, and his arms were numb from the shoulders down. He lay there half sleeping for a long time as it grew dark outside.

He hoped to be left alone, but after some time had passed, the door rattled and three men came into the room. One held a lantern. A young, worried face leaned close to him, and he recognized John Surrey. The agent was with him. A soldier held the lantern. Surrey's hand felt at the back of Charlie's head where the blood was sticky and clotted. His fingers probed, and Charlie moaned and turned his head away from the light.

"I'm taking him," Surrey said flatly. "He could die, Mr. McChesney."

The agent seemed uneasy. "If what you told me is true . . ."

Surrey stood up. "He's just a boy, fresh from school. He knows nothing of what's going on here. I'm sure he has no idea how serious his actions were. And I think you'll agree the soldier's response was too strong. Ambrose doesn't have a scratch on him."

"You'll take responsibility for him."

"Yes. Until someone from Little Chief's Cheyenne band can take him down to Pine Ridge."

"Very well. I'm not sure I like letting him go . . ."

"You have bigger things to worry about, sir. Kicking Bear's stories, and the dances. Don't waste your time on little Charlie Gray Stone. He's no threat to anyone."

"You're right, you're right. Get one of the soldiers to help you move him. Good night, Surrey."

"Thank you, sir." The doctor knelt by Charlie again and said, "Can you get up? I want to get you to my office."

Though he would like to lie still in the dark, Charlie rolled to his knees and let Surrey help him to his feet. The doctor was stronger than he looked, and supported him until some of the vertigo had passed. They walked slowly out the stockade door and down the dark street, Surrey's arm firmly under Charlie's shoulders.

The office was lit with oil lamps. A young Sioux woman sat in a chair by a sick child on a cot. She was singing softly to her son, stroking his forehead with one hand. Surrey murmured a greeting to her and led Charlie into the back room to lay him down on his own bed. There were bookshelves and a desk and a camp stove for cooking. The doctor closed the door to the outer room and came to sit by Charlie's side.

"Angry Dog told me what had happened and said I had to get you out of there. How could you have done something so idiotic? You're no fool, for all I made you sound like a child to McChesney."

"They had no right to make us leave." Charlie gasped as Surrey's hands went to his head again and probed even more firmly than before. "It is his land, sacred land. . . . Stop, that hurts."

"How's your vision? Blurry, spots?" the doctor asked coldly. He took his hands away and went to a washbasin to wring out a cloth. When he came back he began to soak the clotted blood at the back of Charlie's head.

"Better now than at first. Can't you . . . leave that alone? I want to sleep."

"Be quiet. I'll be finished soon. It isn't bad, probably a mild concussion. You'll have to stay in bed for a week or so. I want a look at your back too. Maybe a cracked rib, where he kicked you. You're a lucky idiot. Williams would have shot you if he hadn't been worried about hitting his commander. I heard him say so, bragging in the street."

"Bastard . . . I'd like to . . ."

"Not another word. Understand? It isn't our land anymore. It's theirs, all of it, even on the reservations. If you try to fight them you'll die. No, don't try to argue. It's true. I'm going to bandage this now, and get to work on your side."

# CHAPTER TWELVE

For the next four days, Charlie lay on John Surrey's bed and wandered from restless waking to restless dreaming. Coyote came and spoke to him, some kind of warning, and for the first time in his life the wendigo spoke to him too. It was as if the blow to his head had made a doorway they could pass through. Their voices in his dreams were cajoling, flattering. They were Indians like himself. . . . They had learned from their exile. . . . If he would only let them back into the world, they would help him drive the whites away. . . . They loved the land as he did. Listen to the words of the prophet, the voices whispered. He is a prophet, but you could be a savior.

Surrey was in and out of waking and dreams, replacing bandages, tightening the wrap that kept Charlie's ribs compressed and made every breath painful. "You have a fever," Surrey told him once, as Charlie tried to push his hands away. "Hold still. You've been saying crazy things, about killing all the white people, about ghosts. People heard you in my office. They're talking about you. If those crazy Ghost Dancers hear, they'll think you're one of them. If McChesney hears he'll probably arrest you again."

"They're at the border," Charlie shouted. "Waiting for me. I can open it, I can let them in."

"Be quiet. I'll put a gag on you if I have to. You'll get us both in trouble. There are soldiers everywhere." Surrey wiped Charlie's forehead with a cold, soothing cloth, until Charlie closed his eyes again. But then the dreams returned.

"White man's medicine," said a voice, making the words a curse. "It's no good for Indians. The boy needs the dance."

"He's been crying for it, John Surrey, but you've turned too white to hear." Noise came into the room and Charlie opened his eyes. He felt terrible.

Five middle-aged men crowded in beside him, with Surrey shouting at them to go, to leave his patient alone. The Indians were Oglala Sioux, their faces painted, not for war, but for some sort of ceremony. They wore bright breechclouts, furred moccasins with dance rings on their legs, and long-sleeved white shirts with painted sun, moon, and animal designs. It was late in the evening on the fourth day Charlie had been at the agency.

"They say you cry out for the prophet's words," said one man eagerly, his eyes searching Charlie's face.

"Someone said . . . in my dream . . ." He shook his head, trying to remember. "But I don't know who the prophet is."

"We will teach you." They were all smiling now. "Come with us. Surely the dance will heal you."

"No!" Surrey took one man's arm and was pushed down. He tripped and fell over his camp stove, and cold ashes scattered on the wood floor.

Two of the five men took Charlie's arms and helped him rise. His side ached, but his head seemed clearer. He could stand without feeling dizzy. One man took the blanket from the bed and wrapped Charlie in it. Then they helped him out the door, into the street, and onto a horse that was waiting with four others. The smallest of the Sioux got up behind Charlie to hold him in the saddle, and they rode off at a trot that made Charlie grit his teeth to keep from crying out. They passed the tents of the soldiers, but no one tried to stop them.

He did not really want to leave Surrey. He knew the doctor would be worried. "Did Angry Dog send you?" he asked the man behind him.

"Short Bull sent us, once we heard about you. There's a dance at Pass Creek, near Pine Ridge. We'll have you there by morning. Sleep if you want to." The man was cheerful, and seemed to mean him no harm. Charlie let the rhythm of the horse keep his mind from thoughts. Somewhere inside him the wendigo were glad.

The Indian Messiah had come to earth, they told him in the morning when they reached the dance camp. His name was Wovoka and he was a Paiute, living in Nevada. Eleven men from the Dakota tribes had traveled to where he lived to hear his message. They had seen marvels. In a drought, he had brought rain; he had made animals talk to one another so the Sioux could hear; on their way home they had killed a buffalo, and cut it in pieces as Wovoka had told them, and it had come to life again.

Charlie was not that interested in their Messiah, especially when they told him about the wounds in his hands and feet that proved he had been on the earth before, killed by the white men. He had never given more than necessary silence to the Jesus religion in the school, and it sounded as if Wovoka had been crazed by it. But then they told him the rest of the prophet's words.

The dance was a way to prepare Wovoka's followers for the wonderful time to come. A nation of the dead would rise, and the whites would be pushed aside, leaving the Indians on their land once again to live in the old ways with all their lost kindred. And this was not a vague promise for some far-off future, like the whites' Armageddon. This coming spring, the spring of 1891, the new order would be swept into existence. And the Sioux medicine men who believed the Messiah had been granted revelations: if all the Sioux would gather here, at Pass Creek, at the end of November the earth would shake and the wind blow, and the dead would rise to join them against the whites.

"We have danced for two weeks now," said the man who had ridden behind Charlie that long night. "The power is here, we have all felt it. I had a vision two days ago where I went to heaven and saw the Messiah, saw my dead grandparents and my aunt, and they told me it was all true."

"Many of us have had such visions," said another. "You, too, when you were sick and sleeping, you must have realized the truth. You cried out things about the prophet and about the ghosts."

It was all too strange; Charlie could not fall into the fervent belief of the dancers, but he marveled at the closeness between Wovoka's dream of the white men swept away and his own dreams of opening the border to the wendigo so that those ancient ghosts could help drive the white men from the land. He could not join the dance with his broken rib and cracked head, but he sat near the center of the circle and watched it all from the dawn through the day.

Tipis were pitched up and down the creek, and between stands of cottonwoods the dancers gathered in concentric circles, women, men, and older children. A young tree with many branches had been set up in the center; it sagged with gifts and offerings, bright bits of string and ribbons tied to the branches, small carved dolls dangling. Faces painted, purified by the sweat lodges, the people listened to speeches and sermons of Wovoka's revelations. Charlie learned that they considered their Ghost Dance shirts to be proof against any harm, even the white men's bullets. No one had put that to the test.

The singing began at noon. The sun was high over the cold landscape, and the snow was bright. The songs were reminders of all that the people had lost: buffalo hunts, tipis, the kinship with animals, the many friends and relatives killed by the white men. As they sang, the people danced slowly with bent knees, circling left, until Short Bull, the leader, cried out the words "Weep for your sins!"

Charlie had felt power building in the circle, and now the energy there burst forth as people fell to the ground in trance or cut themselves with bits of glass and stone and ran to smear blood on the prayer tree near where he sat. When the leader called them, those who could re-formed their circles and sat down to listen to his sermon.

"The white men will come!" shouted the medicine man, his arms raised. "They will surround us. Do not heed them, continue the dance. If the soldiers surround you, those of you who wear the holy shirts must sing to them, the song that the prophet taught you. Some of them will die at your feet, and some will try to run, but their horses will sink into the earth. The riders will jump off, but they, too, will sink into the earth. All, all of them will be dead, and only the People will be left. I swear to you, this is as true as the sunrise and the sunset." Another leader, Kicking Bear, spoke of the vision he had in Nevada.

There was more, and Charlie thought that in spite of the power of the dance no such things would happen. But the wendigo . . . the wendigo were great sorcerors, or so the legend said. If he let them free what might they not do to the whites?

The circle began to dance again, faster and faster, singing that the time was coming, the people were coming. O my father, O my mother, the refrain ran, repeated over and over until Charlie felt himself being caught up in the thought; how would it be to see his parents again, to live with them again in the old ways? He could see how beautiful the dream appeared to the dancers. They circled and leaped and grew more and more entranced. Many fell to the ground, this time to lie still and see visions of the life to come. Others kept dancing, leaping in and out of the circle, punishing their bodies in quest of the trance state.

Short Bull sang a song that must have been made before, not received in sudden inspiration; those who were not lost in some spirit world joined in, and the sound was so wistful and yearning that hairs stood up on the back of Charlie's neck. He felt it, he felt all that they felt. They were at the end of things, it must be time for a new world.

"The whole world is coming,
A nation is coming, a nation is coming,
The Eagle has brought the message to the tribe.
The father says so, the father says so.
Over the whole earth they are coming.
The buffalo are coming, the buffalo are coming,
The Crow has brought the message to the tribe.
The father says so, the father says so."

Round and round the circle went the song. The dancers continued through the afternoon, resting when they became exhausted, and Charlie left the circle only when the last dreamers awoke from their trances and went to join the others for an evening meal.

He heard a Brulé boasting at the meal about the scare he had put into a white rancher, Scotty Philip, On his way to Pass Creek the man and eleven others had camped at the Philip ranch. He had carried his rifle and told Philip stories of the days when he had smashed the heads of white children and drunk the blood of white women. The day was coming again, even if the buffalo never returned. The Sioux would ride the horses and eat the cattle of the ranchers like Philip. They would make war until all the whites were gone from the Plains.

He heard, too, a woman repeating the words of a moderate chief, American Horse, warning them in Pine Ridge. "How long can you hold out?" the chief had demanded. The country was surrounded by railroads. White soldiers could be there in three days from any fort in the West. They had no ammunition, no supplies. What would become of their families? He called their dancing and boasting a child's madness.

Perhaps it was mad, but it could be turned into a real war, Charlie thought. With the wendigo as allies they could push the whites, if not off the world, then at least back across the Mississippi River. He would have to wait until he was well enough to ride. The valley of the border was far from Pass Creek and there were soldiers throughout the hills trying to herd all the Indians in toward the agencies to control them. He would have to be well enough not only to ride but to hide from soldiers, or fight them if necessary. He would need a few young men as eager as he was to prove themselves. He only hoped the soldiers would not talk Short Bull's people into surrendering before he could act.

There was only one way Charlie knew of to open the border and release the wendigo. He would have to break the power of the sacred Guardian and empty the grave. It went against everything he had been taught, every instinct but his hatred of the white men; hatred he shared with the four young Sioux who would follow him on his ride. With Angry Dog still waiting at Cheyenne River to be granted another plot of land, and with soldiers everywhere in the Black Hills, Charlie and his small band of eager youths would return to the border valley and free the wendigo.

On November 25, 1890, the Ghost Dancers moved to join Oglala bands at White Clay Creek; women and children and old people walked or rode packhorses and travois while the men and youths made a wide perimeter of scouts and guards. Charlie, still weak and sick and hurting in the side, rode a borrowed pony; he would not seem a woman to his newfound friends. They were Brulé: two cousins, Arrow and Raven; a chief's nephew, Bent Arm; and a boy called Walks at Night who had been some years in the white man's school. They did not know exactly what Charlie meant to do; his Guardian training still held strong enough that he did not tell the great secrets. But they knew he had seen visions of the Messiah and that he meant to act, not sit around singing and visiting the land of the dead.

Soldiers and Cheyenne scouts kept appearing at the White Clay camp, urging all the Indians to return to the agencies or be counted as hostiles. Many did return, but Short Bull's people were joined by others, and at last they marched down White River toward a place called the Stronghold. They raided the agency cattle herd on the way and climbed the high plateau between White River and Cheyenne River to reach the protected place. At the end of the main plateau a small land bridge led out to a triangular outcrop a few miles on each side. Almost sheer drops led to the riverlands below. Two springs and plenty of grass, plus the stolen cattle, meant they could last there throughout the winter.

Charlie could not wait until spring. He had wandered around the camp, talking to boys, old medicine men, some of the delegates who had seen Wovoka in Nevada. A girl his age let him caress her out in the rocks at the edge of camp, but he was too hurt still to do what both of them wanted. While he waited for his bones to knit, two hundred of Two Strikes' people were convinced by a scout to go to Pine Ridge. A civilian militia of cowboys and city men rode back and forth along the banks of the Cheyenne River, and Bent Arm fought in a skirmish with them on December 14. On the 15th eighteen of the militia crossed the river and rode toward the

Stronghold. Charlie joined a large band of men who rode out across the land bridge and down the plateau to drive them back again. Bands of young men had fought shooting battles with ranchers and storekeepers in the land around the Stronghold, but still the government soldiers did not move against them.

On December 22 the first Hunkpapa Sioux arrived from the Standing Rock reservation far to the north, with news that Indian policemen had been sent by the agent to arrest Sitting Bull; there had been a battle; the unarmed old chief and his son Crow Foot were both dead, along with many others. It angered Charlie's friends that the warriors did not ride in force against the soldiers now. The chiefs only sang, and made more speeches, and swore they would never surrender, fearing that they would be killed like Sitting Bull.

"I am strong enough now," Charlie told Bent Arm that night. He felt sure he was, though when he moved too fast he still had a deep pain in his side. Arrow and Raven gathered their ponies. Walks at Night was on sentry duty after full dark, and he let them through the line on the narrow land bridge and joined them on the fifth pony.

It was cold and dry, a stormless winter, as if the earth were holding its breath waiting to see what would happen in the spring. Arrow and Raven knew the lands north of the plateau, and they knew where the soldiers were likely to be holding the passes; they swung wide into the Badlands and led the others through stark moonlit gullies and past cracked outcrops of jagged rock. They rode until a few hours before sunrise. It was a silent ride. The horses were unshod and none of the young men spoke to one another. Charlie had tried to make them understand at least that they were on a serious mission, not to be distracted by raids on farmhouses or war paint or boasting. They had even bundled their Ghost Dance shirts into their bedrolls, and wore cheap cotton plaid shirts bought at trading posts. If soldiers saw them, they could pretend to be friendly Indians returning to one of the agencies.

As Charlie rode he tried to tell himself that Angry Dog would approve, that his teacher would agree with what he was doing. He knew it was not true. Too long, the Guardians had been taught that the wendigo were evil. Angry Dog would not understand that the power of the wendigo must be used against the greater evil of the white men.

They rested their horses for an hour and talked quietly. "A great weapon," he told Bent Arm when the Brulé asked him again what they were going to find. "A weapon of the old ways." He hoped that he could make the wendigo understand what they must do. He had not heard their voices in his head for a week now, since the last of his sickness had gone. But he was a Guardian, born at the border. That should mean he could see them and communicate with them somehow.

"What of our own people who have gone in the white man's way?" Arrow asked fiercely. "Should not they, too, be swept aside in the great battle?"

People like John Surrey, Charlie thought; like himself, as he had been before his three days in Angry Dog's sweat lodge. "When they see the tribes returning they will put all that aside and join us," he said, not sure that it was true.

"Their ancestors will talk to them," Raven said. He was the most religious of them, the most ecstatic in the Ghost Dance. "They will not follow the white men when they see their grandfathers and grandmothers living again before their eyes."

"You are right," Bent Arm said contentedly. Charlie nodded when Raven looked at him, but he wondered how any of them could really believe that the dead would return. He knew the wendigo had power, but they were not ghosts; they were exiles, sorcerors. They had never been dead. The dead were gone. He was certain he would never see his parents again.

* * *

The sweat lodge on the high bank of the river had been torn apart and trampled into a scattering of broken willow branches. That must have happened after Charlie lost consciousness. The abandoned cabin waited silently for someone to open its door again. There was no soldiers in the border valley, and no settlers had arrived yet to claim the land. One of the priests who had come to the Stronghold to reason with Short Bull and the others had said that immigrants were afraid now to come into the Dakotas because of the news of Indian trouble.

The five ponies were turned loose in the pasture, and they huddled together against the chill late-afternoon wind and did not bother to look around the old snowbanks for grazing. Charlie sat by himself while the others ate some dried salt pork they had taken from the dwindling stores of the Stronghold. At the river's edge, he sang softly with his medicine bag cupped in his hands; he could not tell if Coyote answered him or if the power was with him, but he did not have time to wait to be sure. He wanted to open the grave and release the Guardian's spirit before darkness came, and he feared that if they waited until morning someone would find them. Soldiers might come, or white militiamen, or perhaps Angry Dog, who could have sneaked away from Cheyenne River agency, sensing that his pupil was about to destroy everything he was supposed to defend.

Charlie stared at the cold, slow-moving water of the winter river. He had been given a name here, Edgewalker, a name of power and honor. If he opened the grave and emptied it he would not deserve that name; but he did not see that being the Guardian of some ancient magical border was of any use now, when the white people had destroyed his people's lives. When he was an old man, he thought, if he lived that long, would he rather be called Edgewalker and pass on the magic of the border in secret, or a war leader telling stories in a tipi to small boys who had never known white men?

"Come with me," he said to the other four, pulling them away from their meal. They followed him across the horse pasture and up the steep slope of the hill to the ridgetop. They were all weary from their ride, but they were ready to do whatever he asked. It was they who were men, Charlie thought, not the leaders who sat in the Stronghold and swore to one another they would never surrender. It was always so, he supposed. Young men acted and old men feared. The old men would be glad when they knew what these four had done.

On the ridgetop they could see the low sun over the higher hills to the west. Charlie found the painted rocks at the opening to the deep grave. His paint stick and a dried lump of red color lay where he had dropped them when the soldiers came. The patterns of the rocks flickered in his gaze, suddenly powerful against an intruder, and as he began to push them aside he knew that no man not born a Guardian could do this easily. "Wait," he had to say to Bent Arm, who knelt to help him.

When he had cleared the stones he nodded to the others, and they all gathered to pull at the sides of the larger rocks that blocked the entrance. The shadows on the ridgetop were very long and seemed to whisper in disapproval. Charlie worked steadily and tried to ignore them. The medicine bag hanging beneath his plaid trader's shirt was dead, as still as if it truly only held a rock, a chipped arrowhead, a feather, and a piece of fur. Coyote was not with him. If he ever had been; Charlie was not sure in this cold December dusk if he had ever really seen the trickster's spirit, or if he had dreamed him when he was a boy in school and again after the long days and nights in the sweat lodge. He had experienced no grand vision when he had spent days fasting and questing on the ridgetop.

The wendigo were real, though. He knew that more strongly with every effort he made to move the stones blocking the entrance to the grave. As they had spoken to him in his fever, now they clustered around the edges of his awareness, urging him on, promising him things he could not quite grasp, reassuring him that this was what he must do. Only he could do this thing to help his people.

"I could get through now," Walks at Night said, whispering. They had uncovered a hole in the boulders about the width of Charlie's shoulders. It looked as black as a stormy night inside; Charlie was not certain there was not a storm coming. The air felt heavy and alive. The sun was at the rim of the hills now, a cold, gray sunset with no color to it.

He nodded to the young Brulé. "Go on." There was little time left. He did not know why he felt so rushed, but he knew he feared the wendigo at night, and he heard the Guardian's spirit even now. If he were a true leader he would not let Walks at Night go before him; but it would take long minutes to widen the hole any further and he was pressed on all sides by the wendigo's longing to be freed.

The act seemed to take no time, or not take place in time. Charlie crouched at the entrance of the grave and Walks at Night passed up to him the Guardian's weapons: a jagged knife set with sharp stones, a horn bow with a rotted string, the stone point of a lance whose shaft fell away in pieces when Charlie took it out of the grave mouth. Arrow and Raven carried those away, down the slope toward the river, where Charlie told them to bury them separately under heavy rocks in the water. Bent Arm stood watch with a drawn bow over the approach where the soldiers had come before.

There were sounds like a medicine man's bone rattles, and the dried and fleshless skeleton of the Guardian warrior was gathered up into the arms of Walks at Night like a child being carried to bed. When the Brulé passed the Guardian up to Charlie's hands, the bones came apart, losing some memory of oneness that had kept them intact inside the deep rocks. Bent Arm helped them gather the bones at the side of the rocks. When the three young men finished their silent task, the ancient border Guardian was no more than a heap of odd-shaped sticks and a staring skull.

"Go to your rest at last," Charlie sang quietly to the bones. "There is no more need to guard. Let it pass, let it be forgotten. Go to your rest . . ." He felt the ancient spirit like a weathered rock finally slipping from its balanced place. It fell and rolled away along the spirit road to vanish to a place he could not follow.

Then there was a scream like a woman's in childbirth as Walks at Night looked up out of the grave past Charlie where the rocks began to gape open and the madness of the wendigo came through.

# CHAPTER
# THIRTEEN

D arcy had only been to the gravesite once, and she had come up on it from the other side. Now she walked through the deepening dusk with Paul beside her and Dr. Ghormley puffing and gasping behind them with two men she did not know. They had left Ghormley's van back in the parking lot at Vedauwoo, and fifteen Esoteric Society people had taken a different trail from theirs, up one of the boulder mountains. Darcy led the hike for three miles of rough boulder-strewn crevices and hills, keeping the highest Vedauwoo mountains aligned as landmarks behind them.

She wished she had her horse now. This trail would be nothing to Cinnamon. If she had been alone she would have rested a few times already, but Paul showed no sign of weariness and her pride made her keep pace with him. At least she was not out of shape like the professor, who might not make the climb up onto the high ridge. The two men he had brought with him were strong, athletic-looking, older than

Paul. They wore heavy coats, though it wasn't that cold. Darcy did not remember them from the party.

Ghormley had told her some of what he wanted to happen from this night's work. He reassured her that they would rescue her mother, but she learned that all his adult life he had been trying to contact the beings he called demons. His wife had left him because of his obsession with old magic. Ghormley described alchemical experiments in the basement, Latin chants, playing records backward; Darcy did not blame his ex-spouse at all for leaving. She wondered why Laura had never told her anything about this.

The professor brushed aside Darcy's warnings about the wendigo she remembered. The only reason they had seemed so frightening was that they were alien, he said; the Indian myth was obviously an attempt to explain a different race the primitive people could not understand. They had stolen her mother, apparently; but Ghormley reminded her of all the modern tales of UFO abductions, and people reappearing after twenty years or more. Perhaps time was different in the demon world. Maybe from her mother's perspective she had only been gone for a week, and think of the wonderful things she could have learned.

Darcy kept her worries to herself. She had heard her mother's voice and seen the thing in her grave, and this was the only way she might find her again. It did not matter what Ghormley's goals were, or Paul's, as long as they would help her with her own. She had already lost some of her infatuation with Paul. He had been so single-minded since he learned she had this Guardian power he wanted. He did not seem to care who she was herself; he loved her, maybe, but only because she was a thing he had been looking for and thought he could use to reach his goal.

The five hikers scrambled down a narrow gully, dislodging rocks as they went, and then they climbed up a sloping hill in the face of a freezing wind. Darcy began to feel a familiar sensation, as if the boulder outcrops at the top of the hill recognized her and welcomed her. "It's here, I think," she said, breaking into a run to the edge of the hilltop. She was on the high ridge, looking back toward the boundaries of the Kennan ranch. She retraced her steps, remembering the way the coyote had led her, until she reached the dark opening and the hand-painted symbols on tiny rocks before it. "Here."

Paul pushed past her and tried to pull the rocks away, but had to stop. "You need to move the first of them," he admitted reluctantly.

Darcy felt a wrenching feeling of wrongness, of danger, but she pushed it aside. If this was what she had to do to save her mother, she would do it. When the opening was large enough she went inside, crab-walking down into the darkness and then under the low doorway at the base of the boulder cluster. Paul was close behind her, and Ghormley more awkwardly after him. The other two men waited outside. Darkness pressed in on Darcy like a smothering blanket, but she did not feel afraid this time.

The spirit of the dead man was alive. She feel his presence as strongly as Ghormley's, more strongly than Paul's even though his knees were touching her back. "This is the grave," she said very softly. "Do you think it is the Guardian?"

"Oh, yes," Paul whispered, his voice echoing strangely in the darkness. "This is the trap. This is the center of the spell that keeps them bound. Help me, Richard." He crept up to the bier where the dead man lay.

It was nearly dark outside the rock cave where Charlie Edgewalker had been sitting all afternoon and evening, his thoughts bound up in old memories. He had not meant to come back yet. His body was cold and stiff, as if he was really a hundred years old; that was not the thing that had pulled him back.

In his mind's eye he could still see the running, the

screaming, of that evening that had ended his childhood. Walks at Night had died after climbing out of the Guardian's tomb and stabbing himself with his knife. Bent Arm had run down the other side of the ridge; Charlie did not know what had happened to him. Arrow and Raven had been chased by wendigo they could not see down by the river where they had buried the sacred weapons. Charlie, watching in horror, had seen: the wendigo were monsters, remotely human in shape, their long arms and bestial faces pure evil. The madness they brought with them did not enter Charlie. He felt it pushing around his skin, seeking a way, but he was protected. At that moment he had wished to die with his friends. Arrow and Raven both drowned, battling one another in an effort to swim away. Charlie had stopped watching by the time both were dead.

The memory was hard, but that had not stopped his vision. Something here, now, an urgent call that made his heart race with the sense of danger. He stood up, forcing his aching body to move, and left the cold and empty cave to mount the nameless pinto horse and ride toward Vedauwoo Park. The Guardian's grave, he thought; someone was there, perhaps the same person who had taken one of the sacred weapons seven years ago and breached the border enough for a few wendigo to cross. Those had killed Darcy's mother and taken the girl's memories. This time he was closer to the grave. If he could catch the desecrator . . . there was a pistol on the pinto's saddle, and the ritual stone knife in its sheath at his belt was meant for wendigo, but it would work as well on human evil.

The ancient bones had been thrown over the side by Ghormley's helpers, and Paul and the professor had divided the Guardian's weapons between them, grimly elated by their evening's work. Darcy felt sick. She did not know what she had expected, but it wasn't this. Maybe some kind of dignified ritual dismissal of the Guardian spirit. Instead they were simple grave robbers, destroying something that had been powerful for hundreds of years.

As they walked back toward Vedauwoo she felt the earth shuddering under her. Rocks quaked in their beds, trickles of earth fell down the edges of gullies. Ghormley pulled her on impatiently when she stopped once to cling to a tree, certain she would be dashed to the ground. "Don't you feel it?" she cried. He did not know what she was talking about. His two companions walked steadily on.

"The border is opening." Paul had moved far ahead of them. She heard his words drift on the night air, but he was only a silhouette on top of the next rise. Darcy could feel the rift in the world ahead of them now, the swirling, sucking hole that had swallowed her mother seven years ago. She had barely escaped then. Now she was headed toward it.

It was Monday night in a cold October. There was no one at Vedauwoo but the Esoteric Society, and Darcy heard screams as she struggled along the rough trail. The wendigo must be coming through, and the students of magic greeting them hadn't been prepared for what they found. She wondered if they could see the creatures. Her mother had not been able to. The two nameless men looked at one another worriedly.

"Faster, girl," Ghormley gasped. "Paul will be waiting for you at the border ... you and he must go through it, into their world, to find your mother."

"Go through?" She trotted with him as the trail grew more level through a rustling aspen grove. "How can we ... can we be sure we'll get back?"

"You're a Guardian," Ghormley said. "You should be able to withstand it, manipulate it. I don't know how it works."

"But how can Paul ..."

There were footsteps on the path ahead of them, and fierce weeping. Darcy stepped behind the thin bole of a tree, feeling the smooth, flaking bark against her hands, a reminder of reality. A blond woman came running past them, and Darcy saw the wendigo chasing her, a small creature, now running, now hopping in leaps like a flying squirrel. The woman was Ariadne from the party, but there was nothing in her eyes but insane fear.

"Ariadne! Over here, we can help you . . ." The woman did not seem to hear her. Darcy looked back after her and stood still for a moment. Adriadne had started to climb a lone boulder sitting among the aspens. One side was rough, sloping enough to scramble up, while the other side was a sheer concave drop to a scattering of rocks below. "We have to stop her," Darcy said. "She'll jump, kill herself!" Ghormley held her by one arm, preventing her from following the desperate woman.

"There's no time, nothing we can do," Ghormley said. "I don't see the demon chasing her, but I feel it . . . hot, that sulphur smell again, just like in the books. Could you see it, Darcy? Did it have horns, hooves?" He had hold of her hand again and was dragging her away, up another slope onto one of the regular hiking trails of the park. Now his two friends fell in behind them, trudging along with their hands in the pockets of their heavy coats.

"It's a wendigo, not a demon," she said. "Like a beast man. Fur, but no horns or hooves." She heard a shriek and looked back fearfully. She could not see Ariadne on the rock anymore. All was quiet in the aspen grove.

"Hurry, we're almost at the border," Ghormley said.

Her body was exhausted after the long hike out and the forced rush of the way back. She tried to search for courage and strength; she had to find her mother and bring her home. She mustn't think about anything else.

"Do you have Darcy?" Paul's voice cried from a ledge above them, partway up the highest boulder mountain. "Bring her up here, don't waste time, man. Our enemy is at the gravesite, he may be able to close the border from there for all we know. I tell you, I can feel him now."

Charlie, Darcy supposed. Would she have to think of him as an enemy? Nothing mattered but her mother. "Help me up," she said to Ghormley. The path was too slow. He gave her a base with his hands to reach past the first sheer part of the rock face, and six feet up she found footholds, handholds, and climbed steadily toward Paul. She could not fear. Fear would not save her mother. She have never climbed before, not like this, except in her strange dream as an Indian in an alien world. Charlie had told her if she dreamed about it she'd have to do it someday.

Paul pulled her onto the ledge with him, roughly, and her knee banged on a sharp rock edge. She had to sit holding it for a moment, while he said no words of comfort. "Ready?" he urged.

She nodded, stood up. He led her along the ledge to a broad slope of slippery granite. Quickly, on hands and feet like monkeys, they ran up the slope in the near darkness. Darcy was glad she could not see the drop below them. If she slowed down or looked back she was sure she would fall.

Loud voices rang from the mountain above them, shouts and screams and even laughter, sounding like the worst horror-movie madhouse. Two gunshots in quick succession made Darcy freeze, refusing to let Paul tug her along. She heard a weird bubbling cry and hysterical weeping, a man's voice. She could hear wendigo voices too, cajoling and mocking, not saying anything she could understand.

Halfway up the mountain in a cracked seam of rock was a shallow cave, blocked from outside view by a huge fallen boulder. At the lip of the cave were seven Esoteric Society people, Ephron and Dion and others she did not know, silhouettes in the dusk, surrounded by prancing wendigo who tugged at their arms and legs and climbed on their shoulders. Some of the people were down on their knees; two were still, broken over the rocks, surely dead. Now Paul put a hand on Darcy's shoulder and stopped climbing.

"Wait just a bit," he said softly.

"Can we help them?" she whispered. "Paul, they'll die, they'll kill each other."

As she spoke she saw Ephron's large body go down, his throat cut, sprawling on the rock ledge in front of the cave. A slightly built man, perhaps Dion, flung himself off the ledge into midair and fell past Darcy and Paul, eerily silent. Darcy bit her tongue in reflexive horror when she heard the thud of his body hitting and breaking against the lower rocks. Blood seeped into her mouth.

"It will be over soon," Paul said. "We have to wait. The wendigo will leave and we can cross the border. Try not to watch, Darcy."

Half a dozen wendigo clambered down the rocks near them, ignoring Darcy and Paul. Their nearness was an invitation to madness; Darcy could feel her thoughts whirling, her body curling up into itself in desperate defense; and then they had passed, and the feeling was gone. Paul started climbing again. It would be worse to stay alone clinging to the rocks than to see clearly what had happened on the now quiet ledge. Darcy followed him.

The Esoteric Society people made bulky contorted outlines, smelling of death in the night. They had been carrying weapons, which had made it easier to kill in their madness. These were supposed to be psychically trained initiates, more prepared than most to deal with the supernatural. They had not been any stronger than ordinary people against the wendigo. Skulls smashed beyond recognition from gunshots, knife wounds in throat and chest, one obviously strangled. Darcy fought back nausea as Paul led her through the maze of bodies on the narrow ledge.

"It must have been hard for them to get up here," she said, looking back at the bodies of fat Ephron and forty-year-old

Lucretia. "They were so hopeful for the magic they thought they'd find . . ."

"There's an easier path than the way we took," Paul said. "Don't waste time. We must go through quickly. I can't tell what the living Guardian can do now that we have destroyed the dead one."

This cave was one edge of the border. On the other side of this mountain was where Darcy had lost her mother seven years ago. The gaping hole inside the cave sang to Darcy through the rocks. Her eyes strained into the black corners of the cave. This was where she had been born. She remembered a cheerful morning hike with her mother and father on her eleventh birthday, when they had shown her the cave. Her mother had been embarrassed at some of the stories her father had told.

At the back of the cave the wall was gone, replaced by a whirlwind shimmer of energy and power, a terrifying thing; Darcy closed her eyes, holding onto Paul's hand, and stepped toward it, wondering once more how he could cross with her if he was not a Guardian as well. The vortex reached out for them, clutching, pulling them apart, and Darcy screamed as her feet left the dry rocks and she began to twist and tumble through rushing, wailing air. She had lost Paul's hand. She felt torn open, dislocated, horribly changed. It went on and on.

If he had been the boy he was before, he would have wept, feeling the desolation of the gravesite, the emptiness of the burial chamber. For this he had watched for so long. So many years, repainting the stones, even replacing the stolen knife when he discovered its loss. He had chipped one himself with every ancient ritual he could find to give it power. Who could have done this? He knew that very few people could get past the painted guards on the entrance. Most would not even see the hole in the rocks. The face would look sheer to them.

He had no tears to shed, but he had anger enough. A finger bone, as small as a pebble, had first told him what had happened as he rode along the foot of the ridge. He had picked up the bone and listened to its remnant of old power; it lay now in his medicine bag with the new magic he had gathered over the past ten years. He had given his old medicine bag to Darcy in the Black Hills, knowing she needed the protection. And it was safer to have it away from him. If an enemy guessed . . .

He thought of going back to the ranch. If Darcy was there, she could hunt the enemy with him. No more quiet hints for her; show her the evil and let her remember if she could. But the trail of the thieves ran the other direction, and it was fresh. She night not be home. He did not have time to go out of his way for the sake of her training.

Climbing back out of the tomb, Charlie called to the pinto, who had wandered a little to graze in the shelter of another mound of boulders. The horse trotted over to him willingly. He mounted and turned its head down the slope toward the back of the night-outlined mountains of Vedauwoo. The border was open, he sensed now, and some wendigo had crossed. The trail of the thieves was easy to follow. The sacred weapons' power was lessened every moment they were away from the Guardian's grasp, but Charlie could track them by a faint glow left by their passing. He tried to seek ahead and find the minds of his enemies, but they were blocked from his sight. That was rare; he could sense at least a presence from most men.

He wondered if he faced someone with shaman training. He had been warned a lifetime ago by Angry Dog that sometimes outsiders caught a scent of the wendigo power and sought it for themselves. A renegade Guardian was possible too, if there were any other Guardians left. Charlie had never met one in this time except for Darcy. But there might be someone who belonged to the Black Hills or the Medicine Wheel in the Bighorns.

He had been a renegade Guardian himself, that terrible night when dozens of wendigo scattered across the Dakota country spreading madness and death. Angry Dog had found Charlie on the ridgetop two days later and told him what the creatures had done, the violence they inspired, the madness of Wounded Knee. And then Angry Dog had showed Charlie the only way to close the border and force the wendigo back inside.

Charlie shivered, remembering. He had dug up the sacred weapons from the riverbed near the bodies of his friends Arrow and Raven. With his arms crossed holding the weapons, Angry Dog had lain down in the Guardian's grave and ordered Charlie to seal it up over him. For three days and nights, crouched by the rocks, Charlie heard soft chanting, the weaving of the ancient curse as well as Angry Dog could reconstruct it. The voice was silent in the middle of the third night. At dawn, the wendigo were pulled back inexorably by the Sioux's death. Charlie had fasted, miserable, the whole time, and he had no defenses when the returning wendigo attacked him. As the border closed he was pulled in their arms, sucked into the otherworld and trapped there alone.

A woman's broken body at the foot of a tall boulder stopped his horse just before a grove of aspens inside the park. Charlie looked down at her. She must have climbed the rock just to jump off when she reached the top. He smelled a lingering trace of the wendigo odor, like wet animal fur. He had seen too many such sights. The worst, after his friends the first time, had been a group of hunters who had killed one another with guns and knives in the Black Hills. The wendigo who caused it had fled from Charlie and when he found it he had also found the child Darcy.

Maybe this dead woman had been one of the thieves. He had no time to sing over her and send her spirit gently on.

The pinto shied, but he forced it to pass, and rode through the aspen grove warily. The trail of the weapons led up the side of the largest mountain, the back side where few climbers or tourists ever hiked. Now Charlie knew that many wendigo had passed through. He would hunt them after the thieves. The pinto could not climb the rocks of the boulder mountain, so he picketed it in the grove of trees where it would be hidden from his enemies' view.

Stroking the animal's head to calm it, he sang his call to Coyote to help him. There was no response. That troubled him; the spirit animal had never failed to come to his side ever since the seven years they had spent together in the wendigo world. Coyote had saved him then, and he had done the same, if you could save a being who had already died centuries ago. He would not have survived those years without Coyote.

In the year 1960 when an anthropologist had dug up Angry Dog's bones, photographed them, and put them back in their resting place, the border had opened long enough for Charlie to escape. The anthropologist must have thought he was a ghost. The white man had run down the hill, leaving a twenty-four-year-old Indian blinking in unaccustomed sunlight wearing a ragged plaid shirt, a breechclout, and moccasins. Charlie had wandered for days, finally reaching a Pine Ridge reservation town.

The wendigo world had changed him despite his Guardian protections; he had been insane, probably, when Dave Little Owl pulled him away from barking dogs and took him into his home. Charlie had been lucky to find Little Owl. The man was the leader of a revival of the old religion, and he took Charlie through the healing songs and sweat lodge rituals that were what he needed to slowly come back to himself. If a more modern Sioux had found him he would probably still be in the violent ward of some asylum. They would have wondered by now why he had never aged.

This might be the end of his strange second life, Charlie thought. He knew of no other way to close the border than to take the place of the old Guardian, as Angry Dog had done. But first, the thieves, and the wendigo who had escaped. And Darcy—he could not leave her not knowing her duties, not knowing what she must guard and why. "Coyote, why do you not come?" Charlie murmured in Cheyenne, but the spirit animal was silent. He did not want to die. If there was a way to close the border without that final answer . . .

It was time to face the thieves. He took the holster from the pinto's saddle and slid it onto his belt. The pistol was an unfamiliar weight at his side. He had never killed a man, in all his years as a hunter. Only wendigo. It should be easier to kill a man, but he did not like the necessity. He would have been eager when he was seventeen. Now he had seen too many die.

"Wait for me," he whispered to the horse, who flicked his ears in answer. Charlie started up the trail, seeking cover to keep out of view from whoever might be waiting up above. If they had been watching, though, they could have seen him riding until he reached the aspen grove. Still he would be as cautious as he could. His moccasin boots were quiet on the rock faces and he stepped squarely on each foot so no gravel shifted to fall and betray him. The border was up ahead, gaping open. He could not sense any individual minds around it, either because the power of the place was masking them or because they had their own ways to keep hidden.

Slowly, from crevice to chimney, he worked his way up, keeping the trail of the sacred weapons as his beacon line. He passed another rock-torn corpse, another wendigo suicide. He had to stop this now, close the border however he could. No more people should die because he had failed as Guardian. Find the thieves, find the sacred weapons. He climbed steadily in the darkness among the harsh rocks.

Charlie was breathing hard, scratched and bruised, when he

finally hauled himself over a lip of rock and found the muzzle of a pistol pointing at his face. He froze.

"Charlie Edgewalker?" said a bearded white man. He was seated on a boulder beside a stinking group of dead bodies, women and men. The man who held the gun did not speak, nor did another man with a gun who was outlined against the night sky near him.

The bearded man knew his name. Charlie said nothing. He slowly pulled his legs up and sat cross-legged at the edge of the rock face. The weight of his pistol was useless against his hip. The man with the gun motioned to him to keep his hands up. He could tell that one of the sacred weapons was in the coat pocket of the man who had spoken. The open border pulsed and whirled in the cave behind them, making his head ache and distracting his thoughts.

"I was afraid you might be able to do something from the old grave," said his enemy nervously. This man was no master shaman, Charlie realized. More a charlatan who had picked up a few tricks and techniques somewhere. "But it seems you need what we carried away with us." He smiled in the darkness, a gleam of teeth.

"You said we'd have to kill him." Now the closest gunman took a step forward. "Just tell me when, Dr. Ghormley."

Ghormley . . . "You're the man at the university. The UFO and hypnosis man." Charlie kept his voice even. "I have heard some things about you."

"I'm more than that." Ghormley was filled with pride. "The demons have promised me great mastery. I will be an adept of the first rank."

Charlie felt the bullet in the gun waiting for him, the eagerness of the man who wished to kill. "The wendigo are great promisers," he said. "They know what you want most and they offer it." How many wendigo had come through? It would not take many to have inspired the madness that had killed up here.

Ghormley glanced away from him, not listening. "I think . . . I think we will wait to kill him," he said. The gunman was visibly disappointed. "Tie his hands and take his weapons."

The only route of escape would be to fall backward over the lip of rock, and Charlie was not sure how quickly he could recover from such a fall. They would probably shoot him when he moved, anyway. He sat still. They took the gun, his stone knife, and a roll of fence-mending wire from his belt; one of the gunmen bound his hands behind his back with the wire, pulling it painfully tight. Charlie felt blood oozing from his wrists as the man pulled him to his feet and walked him over near the university professor. He was made to sit down again beside one of the bodies, a heavy man wearing a loose robe.

"Why not kill me now?" he asked.

"If Paul and Darcy don't come back out soon I may have to have you take me in after them," said Ghormley.

Charlie's head whipped around to look up at the man. "Darcy?"

Ghormley smiled again. "Yes. You didn't know she was with us?"

"With you? I . . ." The shock built in him slowly. "No. I did not know."

"She led us to the grave. She remembered quite a bit under hypnosis last night. She's in love with Paul, who's one of my colleagues. She went with him into the demon world." The man seemed pleased to tell Charlie these things.

Charlie felt hollow, beaten. His failure as a teacher had brought Darcy to this. When Angry Dog had failed with him a hundred years ago, he wondered if the medicine man had felt this way. He had no tears, but if he had he would have wept without shame. Darcy . . . he should never have left her alone, he should have kidnapped her when he came across her at the age of ten, taken her as an apprentice then, never given her back her name, her life. Then she would have been safe. Now she was lost to him . . . unless he could get her back.

He looked at the triumphant white man. "Will you unbind my hands and let me follow them in there and bring them out again? They will not survive. I know. I've been there."

The professor laughed. "I think they'll survive. If they aren't back by morning we'll go in after them, you and I. But even then I won't unbind your hands. And that reminds me . . ." He leaned down from the rock where he sat, parted Charlie's shirtfront with his hands, and ripped the medicine bag from its thong around Charlie's neck. "You won't be needing this." He poured the contents out into the palm of his hand, stood up and went to the edge of the rock face, and threw them out to scatter in the darkness.

# CHAPTER
# FOURTEEN

────────

he sky was wrong. Pink and orange streaks from horizon to horizon colored the jumbled mountain rocks
with lurid reflections, giving Paul's face and her own
hands a ruddy glow. At least the ground was solid earth, and
Darcy stood very still for a few minutes after they reached
the wendigo side of the border. Wendigo were approaching in
groups, getting ready to cross, but the creatures ignored the
two humans. Darcy smelled their eagerness, their bloodlust.
She hated them with more passion than she remembered feeling about anything before.

A chasm on the scale of the Grand Canyon gashed open
the earth to the right of the border, and beyond it rose high
mountain peaks. Paul led Darcy the other way, their feet
crunching in gritty sand, into clustered hills beside a rocky
plain, with boulder mountains behind them like those at
Vedauwoo. She wondered if that was why the borders were
where they were, because the mountains were the same shape

in one world and the other. From the wendigo side the border was the same, a whirling chaos of air within a dry rock cave.

"Cover your face," Paul said suddenly, turning her by the shoulders. A dust devil whistled toward them out of nothing, picking up pieces of gravel and bits of orange grasses and bombarding them suddenly with its weapons. Darcy crouched with her arms over her face, as flying dust and rock scraped her hands and tangled in her hair. Then it passed, and Paul took her hand and pulled her onward. Where the dust devil had been the land had made an unsettling change. A ravine she had noticed was now flat prairie land, and a new spur of rock had thrust out from the soil beside it.

"This place . . ." Her voice was quivering. She was on the verge of tears, for all her attempted courage. She stopped walking.

For the first time that day Paul looked concerned for her. "It's affecting you?" He stopped and gazed at her face. "It isn't supposed to if you're a Guardian. You should be able to block it."

"Maybe I knew how once . . . I can't remember." She thought of the way Ariadne had looked, running mad. She didn't want to lose herself like that. Is that what the wendigo did to people? They were nowhere near any wendigo now but she still felt unbalanced, ready to scream or run. "How could my mother be here?" she whispered. "How could she have survived? She isn't a Guardian. I think . . . I think you lied to me, all of you. You wanted me to help you open the border. You wanted me to go with you here, maybe because you couldn't cross without me. You don't love me at all." Now she was crying, tears running down her cheeks.

Paul touched her gently with both hands on her face. "This place will twist your thoughts, Darcy. Of course I love you. And as for your mother, you heard her voice. We all did. No one expected that, no one planned that. She is here, you know. She crossed when you were attacked seven years ago.

Does it matter if I have some other quest? You can still save her."

"She couldn't have survived." Darcy looked wildly around at the bizarre rocks, the painful colors of the sky, the wind that swirled in clouds of dust. "I can hardly bear it here."

Now he turned and walked away from her. "Go back if you want. I'll search for her myself."

"No." She followed him, fighting the tears, the hysteria the place was causing in her. "No, I'll go with you."

They began to climb on the low foothills, crossing narrow rock bridges over dry ravines that might once have been carved by swift rivers. It was nighttime back in her own world by now, but here the streaked sky gave off its harsh light without a sun that Darcy could see. Her hiking boots gripped the stones well enough, but she felt dizzy and unbalanced and it was terrifying to walk with thirty- or forty-foot drops on each side of her.

Far below on the prairie she could see a kind of town, mud huts like early Indian dwellings, and wendigo moving about like insects. Could she fight off the madness, she wondered, if she was in the midst of dozens of them? If the wendigo decided to pursue them . . .

The land was familiar from her dream. She remembered the desperate, hungry boy and the Coyote spirit that helped him. Where did the dream come from, she wondered, and why was it so real? She knew she had never been here before, or imagined it. Coyote she could explain, from her imaginary companion when she was a child. She had never believed in premonitions, but here she was now. She found herself looking for the cliff she had climbed in that dream.

Paul moved swiftly, never varying his speed, waiting impatiently for her, sometimes reaching back a hand to steady her. The thought came back stronger: what was he doing here, obviously unaffected by the place, untouched by the wendigo's madness? He had said he loved her when she accused him; he valued her for something, but she did not believe it had anything to do with her mother. He led her so quickly through the ravines and ledges, as if he knew where he was going. Had Ghormley's research in old demon lore turned up a map of the wendigo world? Treasure, she thought with weary amusement, maybe they were hunting for treasure, some kind of magical trove left by demon pirates.

Strength grew in her as she walked, until she felt her emotions steadying and her mind growing calmer. After two or three miles, the influence of the place was no more than a heaviness outside her, a weight like extra gravity against her body. "I haven't remembered anything," she said to Paul ruefully when he paused to let her climb up a steep five-foot boulder to the next ledge. "I've done it unconsciously somehow. But I'm all right now. I'll last until we get it done, whatever we're doing."

"Good." He did not smile. She had the weird feeling that he had forgotten, that smiling was something he did only when he remembered he was supposed to.

They were high on the slopes now, and Darcy could see for miles. Two more wendigo camps clustered in the distance, hazy with orange light, just as distant objects turned purple in her own world. "A lot of the wendigo are staying where they are," she observed. "Only some of them are going to the border to go across. I wonder why."

Paul looked back at her, seemed to consider a moment, then answered her. "It's because it's dangerous to go to the human world. The wendigo are immortal here. Something they've discovered—well, you can only do it here; they separate their souls from their bodies and keep them in a talisman, a stone or a carved knot of wood, something that will last. But to cross into the human world they have to take their souls with them, and it makes them vulnerable to someone who knows how to kill them. And when the border closes they have to return, that's part of the curse. They can't ever be truly free as long as it can close again. The oldest wendigo, the most powerful, don't want to take the risks."

They walked along a hillside, headed toward a box canyon where whirlwinds of dust rose and fell like pistons. "So to kill them you'd have to kill their body and destroy their soul as well, the thing they keep their soul in," Darcy said. It sounded like a lesson she had learned before.

"Yes. And the Guardians, men like your friend Charlie Edgewalker, can see wendigo and track them by the power of the soul talisman. So any wendigo on the human side is in danger as long as there are Guardians."

Paul led her on a sliding descent into the canyon, over loose thin rocks like shale and mica, gleaming with reflections of the pink-and-orange-streaked sky. The air was so dry it was making Darcy's throat hurt. She still tasted salty blood from her bitten tongue. Was there any water here at all? "When we broke into the Guardian's grave and opened the border," she said, "did we open it so it couldn't be closed again?"

"No. That's only one part of the curse, the spell the medicine men set long ago. The borders have opened before that way, and closed again, pulling all the wendigo back."

They reached the bottom of the canyon and Darcy stopped to catch her breath. How did Paul know all this? She was certain Dr. Ghormley knew none of it. But then, Ghormley hardly knew Paul. None of them did. He had only arrived in Laramie a month and a half ago, charming and handsome, with his odd accent no one could identify.

"You aren't calling them demons anymore," she said.

He laughed softly. "No."

The dust devils were hard to pass; they had to run out of each one's path and try to time it when the little whirlwind had lifted itself out of the canyon, before it came down again. "Where are we going?" Darcy demanded, tired of grit in her mouth and eyes, thirsty and footsore.

"We're here," Paul said. "Look."

On a barren mound at the back of the canyon, like a shrine, was a circle of small stones in the shape of a wheel. Four spokes cut it in pieces, and the rim was fifty feet or so in diameter. In the center of the wheel, half-buried in dust, was a small pale object. Darcy moved closer, as Paul slowed and walked behind her. It was an animal skull. The wheel was like the Medicine Wheel in the Bighorn Mountains, another of the borders. The skull . . .

"It is Coyote's skull," Paul said in a hushed voice. "The keystone of the spell, the center of the curse on the wendigo. That is what keeps drawing them back every time they manage to leave for a little while. That is what keeps them exiled here forever. We have to bring it with us back across the border."

"This is where they killed Coyote," Darcy said, remembering the legend. "They killed him and that was the final evil, dooming them, because he was an Ancestor, the true Coyote, and he should never have died . . ."

"Take the skull and we'll go," he said eagerly.

Darcy felt tired and dull, as if she had not slept for days. She did not need the wendigo madness to feel an exhausted despair. "My mother isn't here."

"She might be somewhere." In his impatience he pushed her toward the rock circle. "Get the skull. When the border is finally open she can cross back as easily as the wendigo can. You can help her if you need to. Go on, Darcy, we've got miles to go before we reach the border again."

"Get it yourself," she said angrily. "I don't care what you do. I just want to find my mother."

He stayed outside the wheel of rocks, glaring at her. "Pick it up. That's what I brought you here to do."

What did it matter? she told herself. Her mother was probably dead after all. She could not trust anything Paul told her now, if she ever could. She walked onto the mound, knelt down, and brushed dust away from the fragile bones. The skull was perfect, all the jagged sharp teeth intact, only a little larger than a real coyote's skull would have been. Paul watched her like a predator, fiercely triumphant. She looked up at him once before she put her hands around the cool, smooth skull.

"You can't touch it yourself," she said quietly. "None of the wendigo can, or they would have moved it long ago. You must be one of them somehow." She did not understand it, but it made sense.

She stood up with Coyote's skull carefully nestled between her palms. It weighed almost nothing, but the power it contained was the strongest Darcy had ever touched. She almost expected to be struck dead for what she was doing, but instead she felt a new strength and energy coursing into her.

"Coyote," she whispered, "help me if you can." Wendigo were coming down from the high places of the canyon and crossing under the dust devils toward her. There were twenty of them. Paul was waiting for her to come out of the rock circle. She still bound them, she still held them with the power of the curse.

There was no need for her to forget anymore, something told her, a gentle thought touching her mind. She should let the heavy madness of the wendigo's presence reach her a little, to clear her mind. She should close her eyes and stop fighting it. Now, Darcy.

She felt herself crumbling, as if she were made of soft clay. She sat down not caring what she sat on; it was a harsh-textured rock the size of a picnic hamper, part of one of the wheel spokes. Just let it come in, the low voice told her.

She wept bitterly, tears running over her skin, leaving tracks in the dust on her face. Places inside her that had been hard as stone began to soften, and ravines filled in, like the shifting landscape of the wendigo world. A hard knot of memories burst open like a flower and she saw the night on the mountain again, the night she had thought her mother died. The medicine bag in her hands had power she recognized this time. Where was Charlie—that had hurt the most, that he did not come to save her as he had before. As he had before . . .

She remembered sneaking away from the Girl Scout troop because the pine forest below Mount Rushmore was so beautiful. She had wandered through the forest and then followed an odd creature she saw, followed it for hours until it turned and attacked her. It tried to kill her, but somehow she held it back, pushing against sharp teeth and strong furry arms, until a man with long braided hair ran into the clearing and dragged the thing away from her. He killed it with a stone knife, she remembered, and then he took something from around its neck and burned it with matches from his pocket and crushed it under a stone. Then he turned to her and picked her up and carried her away through the woods, and she felt safe as she had never felt safe before. Charlie . . .

She remembered everything. Her vision quest at the camp where she and Laura were counselors, when Coyote came to sing to her and tell her about her medicine. Charlie, proud and eager to teach her more when she came down from the hilltop where she had spent the night; then back to the camp, waiting for him. But he had to go off and chase wendigo that had escaped and he would not take her, even though she begged to go. Then her mother, and the wendigo, and the crash . . . oh, Laura . . . and the night on the hillside when Coyote had come and brought back her medicine bag and taken away her memories. After that she remembered Charlie in the hospital, not recognizing him, the anger and hurt and fear in his face as he left her . . .

She opened her eyes abruptly and looked at Paul with horror. "I've betrayed everything. I am a Guardian. I've opened the border. Charlie will be in danger . . . everyone will be. I have to go back. Go back and try to close it with him, and hunt the wendigo that got out."

He was a wendigo himself, she remembered. His face did not change, did not transform into a bestial mask as she half expected. He was still beautiful. "What about your mother?" he said. "You did hear her voice. There was a wendigo corpse in her grave. You can't take back what you've done, but you can help her. Come out now and go to the border with us."

She shook her head and stood up. A dust devil was spinning toward them, but it veered away from the circle of rocks. "I can't do this." The guilt, the shock, grew within her. She had betrayed Charlie, betrayed her own people . . .

But the low voice, Coyote's voice, whispered to her again that she must, that Charlie needed her help, and she could not fight them all. She would die soon if she stayed within the circle with no water or food. They would just get some other human to take away his skull. Ghormley, maybe. He had some magic, maybe enough to get him this far and back without the madness. She had to go with the wendigo now. Coyote would be with her.

"Come out now," Paul said. The wendigo murmured around him, looking at her with hatred and longing. "No one will hurt you."

Darcy took her bandanna from around her neck and carefully wrapped the skull to protect it. Then she took a firm grip on the skull and tossed her head back and walked out of the stone circle to Paul. He flashed a smile at her and motioned for her to walk with him. The wendigo creatures clustered close around them, but never touched her. It was horrible enough without the remembered feel of their cool fingers on her skin. She noticed that Paul never touched her either. The skull, she guessed. They were still unable to touch the skull.

The walk back was across the open plains, through dust storms and broken badlands like lava flows. They hurried

Darcy along, chattering in their own language, loping on their short legs with their long arms touching the ground sometimes. They wore ragged bits of clothing made from animal skins and dried grass. She could not tell male from female; the hair on their heads was longer than their body fur. She noticed medicine bundles around their necks now, the things that held their souls. Paul did not wear one. She knew that. She had seen him naked.

Curiosity overcame her fury at Paul, and she asked him, "How did you pretend to be human?" A dreamlike mood possessed her so that nothing seemed strange anymore. Coyote's skull was a friendly presence in her hands.

Paul glanced at her with an odd look in his eyes. He had never seemed less alien than he did in that moment, with the odor and the massed power of the wendigo around them. "I am human," he said. "Not immortal, not even very powerful."

She shook her head. "No, I don't believe that. You're a wendigo. You must be."

There was laughter, harsh and mocking, in the crowd that rushed along beside them. Paul did not laugh. "I was one who got out seven years ago. One of the weapons was taken from the Guardian's grave . . . it was enough of a breach for a few young ones to dare to try a crossing. The others were fools, they stayed near the border, looking for humans to torment. But I knew the border would close again soon and I'd be drawn back. And I knew our enemy was here, one I'd heard of, but I was too young to have known him."

"Charlie," Darcy said.

"Yes, Charlie Edgewalker. We never knew his name before. We can do nothing but run from him. He's so well protected by his medicine power that we can't hurt him much, not our way. I was afraid of him, and I left my companions and ran as far from that place as I could, avoiding humans, thinking of nothing but escape. He didn't follow me. The others kept him too busy, I suppose."

"And you changed yourself somehow." They were nearing the first wendigo village Darcy had seen from the hills. Coyote whispered to her that the central hut of the village, a low stone building like a beehive, was the place where the old wendigo kept their soul talismans, guarded and safe. The knowledge was warm inside her, arming her like a warrior before battle. If she could destroy the stored talismans . . .

"Something I thought might work . . . I could never have done it in this world." Paul looked proud, and he seemed to want to impress her, to want her approval. "I took my soul back into my body. It hadn't been separate long anyway; we wait until we're grown, at least eighteen or twenty of your years, before we separate. The wendigo are human, you know, we all were once. In the human world I found myself becoming human when I took my soul back. It was hard . . . oh, it was painful, I'd never felt such pain. But I did it. Now I'm like you. I'm aging, I'll die someday."

Darcy glared at him. "It didn't give you any sympathy for humankind. You're still a monster inside."

He grinned. "I taught myself your language and customs and waited to see what I could do. I stole money, I went to schools in Canada, as far from the borders as I dared to go. I looked for people who were searching for magic and power, and who weren't too cautious about where they sought it. That led me to the Esoteric Society and our friend Richard Ghormley, and then to you."

They had almost reached the border. Darcy felt worn out, too tired for fear or hatred, resigned to the consequences of the terrible things she had done. "Now . . . once we've crossed with the skull, what will you do? What will they do?"

"I don't know. Most of them will wait to see if it's really safe. The braver ones will be free to do what they like. Most of them have revenge in mind. Can you blame them after our long exile?" He gave her his most charming smile as they walked up the trail to the border cave. Wendigo pressed in behind them, still keeping careful distance from Darcy and Coyote's skull.

Revenge. Darcy thought of Laramie, of all the people there running mad with wendigo invisibly haunting the streets. She knew of no way to stop it. Coyote insisted she must go on. "What will you do with me, once I've done this thing you wanted?"

"You won't be harmed." He was gentle, reassuring. "You're a hero to us now. The Guardian who broke the curse. You can stay with me, if you want. I'll keep you safe."

The border reached out for them and sucked them into its tearing vortex of wind and power. Darcy felt Coyote with her, steadying her; it was not as bad as before. But it seemed to go on forever before she was out, standing on the floor of the cave in her own world with Paul beside her.

The Wendigo Border 199

in Charlie's stomach. Darcy weakness filled her. "Charlie

# CHAPTER
# FIFTEEN

W e're back!" Paul called as they walked forward, wendigo passing swiftly on every side. They walked out onto the overhang of rock in front of the cave. The wendigo raced by without taking any notice of the four men there; Paul must have told them to leave them alone. Darcy saw two seated men, and two standing, holding guns on one of the others. The prisoner was Charlie Edgewalker, she realized with a sick feeling. She had brought Coyote's skull out of the wendigo world; he would surely hate her now.

"They're safely through." Dr. Ghormley stood up in the darkness. "Shoot him now, we don't need him."

Darcy screamed "No!" as the gunshot echoed and Charlie was knocked back from his seated position like a rolling boulder. A rending pain doubled Darcy over and drove her to her knees, still clutching Coyote's skull. She could smell the smoke from the gunshot and the stench of the horrible wound in Charlie's stomach. Dizzy weakness filled her. "Charlie . . . no . . ." she whispered.

Ghormley strode in and bent in front of her. He took Coyote's skull from her weak grasp. "What's wrong with her?"

"She feels the other Guardian's pain." Paul knelt beside her. "Darcy, you can block that, you should know how. Try to find it in your memories."

She hated him, hated them all, she could not think, could not feel anything but the gaping wound, the pain, shadows closing in. But then something moved within her, clicked into place, and she was left shuddering and weak in Paul's arms. She could smell the dead people, and see the silhouette of the man who had fired the gun looking down at his victim. Charlie lay bent over on his side with his eyes closed, making no sound but breathing in shallow gasps. Dark wetness pooled beneath him.

"What do I do with this?" Ghormley asked. He held up the coyote skull.

"Smash it," Paul said. Darcy watched the fragile skull fall and shatter on the rocks; Paul and Ghormley kicked the fragments over the side. More wendigo came through: they swept past with shrieks of delight and dragged the standing gunman over the edge of the rocks. He fell a long way before he stopped screaming. But the wendigo did not stay long enough to do any more damage here. They rushed on into the night and left the little group of humans alone on the ledge in the sudden silence. They must be stronger now, Darcy thought. It was the first time she had seen wendigo directly kill a human.

"I don't understand," Ghormley said to Paul. "They promised me . . ."

"They'll speak to you later," Paul assured him. "Don't worry. They're grateful to you and to Darcy for what you've both done for them. We should all go back to Laramie now and wait for them. Leave this carrion here." He kicked at

Charlie in passing, but got no reaction. "Come with me, Darcy. There's nothing for you here."

Charlie was still breathing; she could not leave him. She had no desire to go with Paul anyway. He was inhuman, a monster in every sense of the word. She searched for excuses. "My . . . my mother," she said, "I have to go back and search for her."

"That can wait until tomorrow. You're exhausted. She's lasted this long. She'll be there when you feel better." His voice was soft, kind, soothing.

"No. I won't go with you. I'm going back in."

He finally said, "Whatever you want. I'll be at Ghormley's house in Laramie. If you need protection, come to me there."

She did not answer him again. She waited until Paul, Ghormley, and the remaining gunman had gone, and the sound of their footsteps on the trail below dwindled into the silence of rocks and forest. Still, she waited, sitting quietly beside the piled corpses, until she heard the faint roar of an engine and knew they were driving away in Ghormley's van. Then she moved to Charlie.

"Oh, dear God, I've killed you," she whispered. "I did this to you . . ." Her voice broke and tears fell on her hands as she reached for him.

He took a breath as if to speak, but the effort made him wince with pain. She unwound the cruel wire from his wrists, feeling more blood there. If she could get him to the hospital, maybe . . . she pulled his jacket off him, and his shirt. He had begun to shiver. She needed a bandage. There were plenty of clothes around, unneeded. She ripped the front of the kaftan away from Ephron's body and bound it around Charlie's waist, her fingers briefly touching the two-inch hole the gun had made, pressing the softness of muscle and intestine back inside. She would never have imagined she could do this, feeling around in a gunshot wound in the dark, but it was Charlie and she had no choice. At the exit hole in his back she felt fragments of bone. Probably bits of shirt and jacket fabric were inside him. She tied the bandage around five times, as tightly as she could. It would be blood-soaked in a moment. Then she struggled to put the shirt and jacket back on him.

"Don't die, don't die," she murmured. "My teacher, my brother, don't die ..." The words were Cheyenne, a few he had taught her when she was thirteen. "The pickup at the ranch. If we can get you there, I can take you to the hospital."

"Can't ... kill me like this ..." he said, a rasping voice with pain shot through it like knives. "I'm not ... dying, won't die. My soul ... wouldn't have survived if I hadn't ... Seven years in ... wendigo world. Had to do it." He began to cough, and then he pushed himself up until he was sitting against a rock, his arms wrapped around his stomach, his head bent.

"Your soul? You separated yourself from your soul, like the wendigo? That's why you're no older now than when we met."

He nodded, sought more words. "Coyote helped me ... would have died. I need it ... the stone ... to help me heal. In the medicine bag ... your medicine bag. Gave it to you for safekeeping. Is it ..."

"It's at the ranch. How can we get you there? You may not be dying." She could scarcely believe that. "But you're losing so much blood you'll never walk that far. It's ten miles." She tried to stop crying.

"My horse. The pinto. Down below, in the aspens. Go get him, ride him ... as far up the mountain as he can go ... then come get me. Go on, I'll be ... here when you get back." He leaned his head against the rock, his eyes closed. "Go." Darcy obeyed, though she hated to leave him even for a few minutes.

It was full dark now, with clouds over the stars, and Darcy's legs shook with exhaustion as she slowly felt her way down the rough hiking trail. There were places on the trail that were fun in the daylight; little boulder crevices, carefully planned to give the average hiker a challenge; they were frightening in the dark. She felt her heartbeat pounding in her neck before she reached the bottom.

In the aspen grove the trees whispered and leaned around her as if telling secrets. The pinto tugged against its reins, its eyes wide and ears pulled back. The wendigo had been here. Ariadne's body was a little distance through the trees. "Hush, softly, it's all right," she soothed the horse, keeping up a murmuring as she approached. It was lucky the pinto hadn't broken the rein and bolted. It was glad to see her, snuffling in her hair as she untied it and led it toward the mountain.

When Charlie could think of anything but the pain of his wound, he would certainly hate her for what she had done. She hated herself. It had been too easy to believe Paul's handsome face, the flattering way he spoke of her power. She had let him manipulate her as if she were a child. Even if she believed her mother might be alive across the border . . . Darcy's throat choked again with tears.

She should have gone to Charlie for help, not the Esoteric Society. Especially after she regained some of her memory under hypnosis. She had remembered enough to realize the wendigo were evil, and Charlie was her friend. She should never have told Paul and Dr. Ghormley about the Guardian's grave. She should have gone straight to Charlie and asked him to fill in the gaps in her memory, and if he knew any way to look for her mother without letting the wendigo through.

What if her mother was still alive? She had to find out . . . but Charlie was more important now. Paul had been right when he said that Sarah Jacobi could last one more night if she'd lasted seven years. Still it hurt, it was like a rock in her stomach, to think of leaving with Charlie and not going back into the wendigo world to search.

The slope was too steep for the pinto fifty yards up the mountain's foot. Darcy left it there with a dangling rein, hoping its cow-pony training would hold it on a night of such strangeness. "Charlie?" she called softly upward. "I'm coming back. Get ready to go." There was no answer, but she could feel him still there, holding on grimly to consciousness.

Climbing again, the boulder ledges and cracks were a little easier going up in the dark than they had been going down. How she would get Charlie down them.... Darcy felt her muscles cramping, sharp pains running through her arms and legs, warning her to stop; she had hiked more than ten miles already tonight, here and in the wendigo world. It did not matter. She made it back to the border cave, gasping for breath, her body shivering with the gathering cold.

"Charlie?" She peered at the lumps of bodies in the darkness. One raised a hand slightly. She hurried to him. He had managed to pull a warm parka off one of the dead people, and he was huddled into it with his knees against his stomach.

"Not much time," he said very softly. "I think ... it's possible for my body to die. I feel so cold ..."

"You can't. You're immortal. You said your soul was separate so you can't be killed," she said as she knelt and put her arms around him to help him stand.

"I wasn't thinking about the kind of wound ..." He stopped talking for a few minutes while they struggled to get him upright; he inched his way up, leaning on a boulder and on Darcy, almost too heavy for her to support. When he was standing with an arm around her shoulders they waited for a long time for his harsh breathing to soften.

Blood had seeped through the parka already, front and back. The smell was strong. From deer-hunting with her father, Darcy knew that it should be a death smell. When the intestines were torn, bacteria got into the bloodstream, poisoned it, and Charlie was losing so much blood anyway. She wanted to believe that he couldn't die, but he might, at least his body, and what would that do to a surviving soul . . .

"It will take us hours to get back to the ranch," she said as they started to walk. "We can't both ride, not all the time, the horse won't stand it. I'd go on, as fast as I could, but I can't leave you here. What if they come back? They might, to bury their dead or just to see if they really killed you."

Moving at all was a slow, torturous process. Charlie was not much taller than Darcy, but his weight across her shoulders was so solid she could hardly bear it. The footing was bad for both of them, the rocky slopes no place to descend in the dark, and if Charlie fell, Darcy did not think she could get him up again. She could not see further than a few feet in front of her face. If the pinto decided to break for home . . . She had not seen anything to tie its reins to. She had to trust to its training, trust that it would stand.

The horse was there when they were down at last. Charlie mounted with Darcy's help, from a boulder on the upslope onto the animal's back. Once there he slumped forward, one hand gripping the saddle horn. His feet were in the stirrups. Darcy guessed he would stay on until she dragged him off. She led the horse down the slope until they reached the level ground again, then mounted behind Charlie. The reins were hard to handle around Charlie's broad back, and her seat on the cantle slipped and rubbed her legs with each step the horse took. The pinto was strong enough at least to begin with, and it could move faster than Darcy's exhausted walking pace.

Every hoof that fell sent a jolt through Charlie, and Darcy could feel bursts of pain in the tightening of his muscles. "How can you last all the way to the ranch?" she said hopelessly.

He shook his head. "I guess I can't . . . we can both ride to the Guardian's tomb. The wendigo and their allies . . . would not go there. You could ride on, come back with the medicine bag and . . . something to sew me up with. Penicillin if you can find any."

"The broodmare's tack room, there are antibiotics in there. Vials of penicillin, syringes. But I don't know the human dosage." She didn't like the idea, but it was better than riding slowly like this until he died.

"A good light too," he said. "It will be close work."

"Stop trying to talk. I'll get what's needed." She would agree to whatever he said, do whatever he told her. The thought of trying to repair the damage the bullet had made was terrifying. She hoped his healing magic would overcome her utter inexperience as an emergency surgeon. Would there be an anatomy book at the ranch house? Probably one on horses.

A little more than an hour later she loped into the ranch yard alone on the lathered, blowing horse. It stood with its head down, shaking, as she dismounted in a pool of light from one of the big spots. She had to get back right away. She could not bear to think of Charlie hidden in the dark beneath those rocks, as if he were dead and buried already.

"Girl, you know better than to ride a horse that way," said Ed Kennan, startling her so much she almost screamed.

He had been standing out in the yard in his pajamas. His thin, wrinkled face glowed with a believer's vision, the irritation of his words aside.

"It's an emergency, Ed. Is Alice here?" She didn't see the pickup where it was usually parked.

"No. She spent the night with Mrs. Argyros in town. They're going to Denver tomorrow to look at English tack for the new 4-H class." He grinned at Darcy. "But all that's unimportant now. They're here."

She walked past him. She had no time for his fantasies now. "Your aliens?"

The old rancher followed her closely. "You didn't see

them? I did. Not quite seeing, really, but one of them was here. Standing here right beside me and talking to me. The time has come, the world is ready for change. That's what he said."

The realization was late in coming. "Ready for change . . ." She paused in the doorway of the porch. "I've seen your aliens, Ed. They killed half a dozen people already and there will be more. Charlie Edgewalker is dying because of them, only I can't let him die, he's the only one who knows how to stop them."

"Charlie . . ." Ed was confused.

"Charlie Stone, the wrangler," she said, remembering. "He's badly hurt. I have to go back to him, I only have a minute. Ed, listen to me." She gripped his thin shoulders with both hands. "Your aliens are evil, they're ancient evil spirits, monsters, and Charlie and I have to try to stop them. Destroy them."

"What do you mean, Darcy, you have to destroy them?" He was suddenly angry. "What kind of lies has that Indian told you? He's a suspicious one, that's what I thought all along."

"Oh, never mind." She turned away from him into the living room and crossed quickly to the stairs. Ed called after her.

"They're good! They're perfect beings. I thought you'd understand, when you saw them . . ."

Darcy ran up the stairs into her bedroom. Thank God the medicine bag was there on the bedpost. She tied it around her neck, hiding it under her shirt. The warm weight of it felt comforting. It was amazing to think that all this time she had been guarding Charlie's soul. She wondered which of the objects inside was his talisman. How could he have trusted her with it? She had proven herself not worth his trust.

Blankets . . . she pulled one off her bed, found two more in the closet, and rolled them tightly to tie across a saddle. With the roll under her arm, she searched her desk drawer for her small sewing kit and put it in a jacket pocket. What else . . . something to boil water with. She'd have to sterilize needle and thread. She hurried down to the kitchen, almost bumping into Ed. He was talking on the telephone.

"She's here now. Yes."

Who could he be talking to? She reached into a high cabinet for the butane camp stove Alice had bought for winter fence-riding. It folded up like a small thermos, small enough to stuff inside her blanket roll. Food and water. Charlie couldn't eat, but he'd be thirsty, and she was starving. She found a canteen in a cabinet and began filling it from the faucet.

"No, he's hurt. Not dead, hurt. She's bringing things to him. I don't know where."

Darcy whirled. "Who are you talking to?" she demanded. "Ed, what are you trying to do . . ."

She grabbed the phone from him and heard a laugh, a voice saying, "Darcy?" It was Dr. Ghormley's voice. She hung up the phone, more angry than frightened. Now they knew Charlie was alive and she was helping him.

"Ed, how could you call them? Do you know what you just did?" she shouted. She wanted to strangle him, this crazy old man she had always loved.

"I knew Dr. Ghormley would believe me about the aliens," he said, backing away from her. "You said you were going to try to hurt them. Somebody's got to do something."

She had no time to try to talk sense to Ed Kennan. He had been dreaming too long about his benevolent aliens. Probably the wendigo had deliberately fooled him, as they had fooled Dr. Ghormley into thinking they were medieval demons.

"Forget it," she said, turning back to her packing. In the refrigerator she found bologna and cheese, two oranges. Meanwhile, Ed had turned and gone down into the basement. Fine, she'd leave him there. The food went into a paper bag and then inside the blanket roll with the stove.

No time, no time . . . Darcy ran out of the house again and to the broodmare's barn. The heated air rushed out at her when she flung open one of the metal doors. Ignoring the low whickers of greeting from the horses in their stalls, she went to the tack room and took three plastic ampoules of penicillin and the smallest syringe, the one used for newborn foals. Those went into a small metal box, then into the blanket roll. Two large camping flashlights were awkward. She tied twine around the handles and fastened them on around the blankets.

After a minute's thought, she reached for the key on top of a shelf, unlocked a small strongbox at the back of the tack room, and took out a .33-caliber pistol, a holster, and a box of ammunition. She knelt there to load five bullets, leaving the firing chamber empty. The holster had a saddle clip, and there was a ring on Cinnamon's saddle by the horn. She did not want to think of using the gun. But if Ghormley came after Charlie, they would need more than magic to stop him.

Now for horses. She ran to the boarding stables, the blanket roll bouncing at her shoulder, the holstered gun in one hand. Sleepy animals looked at her without much curiosity. She pulled Cinnamon out of his stall and bridled and saddled him, tying the blanket roll on with the saddle strings, clipping the holster in place. He pranced nervously, feeling her wild emotions and her haste.

For the other horse she chose a half-Arabian mare named Martha, one of the steadiest working horses on the ranch. Martha wouldn't bolt or run with a hurt man on her back. A saddle and bridle for her, and then she was ready to go. She paused, though, with the horses outside the barn; looked over at the light in the windows of the ranch house.

Poor Ed. He thought she was some kind of murdering, bigoted alien-hater. She had to try one more time to make him understand what was going on. It was dangerous for him out here by himself. No guarantee the wendigo would continue to make glowing promises now that they were free. They might attack him later.

She tied Cinnamon and Martha to a post and ran across the yard, ignoring her aching, blistered feet. "Ed? Ed, I'm sorry I yelled at you . . ." Into the living room, back into the kitchen; where was the old man? "Come on out, listen to me. You've got to understand about the wendigo. You can't trust them for anything. They're evil creatures, nothing like what they pretend to be."

When she was near the door to the basement Ed Kennan ran up the last few stairs. She heard his footsteps and looked just in time to dodge the thrust of a knife in his hand. He didn't say anything, just came at her, trying to kill her with the strangest weapon, a knife with a stone blade like something prehistoric.

So shocked she could not scream, Darcy moved like a numb robot, dodging his thrusts, hearing the thud of their feet on the linoleum. She was stronger and faster than he was, in spite of her shock, and in a minute she had a twisting grip on his knife hand and a knee in his stomach. The old man doubled over and fell like a folding chair, crashing to the kitchen floor. Darcy did not let go of his arm until she had the knife. She knew what it was. The sacred weapon of the Guardian, the one that had been stolen seven years ago.

Her breath came in short gasps. Her eyes were overflowing with tears. "Oh, Ed . . ." He couldn't be much hurt. He was getting to his hands and knees. The knife was what he had hidden in the basement wall. "I suppose the aliens told you to take it."

"And to . . . get it out, just now." His face was sickly pale.

"I'm sorry. When this is all over maybe I can explain to you . . ." She turned and ran from the kitchen out the back door, carrying the Guardian's knife. It fit smoothly in the palm of her right hand, a cold, deadly weight. She knew what it was for; Charlie had killed the wendigo ten years ago with a knife like this. Ed taking it out of the Guardian's grave had opened the border for Paul and the others, the ones who had made her mother's car crash. That good old man, that stupid, good old man ...

Still crying, she tucked the knife in her belt against her jeans. She untied her horse and mounted, and wrapped the other horse's lead rein around her wrist. They left the ranch yard at a brisk trot; as soon as the horses were warmed up they could gallop. Darcy wondered as she rode if she could ever go back to the Kennans'. If the wendigo weren't stopped she supposed it would not matter.

# CHAPTER
# SIXTEEN

―――――――――

"Just take one of your sleeping pills, Ed, and go on to bed," said Alice Kennan wearily. Her husband's call was one of the strangest stories he'd told yet: aliens in the front yard and Darcy stealing one of their artifacts. He said he'd tried to kill Darcy! Alice did not know whether to believe that part or not. If it was true, she should send for the police right now and have Ed taken in. She did not want to believe he had really done it.

There were police sirens out tonight in Laramie, strange on a Monday. Her friends had gone to bed earlier, but Alice couldn't sleep. She pulled back the flowered curtains of the guest bedroom and looked out into the windblown October night. The street was dismally dark between the small circles of light from the corner lamp poles. Marjorie had a split-level suburban house in one of the newer parts of town, every one on her street alike, all dark and blank-faced at night. Alice shivered, and wondered why she was so frightened.

It wasn't just Ed's phone call. It had started before that, at sunset. She found herself thinking that something terrible had happened. And then, a few hours later, the sirens started. She had turned on the radio and gotten nothing but cheerful country-western music. Marjorie and Bill had been uninterested, sleepy from the wine they'd served with dinner. They left her to sit up and feel as if she were caught in the open in the middle of a lightning storm with no cover or low ground.

Resigning herself to her uneasiness, Alice pulled a high-backed chair away from a little writing desk to the window-sill. She sat there pressed against the glass, her hands cupped around her eyes to block the reflections. There was nothing really to see. Leaves blew against the window, a bare willow was swaying across the street, the sky was dark with no stars showing.

But then a car shrieked around the curved subdivision road and skidded to a halt just a house away, in the middle of the street. An old Camaro, it gleamed black or dark gray in the light from the streetlamp. A door opened and Alice saw something fall out from the passenger side, and then there was a gunshot, and then a scream.

Alice leaped up, overturning her chair. She was wearing house slippers but it did not make any difference. She bolted through the house as if trying to catch a runaway horse, past the quiet bedrooms of the Argyros children, through the dark living room, stumbling against a coffee table, and out the front door.

She had expected lights to go on, doors to slam, but the other houses were quiet and dark. A terrified whimpering came from a hunched figure in the middle of the street. The car had gone as suddenly as it came, leaving behind . . .

A young girl, no more than sixteen, wearing a party dress with flounces and stained all over with her own dark, shiny blood. Alice knelt by her and felt a wave of almost uncontrollable nausea; the girl's left shoulder was nearly blown off, her arm hanging by a delicate tracery of tattered flesh. A tourniquet, but where to tie it, Alice thought frantically, pulling off her robe and jerking its terry-cloth belt from the loops.

"Jimmy shot me," said the girl in a shocked whisper.

"Hush, hold still," Alice said, grabbing the girl's arm and pulling it close to her side, tying the belt under and over it. Arterial blood spurted, coating Alice's face and hands so rapidly she knew she'd never get back inside to call 911.

"He was driving me home," said the girl's voice in a faded, dreamlike tone. "Like always, and he got crazy, he turned into somebody else, I mean it. He said he wanted to fuck me and I said no, and he stopped the car right here and pushed me out and got out his shotgun from the gun rack and shot me . . ." She slumped against Alice, bleeding her life out.

Sirens cried like banshees in the distance. Alice thought of her grandmother from Ireland, the way she said one wailed when someone was about to die. This child had a banshee chorus. "Don't try to talk, honey. Quiet, now. You're going to sleep soon, don't be scared." Alice wondered what she'd want to hear if she was dying like this, slipping away so quickly.

"I was scared," said the girl. "Thought I saw a gremlin, or a Bigfoot or something, running by the car before Jimmy went crazy. What do you think it was, ma'am?"

There was scarcely a pulse in her good arm. Alice tried to keep from weeping, not wanting the girl's last memory to be one of sorrow. "I don't know. What's your name, honey? Where does your family live?" She wasn't sure she'd get an answer.

"Here. That's my house." She nodded vaguely at the split-level across the street from Marjorie's. "I was . . . supposed to be home . . . at ten-thirty . . ." She stopped talking and slowly grew very still.

Alice sat with the dead girl for a long minute. A strange brushing sensation against her back made her look up, and she saw nothing, or almost nothing, a shimmer against the streetlamp's glow. It was very close to her. She jumped up and ran toward Marjorie's house, leaving the girl, suddenly convinced she would be killed if she stayed outside.

"Don't touch me," she gasped, running. "Leave me alone . . ."

Screams sounded from down the street, and lights began to go on, and Alice Kennan felt as if she had closed the door on madness as she slumped against it in the Argyros foyer. If there had been something, it didn't follow her inside. She was shaking all over like a very old woman. Ed's alien, she thought with a hysterical giggle, maybe I met Ed's alien.

She had to sit down on the linoleum for a long series of shaky breaths before she was strong enough to go to the phone and call the police about the girl in the street. The 911 operator never came on the line.

With fresh horses, Darcy was back at the Guardian's ridge in less than an hour. She tied the animals to rocks in the ravine at the steep side of the ridge and climbed up the slope, the blanket roll slung over her shoulders. The flashlights bumped against her waist and the buttoned holster she had taken from the saddle dragged heavily at her belt loop.

She was afraid they might be found here. Ghormley and Paul could already be at the ranch by now, and Ed Kennan might have watched to see which way she rode. They would have to follow on horseback, or drive around to the Vedauwoo side and come in on foot. They could guess where Charlie was hiding if they knew her direction from Ed. Darcy would have to move him to some other sheltered place, and quickly.

It was quiet in the burial place, empty of spirits, but she felt a lingering awe as she crept in the low entrance.

"Charlie?" She untied the flashlights and switched them on. The beams of light made the paintings on the rock walls seem to move. Stylized figures; she recognized Coyote by his ears and tail, and a line of horned dancers that must be medicine men. An owl stretched across the stone over the damaged bier. Paul had not been satisfied with scattering the Guardian's bones; the rocks that had been neatly laid together for his resting place were scattered too, strewn throughout the chamber, flat boulders like tires.

Darcy knelt down by Charlie on the earth floor. He lay still, on one side, his face upturned into the light. His face was empty except for the thin set of his lips, a line of pain. She touched him gently; his skin was warm. He must have passed out. His breathing was so shallow she could hardly see it condensing in the cold.

He looked very young with his eyes closed. The sense of threat, of ready violence, was gone. Darcy remembered how deeply she had once trusted him. There was a bond between them; wakened to herself through Coyote's magic, she wondered how she could have forgotten that she loved him.

"I can't get you out of here by myself." She took the medicine bag from around her neck and tied it around his, under the four braids of black hair. It rested against his skin at the hollow of his throat. "Wake up and help me, Charlie Edgewalker."

No response at all. She brought the flashlights closer and took off her gloves. At least she could begin the part of his healing that she understood. Her fingers grew cold quickly as she took out the box with the penicillin and the paper-sealed syringe. One of the plastic vials slid into the back of the syringe, and a needle from the wrapping clicked in at the other end. The needle was long and thick, meant for a horse's hide. Darcy pressed a little of the liquid through to get rid of the air. She had done this to foals, a quick and cheerful job in the minutes after birth, with the mother horse nudging at her hair in worry.

Glad he was unconscious, Darcy unbuttoned Charlie's

blood-soaked jeans and pulled them down off one hip. He had a scar there at his belt line like a slash of claws: old, seamed flesh. Taking a deep breath to steady her hand, she popped the needle in three inches below the scar, through skin and deep into muscle. Half the foal's dosage, she guessed, for now. More later. She withdrew the needle, capped it, and put it back inside its wrapping. Blood trickled in a thin line from the tiny wound she had made. She pulled the denim back up over his hip and buttoned the jeans again.

They had to get out of here. She thought of spilling water on his face to wake him; then something made her sit upright and listen hard. A whisper, a touch of presence. Coyote? It was gone, but something told her she had to go up and look for their enemies. She turned the flashlights off and left Charlie in the dark burial place, taking her knife and gun with her as she climbed out of the jumbled boulders as quietly as she could.

It was pitch-black outside. The horses were undisturbed below in the ravine. She stayed against the rocks, not wanting to outline herself to anyone who might be watching. Someone was out there, she was sure of it now. On their trail, on the Vedauwoo side. She heard a distant scuffing of feet against rocky earth.

Darcy crouched in a cleft of rock near the top of the boulder pile and took her pistol out of its holster. She clicked the hammer and eased the chamber around so it was ready to fire, then she wedged herself back against the stones with the pistol resting on her knees. There . . . a half-mile away, hard to tell in the dark. A flicker of light, maybe from a cigarette lighter. She listened hard for the whispered voices.

"All these rocks look alike to me." The words were clear, on the edge of her hearing. She tried to concentrate. It was a man's voice.

"I can't see anything. You're sure they went this way?" A woman. After a moment Darcy placed the familiar voice.

Roxanne. She felt coldly unsurprised. Her friend might have felt she had to prove herself to Ghormley now that Darcy was considered an enemy.

The man, she guessed, was the second gunman, the one who had survived earlier that night. There might be more searchers out there. Ghormley and Paul should have come themselves. They would not have been so uncertain of the way. Maybe they were afraid they'd get shot from ambush. Ed could have seen her go into the broodmare's barn; he might have checked the gun box, told them she was armed.

No. No, suddenly she hated the feel of the weapon in her hands. She could not fire a bullet into someone, tear their flesh apart like Charlie's. Besides, if there were other searchers a shot would end whatever confusion they had as to the right hilltop. Her hands were getting cold on the metal of the gun. She had not bothered to put her gloves back on.

Her vision quest was part of the memories she had regained. Coyote had been with her that night on a sagebrush-covered hill ten miles west of here. He was her spirit guide, her totem animal. He had taught her songs about the way of the Coyote. She could barely remember them, but the meaning was clear. Coyote would never lie in wait to shoot someone in the back. He was Wihio, the trickster. He would trick them.

How? She could lead the horses over their old trail, confuse the tracks. Too late for that, they were too close. She could let them see her, draw them away from Charlie . . .

Or she could let them reach the Guardian's tomb and find nothing there but rocks. She couldn't move Charlie. But neither of these two had been inside the grave before. If she could block up the entrance to the lower chamber—let them think that the rocks had shifted, with the Guardian's power removed, blocking the only way in.

The cautious footsteps were coming nearer. She had to move if she was going to without being seen or heard. Sweat had broken out on her forehead and under her arms despite the cold. It would almost take more courage to do this than to shoot them both. She scrambled down the sloping boulder into the bottom of the rock cluster, careful with the loaded and primed gun, afraid the sound of jacking the bullet out would be too loud.

"Charlie." She crawled up to him, touched his face again. His eyes were open and he was breathing. "Stay quiet."

The soft earth made no sound as she rolled two heavy rocks in front of the narrow entrance, one behind the other to block a curious push from the other side. A slit of an inch or so was still uncovered at the top of the entrance. The searchers might have a flashlight they could shine through the crack.

She hid the blanket roll and flashlights behind another of the loose rocks. "Charlie, you're going to have to move." He did not argue or ask her any questions. She took a firm hold under his shoulders and dragged him as he moved his legs a little to help. He curled up on himself again when she had him against the wall by the entrance, where no one looking in could see them.

Darcy knelt by Charlie with the gun resting on one knee and thought about silence, about not existing. She was another rock. Mindless granite. The man chasing them was unlikely to have any sensitivity, but she did not know about Roxanne. Ghormley seemed to think she was talented.

They climbed down, as she had feared, and pushed against the rock at the entrance, and shone a powerful flashlight into the dark chamber. "Nobody here," Roxanne said. "God, look at that wall painting, though. I want to come back here sometime in the daylight."

"It would take a rock hammer and all day working to get inside there. They couldn't have gotten in. And how could a wounded man get down these rocks?" The man's voice had an East Coast accent.

"The Indian guy can't be alive anyway. No one in Laramie ever believed Ed Kennan before." Roxanne sounded amused. "I bet his aliens told him the guy was alive. You said you saw him shot in the guts."

"He's dead by now, that's for sure." The man's voice moved away, and there were noises as the two climbed back up the boulder slope. "Unless the girl got him to the highway and got a ride to a hospital. Ghormley should check the hospitals in Cheyenne. That ranch house again too. Maybe the old man is hiding them both. Maybe he sent us out on a snipe hunt."

"That's the first smart thing you've said." Roxanne's voice faded as they walked away. "Yeah, let's drive out to the ranch. We can call Ghormley from there and tell him they weren't holed up in the old grave. You know what I think? I think they might have crossed over to the demon side up at the cave. But I'm not going in there to look for them. Leave that to the big magicians, that's what I say." Their words faded and were soon gone.

Darcy slumped against the stones and closed her eyes, then forced them open when she realized how easily she could fall into an oblivious sleep. She couldn't rest yet. She crept over to the supplies hidden behind rocks and took a drink from the canteen. Their enemies had been gone long enough. She turned around to see Charlie watching her, a glimmer of eyes in the darkness. "Thirsty?" she asked.

"My throat's dry." She brought him the canteen and he took two careful swallows. His eyes closed again and he leaned back against the boulder wall with a sigh. "You can help me now. I don't think you'd better try to stitch anything up, but at least get the wound cleaned out."

"It will take me a few minutes to heat the water." She brought the camping stove kit over to the wall and took it apart. The lid became a pot. She found a match, turned on the butane, and lit the little flame, like a Bunsen burner at school.

Water from the canteen filled the small pot and she knelt there waiting for it to boil. At this high altitude water behaved differently, reaching a boil more rapidly.

"Heat a knife too," Charlie said weakly.

The work would have been difficult and frightening even in daylight. The two flashlights and the camp stove cast strange shadows, and when Darcy moved she often blocked the light to the wound. Charlie lay still on top of one of the blankets, breathing in shallow, steady rhythm. The parka covered his legs, and the other blanket wrapped his shoulders and upper torso.

She had to soak the stiffened bandages before she could peel them away from his skin. Pieces of the cotton fabric that were not bloodstained she tore up and boiled in the pot to use as swabs. She cleaned the wound, soaking off clotted blood and pieces of charred fabric, cutting with the heated blade of her pocketknife to free bone fragments and bits of blackened flesh.

The worst was holding the hot knife inside the wound to cauterize whatever blood vessels the bullet's heat had missed. The smell sickened Darcy. Charlie swore steadily while she did this, sweating as if it were not cold enough to see your breath in the flashlight glare. They were both exhausted by the time she was finished. She bandaged him again with torn strips of blanket and helped him get back into the parka, then wrapped him in blankets and let him lie still.

In the old stone tomb, an hour passed endlessly. Charlie lay with his hands resting on his bandages, drawing strength and healing power from the talisman in the medicine bag. They stayed out of sight by the blocked entrance, and Darcy had turned the flashlights and the stove off. Their enemies might come back. Charlie was so concentrated within himself that he would never hear them or sense their coming until they were within the chamber.

Darcy fought sleep, drifting in and out of a light doze and shaking herself awake a dozen times. When she was awake her thoughts ran in a circular pattern: she had betrayed Charlie and her Guardian duties; she should have stayed in the protected wheel in the wendigo world and starved there rather than take Coyote's skull out to be destroyed; Charlie must hate her for what she had done; if her mother was still alive she had to go back into that terrible place.

Her head snapped up from a doze when the silence in the chamber was broken. Charlie was sitting up, singing a low, hoarse-voiced chant in which she recognized the word Wihio for Coyote. His legs were crossed and he rocked back and forth as he sang. Wrapped in a blanket, his long braids down his back, he looked like an Ancestor himself, an ancient sorceror from cave-dwelling times back in the Ice Age. Darcy felt her bones tingling with the power of the chant, the power of his fierce concentration.

She found herself wondering for the first time just how old he was. Seven years in the wendigo world, he had said, and she knew that time was different there. Paul had told her he was too young to have known Charlie, presumably meaning when Charlie was in the wendigo world. Paul was as young as he appeared, she thought, and that would mean Charlie was there more than twenty years ago.

She remembered the dreams that had puzzled her. One about a young boy at a strange boarding school; Coyote had given him a ride on his back and had taken his medicine bag off for safekeeping. The other dream was the nightmare of the wendigo world, being hunted, chased, with Coyote as the only companion left, and even Coyote little more than a ghost. The boy in that dream had been sixteen or seventeen years old. She guessed now that she had somehow dreamed of Charlie's past, or shared his dreams. The memory of the first dream even gave her a name: Owl Child, that the school had changed to Charlie Gray Stone. She did not think that any school for Indian children in modern times would change a boy's name like that. And the school had felt more like a prison.

If the Guardian spirit were still here, Darcy guessed that Charlie would have found an easy source of healing power. She had watched Paul and Dr. Ghormley destroy the power of this place. The thought reminded her of the stone knife she had taken from Ed Kennan. It had been one of the sacred weapons of the Guardian. It had probably been buried with him centuries ago when the wendigo were banished. She drew it out of her belt; the serrated edge was wickedly sharp, small stones inset like saw teeth along the larger flint of the blade. It was pale and heavy, and she could see it clearly in spite of the thick darkness in the chamber.

The chanting stopped. Charlie turned toward her; she saw a glint of eyes. "Let me see that," he said, reaching out one hand. She put the knife into his open palm. "The blade that was stolen . . . where did you find it? Across on the wendigo side?"

"No." Darcy was reluctant to tell him, but she decided she had better not keep anything from him again. "When I went to the ranch for the supplies, Ed Kennan tried to kill me with it."

"He was the thief seven years ago?"

"He thought it was some kind of evidence of his aliens. He stumbled onto the grave once, and took that, but he wasn't ever able to find it again." The day Coyote had led her to the grave, Ed Kennan must have been riding aimlessly just over the hill, searching for this place.

Charlie nodded, holding the knife now across both palms and staring down at it. "And the other deluded fool, Ghormley, he has the lance head. I could see it glowing through his coat while he sat on the rock waiting for you and Paul to come out. We'll have to get it back from him to close the border again. We can do it, with both weapons. It would be

faster to go after Ghormley than to make a new lance; the
ritual takes four days." He was quiet, thoughtful.

"You're in no shape to go after anyone," Darcy said.
She covered up a deep yawn, wondering how much longer she could think at all. She was tired and miserable, and
all she wanted to do was to crawl into her bed and pull the
quilt up to her eyes.

"If we could lure him here . . ."

"How can we close the border even with both of the
weapons?" Darcy said. "The Guardian is scattered all along
the ravine, and his spirit is gone. We won't be able to get
him back."

Charlie's voice was very soft. "So we will make a new
Guardian. But I need both of the sacred weapons for the
curse to be complete, for my death to have any meaning. If
you can ride to Laramie, get to Ghormley, lure him with
some wild tale of demons or even with the chance to get at
me again . . ."

"Your death?" Darcy stared at him. "For your death to
have meaning? Charlie, I've been trying to keep you alive.
You've been healing yourself. You're stronger now, and you
have your soul talisman back. Why would you want to die?"

He turned the knife over and over in his hands. "There
has to be a Guardian, a spirit Guardian, to keep the border
closed. It is what my teacher did a hundred years ago." His
words were slow and heavy. "I watched over the grave for
three days. When he died, the border closed and the wendigo
were pulled back to their world. I have to keep myself alive
long enough to get the other weapon, the lance, or it won't
work. Once I have the lance it can be quick, much quicker
than it was for Angry Dog. All you need to do outside the
rocks is smash the stone that holds my soul. I'll slit my
throat with this knife. I've already done some of the chants,
the first part of the curse."

A hundred years ago? Darcy brushed that aside, unimpor-

nt now. "I don't know how it worked with your teacher.
ut it isn't the same now." She swallowed hard, her throat
onstricting again with tears. "You were shot before they
mashed Coyote's skull, from the wendigo world. It's de-
royed. Paul had me bring it out for them and then Dr.
hormley smashed it on the rocks by the cave. Paul said that
eant the border would be open forever."

"You did that?" She felt his shock, his horror, through the
arkness. It was like another gunshot. "Coyote's skull, from
e mound in the canyon?"

"It gave me all my memories back," she whispered.
When I held the skull it was all clear again. I remember
ou, and the things you taught me. I know what I've done."

"That was the central piece of the curse, the binding on
e wendigo. The wendigo needed a human to remove the
ull." He was angry now, though his voice was quiet. "All
e years I was trapped over there they tried to get me to do
They promised they'd stop hunting me, they'd leave me
one, but I never gave in to them. They almost killed me.
would have died except that Coyote showed me how to
ke my soul out of my body and put it in the stone."

"It probably doesn't matter why," Darcy said. "I should
ever have done it anyway. If I'd remembered more I
ouldn't have done it no matter what they told me."

His voice was bitter in the darkness. "What did they tell
ou?"

"That my mother was still alive, trapped in the wendigo
orld. I thought I heard her voice, even, at a séance at Dr.
hormley's. I thought . . ." She had to swallow hard against
ars. "I thought Paul and I were going across to rescue her.
at's the only reason I led them to the grave. They told me
at would open the border so we could save her."

"Your mother?" He was silent for a long moment. "I
ought it was because you were in love with Paul." Charlie
ached a hand out to touch her shoulder. She flinched, feel-

eal sobs starting, shaking her body so she could not
that she was crying.

1at was part of it."

'hy didn't you come to me?"

didn't trust you. I didn't remember." She felt tears slid-
own her cheeks. "Coyote took my memories. Did you
 that? He took my memories, just like he took your
:ine bag when you were a boy. For safekeeping, maybe.
ss he didn't know what would happen, how stupid I'd

'hat about your mother?" He kept his hand on her
der in the darkness. "Tell me how they made you be-
 she was still alive."

e told him, difficult as it was to speak coherently. The
e, her hypnotized memory of the night the car crashed,
ody in the grave. At that, Charlie interrupted her.

 wendigo skeleton? I never went to her funeral, or to
ravesite. Surely I would have sensed that . . ." He was
' with himself now. Darcy could understand the feeling.
is afraid of being seen by your father, noticed by some-
 after the scene in your hospital room. When you were
nd I brought you back to Rapid City after three days,
 was a warrant out on me for kidnapping. They had my
iption from the truck stop where I left you. Your father
d have remembered."

nd you didn't look any different." Darcy smiled
gh her tears. "You've never looked any different. You'd
 I could remember a face that never changes."

lame Coyote for your forgetting. He probably thought
uld trick the wendigo, that they'd never find you if you
t use your power. But your mother in the wendigo
l . . . she must have gone across, I think. You saw noth-
/hile you were there?"

rcy shook her head. "How could she have survived?
 seven years . . ."

"Less than that for her. Maybe a few months. I was p
into the wendigo world in December of 1890, and I c
out again in 1960. It was seven years for me. She could
be there. If she was strong enough to find food for hers

"I have to go back and look for her." A few months
Darcy tried not to let herself be too hopeful, remembe
the madness of the place.

"Help me finish my healing, and we'll go back toget
Charlie said.

"Then you . . . aren't going to . . ."

"Kill myself? No. A spirit Guardian won't close the
der if Coyote's skull is gone. There's nothing we ca
now, except search for your mother. Lie down here be
me and try to rest. If you remember everything, you rem
ber how to meet me on the vision road."

# CHAPTER SEVENTEEN

B efore it had always been Coyote who led her onto the vision road. Feeling blind without her guide, Darcy lay down on the cold earth, curled up in a ball with her hands tucked under her arms and her stocking cap pulled down to her eyes. Her throat was still thick from crying. She tried to breathe deeply and evenly, watching the mist of her breath rise in thin, measured streams, following it in her mind to the place where the mist vanished. She remembered the strange artificial trance she had experienced in Ghormley's laboratory. This was different. This was a simple journey, an easy rise out of herself until she felt the bonds of body and spirit stretched thin.

Beside her, Charlie's breathing matched hers, except when it caught with pain. She could see him clearly from the place where she hovered over her body. Blankets and clothing were sheer, almost transparent. The warmth of blood pulsing beneath skin and the strong resting curves of muscles; the cold places in hands and feet where circulation had withdrawn to feed his healing; the broken confusion in his abdomen where flesh pressed against flesh trying to regain connections that were lost; these were what she saw of Charlie on the first stage of her journey.

As her body fell into a sleeping state she felt herself moving further, at a calm, unhurried pace that was like slow flying. Through a kind of hard curtain—the boulder walls?—then awhile through clouds, and then the gentle descent to the road itself, where her altered feet touched quiet earth.

Usually before, she had seen the vision road as a hill to climb, a hill with pine trees near the base and bare rock at the top circled with clouds. Now, maybe because she had journeyed from such an enclosed space, she found herself lightly stepping onto a treelined path with moonlight dappling through the leaves. It was fall here as it was in Vedauwoo, and the aspens were pale and shimmery at night, deprived of their golden color. Her spirit form was very young, with womanly curves gone, with the tangled fine hair of a ten-year-old who could not be bothered to brush it. She always found herself in this form, as she had been when Charlie had first wakened the shaman power in her. She was wearing shorts, a green tank top with a smile printed on it, and sneakers.

The smell of the leaves and the rich earth filled her with each breath. She could not help but be at peace here, at least at first, though later on the road she sometimes had met things that frightened her. But her peace was tinged with sadness and shame. Even in this innocent shape she knew that she had carried Coyote's skull out of its protected place and allowed it to be destroyed. If she had not done it she might be walking with the animal spirit now, one hand resting on the rough fur of his neck, laughing at his jokes and his stories of the past. Further on the road than she had ever gone, Charlie had told her, Coyote sometimes appeared as a heroic warrior, a man wearing ancient garments with a roach of fur down his neck, sharp ears, and a proud-carried tail. In that form he could inspire great, reckless courage. Usually he was a totem for scouts who must be silent and clever, and for medicine men who must seek the secrets of the earth with endless curiosity.

Darcy kept looking behind her, even walking backward some of the time, but she did not see Charlie. He must be coming another way. Usually they met at the top of the hill. The aspen trees opened out around a clearing, where a beaver had dammed the stream into a shallow pool that eddied around the matted brush of his dam. Darcy found a mossy stone by the pool and sat to wait. She would like to see the beaver or talk to him. Unlike the vision quests, where you sang and prayed and pleaded for notice from the spirits, the vision road was a place where you accepted what came to you. If the beaver came out to talk she would be glad, but she would not try to call him.

She began to wonder if Charlie could reach her. The pain of his wound might keep him bound inside his body. But after a long time of kicking her feet against the stone she heard his moccasin footsteps rustling through the leaves on the forest path. She stood up to wait for him. He looked tired even here, but otherwise he was different; his shirt was fringed deerskin with beaded patterns at the breast, and his medicine bag hung outside it without any need to be hidden. He wore a wrapped loincloth and fringed leggings of buckskin that laced to his moccasins. Darcy had thought when she was thirteen that it was strange Charlie's spirit form dressed as an old-time Indian; now she knew he was from that time: 1890. He must have been born in 1873.

He nodded a greeting to her and they sat down together on a fallen log the beaver had stripped of branches. For a while they watched the still pond and the reflected moonlight. Darcy skipped a stone across the surface; it jumped twice, making concentric circles like the rim of the Medicine

Wheel. A fish broke the surface, looking for the large insect it thought must have landed, then it flipped in the water and swam back to the bottom. It was the first animal Darcy had seen here.

"Can you . . ." Charlie paused, began again. "I need . . ."

Darcy shook her head, quieting him. She was angry with herself. She had forgotten little things. Such as this: on the vision road things you wanted must be offered, not asked for. She put one of her hands in his bigger one.

"You can have whatever you need of my strength for your healing." She felt shy, like a wild deer trusting the hunter, but the peace of the journey-place filled her as she closed her eyes. The power, the strength, was like a soft light, a moon's ray slipping out through her fingers into Charlie. She could feel him drawing on her cautiously, afraid of taking too much.

"I have more to give," she said. "Take what you need." She was in no hurry to use it or get it back. Strangely, thoughts of the Esoteric Society people rose in her peaceful mind. Not one of them would think of doing a thing like she was doing, giving away their power to help someone. They would rather hoard power, amass power, and it made them lose track of themselves somehow. Darcy felt more like herself now than she had in years. She was comfortable in her child's skin, in the quiet clearing with this man beside her. This was part of the work she was born to do.

It might have been hours before Charlie let go of her hand and smiled wearily at her. It was time to go back. His hand came up and ran through her hair, smoothing it like a cat's fur; then he stood up and walked softly away, not looking to see if Darcy was beside him. She was.

The darkness had faded a little inside the rock cave. Darcy blinked her eyes twice and shut them again, unwilling to leave the warm place where she was curled up against soft fur. There were noises in the room. In her half-asleep state she recognized them: the camp stove being put back together, someone drinking from a canteen, a bullet being ejected from a loaded gun. She uncurled her legs experimentally and stretched them against cramps. A weight shifted against her side and she reached out one hand to soothe the disturbed animal. It whined and she felt a warm tongue lick her fingers. Suddenly she turned and opened her eyes.

A young coyote lay there on the earth beside her with his legs stretched and his head tilted back to look at her. Both ears were slowly moving upright to see what she would do. Darcy let her hand rest on the tawny brown fur of the coyote's shoulder and met the shy dark eyes; they shifted quickly away, but he did not turn his head. His jaws were slightly parted and sharp teeth showed at the sides of his tongue.

"Coyote?" she said in disbelief. She had thought she killed Coyote by bringing his skull to be destroyed.

"If that's who it is, he won't speak," Charlie said ruefully, rolling up the blankets on top of the old Guardian's bier. "He got in here about an hour ago while you were sleeping. I didn't see the rocks roll away, but they've shifted enough for a skinny coyote to squirm through."

He was right. Dim dawn light showed her that the entrance to the burial place was open again. Not enough for a man, but enough for a man to see through. Darcy sat up quickly, thinking of their enemies.

"Can you travel? We should get out of here. I didn't mean to sleep so long."

"I don't think they'll look for us here." He moved slowly, but the drawn look of pain was fading from his face. "We may find someone watching the border, if they listen to your friend who was here last night. It may be harder to get in than to find your mother once we're across."

"You should ride away somewhere." Darcy shifted the coyote a little to pull an edge of her jacket free. "Get your strength back. I was already planning to go after her by my-self."

Charlie settled his black hat on his head and drew a bent feather up through his fingers so it stood straight in the brim. He was no longer wearing the heavy parka, and Darcy saw no lump of bandages beneath his jacket and shirt. "I'll be all right. You need me along. You gave me enough of your power last night to finish the healing I'd started. There are some advantages to being cut off from your soul." He handed her the medicine bag, which had been resting on the earth by the blanket roll. "Here, you carry this. Safer for me, and more protection for you against the wendigo."

Darcy did not argue. She could feel her own power drained and hidden deep inside her, unlikely to be any use until she had eaten and rested for a few days. The medicine bag was a familiar weight, warm and strong against her skin. She tied its thong securely around her neck.

She was hungry. "I put some bologna and cheese in the blanket roll. Did you see it?"

Charlie tossed her the plastic bag of food and the canteen. "Eat while you ride," he said. "I'm hoping the Esoteric Society has enough to keep them occupied in Laramie this morn-ing, but the sooner we reach the border the easier it will be to cross undisturbed."

The wendigo were in Laramie by now. At least the twenty who had crossed with Darcy and Paul. Darcy forced her mind not to dwell on the probable chaos in her town. She had a task to finish before she and Charlie could ride in that direc-tion.

There was one thing she had never learned in her earlier training. "While we ride," she said as they climbed out of the boulders, "explain to me how you kill a wendigo. I think I'll need to know that before we get very far today."

They found the horses in the ravine, sleepy and stiff with spending the night out in the cold. Darcy threw scraps of bologna down to the coyote, who padded beside her horse like an ill-fed, sharp-eyed dog. Their pace was slow, but they didn't have far to ride. Only back over the path to the mountain where the border gaped open in a swirl of winds.

Ariadne's crumpled body was still where she had fallen, partially eaten now by birds and coyotes. In the cold it had hardly decayed, but still it was a horrible thing to pass by. The horses snorted and shied and acted like new-broken colts until Darcy and Charlie both had to dismount and lead them past. The coyote who was following them sniffed at the body, but seemed more interested in what the two living humans were doing. It trotted after them with its ears pricked.

Once again they had to leave the horses tied to aspen trees. Charlie wore the gun at his belt, and Darcy had the stone knife from the Guardian's grave, the medicine bag, and the canteen. They left all the rest of their gear tied on Cinnamon's saddle.

It was quiet in the aspen grove, as chill dawn sunlight began to color the leaves and the shadowed rocks of the mountains up ahead. It was Tuesday morning. Darcy wondered why it seemed so much time had passed since Charlie arrived at the ranch. It had only been on Thursday afternoon that she had picked him up at the motel in Laramie; the party where she had heard her mother's spectral voice had been Friday night; on Sunday night the Esoteric Society dug up the grave; and only nine hours ago she had been in the wendigo world with Paul. She felt much older, much different, than the college student who had laughed about astrology with Roxanne.

Chipmunks, unafraid and used to generous picnickers, scampered up onto the tops of boulders and peered around bushes at Darcy and Charlie as they hiked past. Darcy threw them her last pieces of cheese. She had made one come to her hand once when she was a child, but her mother had warned her not to touch them because they could be rabid. She had never seen a chipmunk look even slightly dangerous, but still she had not tried to get close to them since. More likely she should be afraid of the coyote who glided behind her like a trained pet. The chipmunks would not come close with him there.

"Anyone up there?" she whispered to Charlie as they halted below the largest boulder mountain. The sunlight gave little warmth on the shaded side of the rocks. She could not see the border cave, and she heard no sounds but the soft wind through the aspens behind them.

"Don't know." They began to climb. The path that had been so difficult and frightening last night was an easy, if steep, set of obstacles now. Darcy felt oddly strong and rested after her cold night on the earth floor of the Guardian's cave. Charlie moved a little stiffly, but he seemed not to be in any pain. He might not have slept at all last night, but then, Darcy did not know how much sleep a soulless man might need.

What did it mean for him, not having a soul in his body? He was not emotionless. She had seen his anger last night when he learned what she had done. And he often laughed. The lack of a soul did not prevent him from spirit travel on the vision road. So what was missing? Change, perhaps, Darcy thought, and growth. He had probably not changed in any real way since he escaped from the wendigo world in 1960. The idea saddened her somehow.

Charlie had to stop to rest halfway up, leaning against a rock. His breathing had grown harsh again, labored. Darcy waited with him, worried, as the coyote jogged impatiently ahead. The healing he had done last night had taken much of his strength, she knew. Could he be much help to her in the wendigo world? Maybe she should have insisted he go off somewhere to hide and rest. She could not have done that easily. One thing she had realized last night, with her re-newed memories and everything that had happened: she did not want to be separated from him again. If nothing else he was like a brother to her. If nothing else . . . she did not even know if he could feel love, if he cared for her as anything but a promising pupil.

For a moment she fell into an amused daydream: her father, the Kennans, all her friends would think she had lost her mind if she chose to spend her life with a long-haired Indian ranch hand. The idea was not strange to her. She must have thought of Charlie that way since she was ten. Probably the reason she had never dated much, never taken anyone seriously all through high school. She had lost her way a little with Paul, but that was over.

They started to climb again. Still no shouts, no gunshots, from the cave up above. Charlie did not bother to take a covered path. He was after speed this morning, not surprise. Darcy was panting hard after a few minutes more, but then they reached the ledge and stood up in front of the border cave.

The bodies of the Esoteric Society people were still intact, lying as they had died the night before. No animals had been at them, not even birds. Darcy felt the reason as she stood there; the atmosphere around the cave was disturbed, altered, as if the wendigo world was slowly pushing out into this one through the open gap. She felt the blocks in her mind rise up to guard against the place's influence, and wondered again how her mother could have taken it even for a few months. Yet she had been alive four nights ago to speak through Dion at the séance.

The coyote whined, then barked sharply once. The sound of a car engine grew in the stillness below. Looking down through the morning mist, Darcy saw Dr. Ghormley's van driving hard around the curves of the narrow Vedauwoo road toward the parking lot beneath this mountain. Whoever was inside would be here soon. "Let's go," she said, and started in at the cave mouth. Charlie and the coyote followed her.

"I never thought I'd willingly go back across," Charlie muttered at the edge of the swirling portal.

"You could wait here. Watch for company." Darcy's body was shaking, almost immobilized from fear, as reluctant as Charlie to go through the border crossing again. Her mother, she told herself. If she was alive, if she could be found . . .

One thing Darcy was sure of was that Sarah Jacobi would never be able to get across the border by herself, even if she could find it from the other side.

The coyote had already vanished into the rising wail of the winds. Charlie looked once at Darcy, took a deep breath, then stepped into the vortex himself. She closed her eyes and followed. It was horrible, nothing she could prepare for even though she had passed through twice before. Her limbs were flung out, stretching muscles, straining connections to bone; the wind tore at her closed eyelids, roared in her ears, her nostrils. She could not breathe. She could not think. There was no time, but it was a longer passage than before, and harder. When she was on her feet again in the orange rocks of the wendigo hills, she could not move at all for minutes while her lungs fought for breath.

It was not much better here than within the vortex. Winds howled, blowing grit and bits of rock. It was cold, colder than the human world had been in the early morning. The alien night had fallen, with no stars or moon, no light but an eye-straining phosphorescence from the rocks themselves. Along the great plain below the hills, pale lights gleamed from the wendigo encampments.

Many of the mountains to the left of where Darcy stood had altered since she was here hours ago. Dust rose from great chasms and she heard a rumble of earthquake in the distance. The rocks trembled underfoot.

Charlie stood a few feet away from her, looking over the plains, while at his side stood a magnificent animal. Coyote, Darcy realized, but younger, bigger, more powerful than she had ever seen him before. He turned his wolflike head toward her and she saw a deep intelligence in his eyes. How could that be . . . she had been sure he was killed, finally and forever. His ragged ear was whole again.

A growly voice she remembered from dreams said, "A good trick, don't you think? Make them think they're freeing themselves."

"You freed Coyote's spirit," Charlie said without turning from his frowning lookout. "He was trapped here all these years, holding the curse himself, the most important of the Guardians. All the time I thought he was dead, and the coyote that hunted with me a ghost . . ."

"Less than a ghost," said the spirit animal, padding over to Darcy and letting her scratch behind his ears. His back reached her waist, bigger than most wolves, twice the size of real coyotes. "A phantom, a vision traveler. Now I'm whole again. But this world isn't."

The ground shook terribly, throwing Darcy to her hands and knees. Coyote nosed at her, grinning with his sharp teeth. "This world . . ." she began.

"Is falling apart," Charlie said. His voice was thin and his breathing shallow. "And myself with it, I think. The magic that let me loose my soul from my body is fading."

Darcy staggered over to him on the unsteady ground. "Go back across, as quickly as you can." He looked no different, but she could see fear in his eyes.

"Wouldn't help," growled Coyote.

"I'd be even further from my source of power," Charlie said. "No, let's go on. Find your mother, if she's here."

Her hand at Coyote's neck, holding onto thick fur as if they were on the vision road, Darcy leaned into the wind and started down the hill. Charlie walked just behind her. The dust was choking, blinding. Soon they lost sight of the wendigo villages, only following where Coyote led. They were going down, that much Darcy knew.

She stumbled and fell often as the ground shook and changed around them. The wendigo world had been held together by magic, by the ancient curse, and now she had broken the curse. What would happen to the wendigo themselves? She heard cries in the distance, choruses of bestial voices, but she saw nothing.

Charlie had fallen back. She stopped and turned, not seeing him. "Charlie!" she shouted.

"We're being followed," he said, running back to them. "Two humans have crossed the border."

"Ghormley and Paul?" she guessed. "If they can follow anything through this storm I'll be surprised."

"No need to follow," Coyote said impatiently. "They know where we're headed. They'll just go there too." He gripped Darcy's jacket in his teeth and tugged her into a run. She and Charlie ran as best they could on the unsteady ground, their eyes streaming with tears from the blowing dust, their lungs beginning to wheeze from breathing it.

"I don't even know where we're headed," Darcy said as she ran. "We'll never find my mother if we can't see anything."

"I showed you the place," Coyote howled over the wind. "When you were carrying me out of here. You remember."

What had he pointed out to her? A hut in the largest wendigo village, Darcy finally recalled. Where the oldest wendigo stored their souls. That didn't have anything to do with her mother. She had thought at the time that she should try to destroy the soul talismans.

"Is my mother still alive?" she demanded, catching up with Coyote with a fierce effort. "You must know. Why won't you tell me?"

He didn't answer, only ran on. Darcy and Charlie stumbled after the flag of his uplifted tail. A wendigo with bloody scratches down its face ran past them through the orange

dust. It saw them, shrieked, and ran in another directio⬛
Darcy felt a passing wave of disorientation.

"He tried to retrieve his soul." Coyote laughed, his he⬛
turned over his shoulder as he barked back at them. "So ⬛
could cross over to your world, so he could survive. S⬛
wouldn't let him inside, wouldn't let him take anythin⬛
She may be mad, but that much she understands. They s⬛
her to guard the storehouse of souls."

Darcy did not ask who "she" was. They had reached t⬛
edge of the wendigo village, and Coyote slowed his pace su⬛
denly so she almost ran into him. Charlie stopped by the m⬛
wall of a hut where the wind was less and took his gun o⬛
of its holster.

"Your mother," Coyote answered the unasked questio⬛
"She's here. You'll have to get past her yourself if you're ⬛
destroy the soul talismans."

"What is it you're asking us to do?" Charlie said, lookir⬛
back into the clouds of dust.

"The wendigo world is breaking apart. They'll all try to e⬛
cape now that they realize what's happening." Coyo⬛
sounded smug, as if all of this had been part of his plan. "U⬛
less you want your world full of exiled wendigo, you'd bett⬛
destroy all their souls before they can get at them. And th⬛
maybe if you can make her understand, you can get Sar⬛
Jacobi back across before the borders close forever."

# CHAPTER EIGHTEEN

Darcy hated Coyote then. Why hadn't he told her about her mother when she was passing the village before? She would never have let Paul stop her. She uld have rescued her. Mad as she is, Coyote had said. How d was that?

The wendigo village was suffering the same disintegration the rest of the world. The mud huts crumbled, shaking art. In the streets, strange little doglike animals barked, run- ng around crazily, attacking one another. Coyote loped past m and sent them yelping away into the shadows. Darcy lowed at a stunned walk, with Charlie's hand on her arm ging her along.

There was no clamoring crowd of wendigo around the rehouse hut. The mud bricks were damaged, and the side one wall had fallen inward. The street up ahead was being ept by a fierce dust devil; other than that, the village emed deserted. Darcy found herself standing immovable a w feet from the door of the mud hut. She had fallen back

the horror of that night when she lay crying with a bro-
leg on the mountainside, her mother lost. She could re-
ber the fierce, determined way her mother had followed
hat night, even though she did not understand what was
ening. It was all a nightmare. She wished she had never
a Guardian, never known what the wendigo were. She
known for seven years that her mother was dead. She had
pted it finally. Maybe she should never have gotten back
memory. If she had moved to Denver with her father,
of this would have happened.

harlie was emptying all the bullets from the gun. She
d at him, shocked. With Ghormley and Paul close be-
them, their ammunition spilled out on the ground, falling
the thick orange dust. Charlie handed her the gun butt-
Then he took a book of matches from his pocket and
them to her. "There will be stones and wood carvings
ly," he said. "Give me the knife."

arcy looked at him without understanding. Stones and
d carvings? He reached for her belt and drew the knife
elf.

he soul talismans," Charlie said angrily. "Pound the
es with the gun butt and burn the wood pieces. I'll keep
from stopping you. Move, Darcy. We don't have time
you to stand here pitying yourself."

e was as cruel as Coyote. All they cared about was de-
ing the wendigo. Darcy looked around, blinking her ach-
eyes against the blowing dust. She did not see Coyote. He
brought them here, then abandoned them.

Move, goddamn it!" Charlie shouted at her and pushed
forward. Then a gunshot rang out and she felt the whirr
bullet going past her shoulder. Chips of mud flew off the
of the building in front of her. She ran inside through the
en part of the wall. Charlie did not follow her. If he was
again . . . She turned around uncertainly.

Get out, get out, get out!" cried a hoarse voice, and fists

like rocks pounded at Darcy's back. She dropped the gun
matches and whirled, trying to catch the flailing, punish
hands. Her mother's face had hardly changed, except for
ers of dust and lines of fear, and the light in her eyes that
iadne had when she ran pursued by the wendigo.

"Mother, it's me, Darcy," she shouted, her eyes hurting
much for tears. Sarah Jacobi still wore jeans and a sweats
from picking the girls up at summer camp. Her hair was
gled. Her hands were claws, her fingernails grown long,
she tried to scratch out Darcy's eyes. Darcy backed a
around the circular room, holding her hands up in front of
face. She tripped over piles of small painted rocks, stack
ornaments, beads, carved totems. Wendigo souls, like C
lie's in her medicine bag.

"You can't take them away. They stay here. No one is
to take them away," insisted her mother in her scratchy,
voice. "I keep them safe." She attacked more ferociously

"Mother, it's Darcy, it's your daughter. I'm here to
you home," she panted between blows. They were the s
height now, but she was much stronger and healthier than
older woman. She wondered what Sarah had found to
here. Darcy dodged and blocked the blows, shouting her
name over and over. "It's Darcy! It's Darcy!"

More gunshots echoed like cars backfiring, muffled by
wind outside and the thick mud walls. Charlie . . . He had
time than any of them if what he suspected was true, i
was doomed with the end of this strange cursed world. Bu
Paul killed him first then none of them might get out. Da
grabbed her mother's arms and pinned them at her si
holding the struggling woman as if she were a child hav
a seizure.

"I'm Darcy. You called me to come get you, don't you
member? You talked to me at the séance. You said you v
still alive. Oh, mother, remember, please remember." 
wondered if this was what Charlie had felt like when he

tried to get through to her in the hospital after the accident. It was a horrible thing to feel.

Hardened, fossilized structures in Charlie's body were softening, losing form. He could feel himself losing control bit by bit, losing the power of the ritual that had replaced his soul with magical patterns like wheels inside his mind. He could still think, could still move, but he was weakening. If he could do nothing else, at least he could keep Darcy's enemies from getting at her while she broke up the souls in the storehouse.

The gun fired again. That was four shots. If he was lucky it was the gun that had shot him last night, and there was only one bullet remaining. Let them shoot. The dust storm hid his movements, and the noises that drew their fire were being made by Coyote. Charlie moved as silently as he could in the soft layered dust, toward the sound of the gun, the soft curses of the two men.

The first to see him was Paul. Charlie had not seen the young man before, except for a blur that kicked him after he was shot last night. He was handsome, that was true. But his handsome face became a mask of hatred and fury, and the gun came up swiftly. Charlie dove face-first in the dust. The bullet whistled above him and he looked up to see Paul throw the gun away and charge toward him. He stood up to meet the rush.

"Don't kill him!" Dr. Ghormley's voice was high, distracted.

Paul bent and ran headfirst into Charlie's stomach, driving the breath out of him and knocking him down. The pain was immediate as the barely healed flesh inside him began to part again. Charlie rolled with Paul on top of him and fought to get his hands around his enemy's throat.

Ghormley made wailing, irrelevant background noise.

"Don't kill him, he might know something. He might know where the demons are hiding."

Paul was agile, but Charlie was heavier and stronger. He pinned his attacker for a moment and drew the stone knife from his belt. Paul struggled out from under him, rolled, got to his feet, but he had been cut along the collarbone. Charlie went after him in a crouch. He had killed wendigo this way before, hand-to-hand, with the knife to finish it. Paul had been too busy becoming a human and hiding himself to do any killing. His instincts were good, though. He broke a wooden slat from a collapsed water trough by one of the huts, and swung it under Charlie's knife hand to sweep at his stomach. Charlie had to fall back, feeling blood begin to seep inside him once more. Ghormley waved his arms and shouted a few yards away.

An earthquake stronger than any they had yet felt shook the earth and knocked all three men off their feet. A crack slid down the middle of the dirt road, and Charlie scrambled against falling rock until he could cling to a damaged outcrop of mud wall. He wondered if this was what it felt like to begin to die. Parts of his mind shut, locked against entry, and he was fighting from sheer will to survive, to defeat his enemy.

When the earth stopped rumbling he lunged after Paul and caught him with the knife in the left side. Blood ran, but Paul brought up his wooden slat again and flung it back and forth with furious efforts, forcing Charlie to retreat toward the crack in the earth. At the edge of awareness, Charlie noticed that Ghormley was across the crack on the other side and headed toward the storehouse of souls where he had left Darcy.

The crack was only five feet across at one point. Charlie ran and leaped it, landing with a dizzy sense that he might not be able to do that again anytime soon. Paul tailed him as he chased Dr. Ghormley down a street that wavered and doubled in his vision.

Wendigo had emerged to gather at the storehouse up ahead. Charlie guessed that meant Darcy had begun destroying souls. Coyote was a growling, barking guard at the threshold, and the wendigo screamed and threw mud bricks at him, but he kept them back. Coyote would have some explaining to do when this was over, Charlie thought. Playing with his and Darcy's lives as he had done . . .

A blow struck him from behind, Paul's length of wood, hard across the kidneys. He fell in a wave of pain, rolling not quite fast enough to keep another blow from striking his shoulder. Some wendigo were coming their way, noticing them now. Charlie felt as desperate as the boy he had been, hunted through the wendigo world. A few of these wendigo might even recognize him as their old prey.

"You aren't going to take them away," said her mother uncertainly. That was the only way Darcy had been able to stop her. She did not respond to names or memories.

"No. The souls will be safer if I break up the things that trap them," Darcy said. She was too exhausted to care if her mother attacked again when her back was turned. Now she could feel the world cracking beneath them, sliding into chaos. She had no time to waste with a madwoman. She knelt down and began to pound on stones.

"Set them free," Sarah Jacobi said unexpectedly. "They were trapped . . ." She sat down cross-legged by Darcy and picked up a talisman.

"Yes." The gun butt made a satisfactory rock hammer. Most of the stones were soft anyway, layered sandstone and limestone. They shattered in pieces with a few blows. A shudder went through Darcy with the passing of each wendigo soul. She felt them rushing out, vanishing into ancient oblivion. The next stack was of wood carvings. She lit each piece carefully, hoarding her matches, letting them reach her fingers before she dropped them. The wood was dry and old and burned easily. That was worse than the stones; more like torturing the souls.

"I should help," said her mother, excited. She began to hit larger rocks against smaller ones. Darcy noticed how cracked and roughened her hands were. "No one can take them away now."

"No, no one can." Darcy could hear wendigo outside, and Coyote howling at them to stay back. They were working up courage to attack the strange animal. Maybe some of them realized who it was, what had happened when the skull left their world.

The room shook furiously and a large part of the wall fell inward. Darcy flung herself over her mother and felt chunks of mud brick bruising her back. Sarah struggled and protested beneath her. Darcy saw her face very close as she rolled off; she was so young. She had married at eighteen, borne Darcy at nineteen. With the strange time of the wendigo world, Sarah Jacobi was still only thirty-two years old. But seven years of horror could have been packed within the three or four months Sarah had spent here. Darcy was grimly certain they had been.

"I'm scared," her mother said now, turning back to her task of breaking up stones. "Everything is breaking."

"We don't have much time." Darcy crushed a string of beads under her thick-soled hiking boots, felt small individual screams.

Two wendigo climbed in over the broken wall and began to search through the remaining piles for their souls, ignoring the women who continued to destroy the rest. Darcy had given up the knife, and her gun was unloaded. She did not try to stop them. After a few minutes, more than twenty of the creatures had come into the chamber. One of them screamed and staggered around and fell dead when Darcy crushed the ornament that had held its soul. Many of the rest found what they were searching for and fled.

Coyote had abandoned his post guarding the door. Darcy guessed what that meant: Charlie was in trouble. She and her mother had crushed, burned, and hammered more than half of the wendigo soul talismans now. She decided that was enough.

"Come on." She put down the gun as a useless burden and lit the last pile of wooden objects with her final match. Then she grabbed her mother by both hands and hauled her to her feet. "We have to get out of here."

"They took them away," Sarah said in misery and fear. "I didn't stop them, they took some away. They'll be angry with me."

"No one will be angry with you. None of them will be left here to care what happens. Come on, Mother. We'll all die if we stay here much longer." She pulled the protesting woman by her bony wrists out into the choking clouds of dust. The ground in front of them had been broken into cracks, and steam and dust rose from deep inside the tormented earth. Bodies of dead wendigo were scattered near the hut. She had killed them, she realized.

Her mother stopped abruptly. "There's no place to go. No place better."

"Yes, there is." Darcy looked right and left for Charlie. She could not see more than a few feet in either direction. "I've come to take you home."

"Home." She seemed to be thinking about it. She let Darcy lead her along the edge of the deepest crack.

The rest of the village hovels were rubble now. Maybe the soul storehouse had stayed intact longer because of the power that still resided there. Streaks of light broke across the sky, but it was too early for the world's dawn. The light was angry red, hot. Volcanos? Darcy shrugged. She could not see much past her hands, much less to the mountains.

The medicine bag was warm against her skin. She remembered suddenly that Charlie's soul was inside. Surely it had some connection still with Charlie himself. She stopped, opened the bag, and took out the strangely heavy carved rock that was his talisman. The carving on it was the Medicine Wheel. With that firmly gripped in one hand and her mother's wrist caught in the other, Darcy suddenly turned and hurried in the opposite direction from where she had been going. "Charlie!" she shouted. A tremor knocked her against her mother, and they both fell. She almost lost her hold on the soul stone. Now that she had a direction, she put it safely back in its bag and pulled the lacing tight.

"No place to go," said her mother like a windup toy.

"We're going home," Darcy said firmly. "All of us, we're going home."

"Pardon me." A bearded man blocked her path. "Aren't you one of my students?"

"Oh, Dr. Ghormley." He wasn't an enemy now. His training had been no use against the wendigo madness. Darcy could see the confusion, the terror, in his face. "This is no place for you. Come on, take my hand."

He obeyed with the trust of a child. "I feel I have lost my way. A few minutes ago I had the delusion I was in hell. But I cannot believe that is the case. Can you explain what is happening, young woman?"

"An earthquake," Darcy said. "I'll take you to safe ground. Just stay with me."

"She says we're going home," Darcy's mother said politely, turning to look at their new companion.

Ghormley stared at her with a shock that had a little more of reality in it. "My God, Sarah . . . Sarah? Is that you? Maybe it's true, then, this is some sort of afterlife. Is Laura here too?"

"No, I'm afraid not." Darcy pulled both of them along, feeling like a school crossing guard with stubborn children to manage. She heard Coyote howling up ahead, an angry, fear-some sound, nothing like the weird song of coyotes in the hills of Wyoming.

"I was trying to talk to demons," Ghormley explained to her mother. "I think perhaps I've taken some dangerous psychoactive drug. I never really trusted that Paul. Maybe he slipped me something. That would explain you, and this place."

At the crumbling lip of a new canyon, Coyote looked like a demon animal, huge, bristling, slavering at the jaws. His howls shook Darcy to the bone. He stood over Charlie, who was struggling to rise past hands and knees. Paul was a few feet away, brandishing a length of wood like a broom handle. He was bleeding from several wounds, and his beautiful face was very pale in the glowing dust.

"Paul!" Darcy did not dare let go of her two charges. She dragged them with her. "Give it up. There's no time left. Do you want to get out of here alive?"

He looked at her in confusion, which was long enough for Coyote to spring and knock the piece of wood out of his hands, and for Charlie to stagger up like a drunken man and leap with a knife for Paul's heart. He knocked Paul down. The knife glanced across a rib, perhaps. Darcy heard a scraping sound.

"Stop it!" she screamed. "Charlie!" Now she let go of her mother and Ghormley and ran to try to drag Charlie off Paul. Too late; the knife struck again, and she knew it had gone in. Paul turned his head a little and looked at her with a thin smile that slowly froze in place. Charlie was a heavy weight; she rolled him off Paul's body finally, and he lay still too. He had left the knife where he had thrust it. Blood was everywhere.

Coyote whined and nudged at Darcy. "Get away from me," she snapped. She closed Paul's eyes. He had been human enough to die like one. More human than Charlie, who was still breathing, though by rights he should have died last night.

"Get up, damn you," she said to Charlie, shaking him. He muttered something in Cheyenne and put one arm over his eyes. "There's no time to rest. Dr. Ghormley, help me, will you?"

He came forward obediently and helped her lift Charlie to his feet, one arm over each of their shoulders. He was limp as a practice dummy. Darcy had once had to take a first-aid class, part of Alice Kennan's requirements for riding instructors, and she remembered the hundred-and-ten-pound dummy she had to rescue from an imaginary burning room. She had thought then that it must be easier with a real human being. It wasn't.

"There's Paul," Ghormley remarked, frowning. "I suppose I'm jealous of him. Subconsciously, I'd like to see him dead. What a bloody mess, though. I didn't realize my imagination was this graphic."

"It will get worse if we don't get out of here," Darcy said. "It's going to be too slow, carrying him like this. Coyote . . ." She turned to look for the huge animal. He was letting her mother pet him and coo over him as if he were a kitten. "Coyote, is the border still open?"

"Yes. It should be open until the very end." He padded up to her and looked at Charlie, his ears laid back. "Can't walk, I see. I think he'll last past the end of this place. Maybe for a while. It might be easier to leave him, though. He's not going to live much longer anyway, without the magic." That was a cold thing to say, Darcy thought. He was Charlie's spirit guide too.

"We can't leave him!" she said furiously. "Think of something, you're the ancestral spirit."

Laughter showed in his cunning eyes. "I just wondered what you'd say. You didn't seem to like him killing Paul."

"That was a waste. Paul had lost anyway, with this world

being destroyed. He might have survived . . ." She stopped and glared at Coyote. "I love Charlie. You know that better than anyone."

"You know, dear, you look a little like my daughter. Much older, of course. She's thirteen." Sarah Jacobi was squinting at her through the dust, smiling.

"I am your daughter, Mom." She was so tired. "Coyote, please, how can we get Charlie out of here? Ghormley and I aren't strong enough to carry him that far."

"I admit he's heavy for a hallucination. But I'll give it my best try," the professor said with a plucky grin.

There was a roar like a hundred thunderstorms and the earth rose up in a wave and rolled over half the wendigo village. Darcy fell to the ground, watching in numb horror as the wall of dirt and rocks stopped just ten feet away from her mother. The ground shook and groaned for long minutes afterward.

Coyote sneezed like a happy dog. "I do have some control left. It was mostly my curse that kept this place going. Left to itself, it would have fallen back into chaos only a few months after the wendigo were banished here." He switched his tail and trotted over to Darcy as she and Ghormley started again to lift Charlie upright. "Put him across my back. Just let him dangle, that's right. You, Ghormley, you run beside me and make sure he stays on."

With Charlie bent like a set of saddlebags over a now larger Coyote's furry back, they set out at a dogtrot around chasms, over new ridges and furrows. Darcy held her mother's hand and Ghormley stayed cheerfully alongside Coyote, one hand steadying Charlie. There was a smell of sulphur in the air and light ash fell, surely from a volcano. The winds had lessened a little, and there were no more dust devils. The land seemed resigned now to its death.

A dozen wendigo, running as fast as they could, passed the small party of humans and Coyote. They must have been the ones looking for their souls in the storehouse. Something would have to be done about them if they made it to the other side. But for now Darcy was more concerned about getting there herself to care if a few wendigo crossed the border.

"You can't be Darcy," her mother said as they paused to find a way around a boiling stream of mud. "I'm sorry, dear, but she's much younger than you, and her nose is different."

"And you, madam, have been dead for seven years." Ghormley brushed ash from the shoulders of his jacket. "I wonder if this is an interaction with drugs and alcohol. I'm fairly certain I had a shot of whiskey last night after I got home."

Coyote found or made an upthrust of rock that bridged the bubbling mud. They all crossed and ran at a faster pace. Darcy kept hold of her mother's hand, afraid she would wander off, but now Sarah Jacobi seemed cheerful about going along with them. She might be regaining a little more of her senses, but the strangest of all the strange things that had happened to Darcy was to hear her mother insist that she could not be her daughter.

The ground began to rise into the foothills, and Darcy recognized the path that led to the border cave. "I hope it hasn't been blocked by an avalanche," she gasped as they trotted uphill, slowing down.

"You can get out." Coyote turned his head to talk and Charlie almost slipped off his back. Ghormley spent a few moments settling the limp form back into place. "It will be hard on the other side, though. I won't be there to help you. Not in this form at least. Not able to speak to you, unless you take the vision road, and you won't have time or peace for that."

"Dr. Ghormley and my mother . . ." she said, panting.

"Will be much the same as they are. This place has damaged their minds."

"Will they get better?" They climbed at a walk now. The

way was steep up to the ledge of the cave. Darcy saw the last of the wendigo vanish in the crossing vortex, and then they were in front of the doorway.

"I don't know." Coyote stood still while she and Ghormley dragged Charlie off his back and hoisted him up between them. "Maybe. Charlie was worse than they are when he left the wendigo world the first time, but then, he was there for seven years. He got better after a few years."

"Oh, Coyote." Darcy looked at him with a sudden feeling of great loss. "I was angry with you . . . I . . ."

He did not speak, but Darcy stopped what she was going to say. He was growing, changing before her eyes, until he was a tall warrior with deep bronze skin and the laughing eyes and pricked ears of a coyote. He bent to her and hugged her, and she returned the embrace with the arm that wasn't around Charlie. "You have the medicine bag still, and his soul?" the being whispered. She nodded. He smiled a sharp-toothed grin and faded away. As he did so, a rending noise rose up behind them, the final death roar of the wendigo world.

Darcy took her mother's hand and shifted her grip on Charlie. Dr. Ghormley nodded that he was ready. They stepped forward together into the tearing winds of the border.

# CHAPTER NINETEEN

T he journey through the border crossing was painful
this time, like being pulled apart and rubbed with
sandpaper. Darcy felt Charlie's arm over her shoulders
and his body against hers the whole time, but she lost her
mother's hand soon after it began. She feared she would lose
her mother again, that they would arrive on the other side
with Sarah Jacobi lost somewhere in limbo, somewhere she
could never be rescued from.

Her mother arrived ahead of her, and Darcy stepped
through with Charlie to see Sarah Jacobi crouched on the
rock floor of the cave, her arms crossed over her body, tears
running down her face. Ghormley came through after Darcy,
not soon enough to help her with Charlie. She almost
dropped him onto the stones. She managed to ease him down
to a sitting position against the cave wall. Behind them, the
wendigo border swirled more and more slowly, quietly, until
at last it was still and dark. Then it was only a slanted rock
wall at the back of a Vedauwoo cave.

"The border is closed," Darcy said to Charlie. "Forever, I guess. That must mean the wendigo world is gone." His eyes were closed and his breathing so shallow she could hardly tell he was alive. She put her hands on the sides of his face. "Charlie, wake up. We're back. We're home." Judging by the sunlight, it was still morning.

"Home," echoed her mother, rocking slowly back and forth. "I remember this place. The cave where I had Darcy. High up in Vedauwoo. Oh, my baby, my child . . ." She was sobbing. Darcy could not leave Charlie to comfort her.

"Oh, please open your eyes," she whispered.

Ghormley had taken a look outside the cave. He returned with a face several shades paler under the layer of orange dust. "I must be jealous of Ephron and Lucretia and Magdela too. They seem to be lying dead out there. I hope whatever this is wears off soon." He sat down near the back of the cave, seeming determined to wait until the drug left his system.

It was cold, but Darcy opened Charlie's jacket and shirt to look at his stomach. It looked swollen, puffy. There were huge bruises that must have been blows with Paul's wooden stick. The puckered black scab that was the healed-over bullet hole had thin red lines radiating out from it. She put her hand over it; it felt hot. From the swelling she guessed that he was bleeding internally. He needed a hospital, but she was afraid he would die before they got there. The power of the wendigo world to sustain him without his soul had vanished.

"Charlie, wake up and tell me what to do," Darcy said in despair.

"Is he your boyfriend, dear?" Her mother was trying to take an interest in her companions. She looked at Darcy brightly through her tears.

"I love him." Darcy buttoned Charlie's blood-stiffened shirt and his stained jacket. "And I think he's dying."

"That must be hard." The words were like butterflies on

the surface of her mother's spirit; they danced across the deep horror and pain that still showed in her face. "I've been away from my husband and my little girl for . . . well, for a long time, I think."

"I know." Darcy had stopped calling her "Mother." It only confused her. "Will you be all right here for a little while? I need to go down the hill and get something out of my saddlebags. I'll be back in a few minutes." The penicillin in the blanket roll was the only thing she could think of, and it was useless against a loss of magic.

Her mother nodded uncertainly. Ghormley spoke up, still bravely facing his hallucinations. "I'll watch them for you. Go ahead." He muttered as Darcy was leaving, "It seems a little more peaceful now. Maybe I'm coming out of it."

Reckless, not caring if she fell and slid, Darcy ran down the mountain path in the clear morning sunlight. The park was lovely, glowing with golden aspens, alive with late season birds. No picnic cars had appeared on the roadsides yet, but it was only Tuesday. She shoved away the thought that with the wendigo in Laramie there might be no more picnickers for a long time.

Her jeans were torn and her hands were a mess, gravel ground into bloody scrapes on her palms, by the time she reached the valley floor. With a stitch in her side, she ran through the aspens to find the horses. Cinnamon and Martha were thoughtfully chewing on leaves, enjoying the crunch if not the taste of the fall crop. They looked at her curiously as she jerked the blanket roll off Cinnamon's back and pulled out the penicillin vials and the syringe. She wished she had not eaten all the food. Her mother looked as if she could use some. She untied the horses and shouted at them until they galloped away toward the Kennan ranch. Ghormley's van would be better transportation for four people.

Something was watching her through the trees. A wendigo. The stone knife was back in Paul's body in whatever non-place the wendigo world had become. They would have to make another one. There must be fifty or sixty wendigo, maybe more, in the human world now. They couldn't be sent back to where they belonged, so they would have to be killed. They could not share the world with humans.

The creature ran off when it saw that Darcy could see it. Only Guardians could see wendigo, at least in this world. In the otherworld, her mother and Ghormley had no trouble seeing them. She couldn't do anything about it now. She went back to the mountain's foot at a run and slowed up only as much as she had to when she started up the slope.

Ten minutes later she stumbled into the cave. Everyone was as she had left them. Ghormley sat glumly watching against the back wall. Her mother had settled into a cross-legged position, rocking back and forth, crying softly. Charlie leaned against the rock wall.

"Will you wake up?" she demanded furiously of Charlie, unbuttoning his jacket and shirt again. She did not know how safe it was, but she was going to inject the penicillin at the site of the red lines that looked like infection.

Ghormley's curiosity was roused. "What's that?"

"Penicillin. His wound is infected, I think."

"Well-prepared mountain," Ghormley remarked, coming over to kneel by her. "Did my imagination put a pharmacy at the bottom of the hill?"

"Be quiet if you can't say something helpful." She was in no mood to humor his madness. But he surprised her by taking the syringe and the vial of penicillin and putting them together with practiced swiftness. He raised his eyebrows at her, and she remembered that to be a psychologist he had probably had a lot of medical training. He wasn't an M.D., like a psychiatrist, but he knew more than she did. "Go ahead," she said warily. "I gave him half a dose before. It's the amount we give foals after they're born."

He nodded. "I'll stay with the half-dose. Can you clean the injection site?"

She unhooked the canteen from her belt and sloshed cold water over Charlie's stomach. Ghormley made a much smoother job of the injection than Darcy had done last night.

"Thank you." She covered Charlie up again. His chest was moving even less now than it had been when she went down the hill. He was not going to wake up, she suspected. That left her only one way to reach him. "Can you make sure my mother doesn't wander over the ledge out there?" she asked Ghormley. "Just talk to her if she needs it. I'm going to try to get to Charlie in a kind of trance." She remembered his hypnosis lab. It did not matter if that was what he thought she was doing. "I'll look asleep, but don't worry. If you need to wake me up, just shake me and yell at me. Definitely wake me up if you see any wendigo—demons, I mean. Or if you think one might be here, invisible."

His sense of amusement at the situation had returned. "Right. Watch Sarah, make sure she doesn't kill herself again. Watch for demons. Anything else?"

"That should do it. Oh, give her some water from the canteen. She probably could use some real water for a change." Darcy hated to ignore her mother now, after so many years, but she had no choice.

Ghormley took the canteen and went to sit by Sarah Jacobi on the cave floor. Darcy took the medicine bag from around her neck, took out the soul stone, and held it in her hands. Sitting by Charlie, she forced herself to let go of worry, fear, everything that tied her to her emotions and her body. To make her mind drift, her body relax, she used the chant he had taught her the first time she went on the vision road. "Coyote my brother, walk with me now. Coyote my brother, walk with me now." Over and over, very softly, three notes in a monotonous cycle.

"Very interesting," she heard Ghormley say. It was only a faint distraction.

When her spirit began to hover and detach itself she was horrified by what she saw from Charlie. Everything in him was fading. Blood, bone, muscle, sinew, all turning into a kind of transparent jelly no more substantial than his clothes. The infection in his wound was one of the only solid places. His lungs, still breathing, could scarcely hold the air. It slipped right through them as if they were woven out of netting.

She hoped his spirit had made it onto the vision road. A trained shaman usually went there when he slept. She did not know if he could be there when he had passed out, or fallen into a coma. She had his soul with her on the journey. In her hand the carved stone had turned into a dimly glowing wheel of silver. It was heavy, almost as heavy as Charlie himself had been to carry.

"Coyote, my brother . . ." her mind-voice still sang, pulling her up through the cave door into the open landscape of the vision road. The aspen grove again, daylit now, and she could see the disturbed leaves where she had walked before only a few hours ago. She was a child again, dressed in her usual clothes for walking this road, but bearing Charlie's soul in her hands.

The sun warmed her through the leaves, and she pushed back tangled hair to squint up at it. An owl flapped slowly overhead, just above the top branches of the aspens. She felt chilled. It was a night creature, a bringer of death; there was an owl feather in the medicine bag she had left behind in the cave. She had thought it was symbolic of overcoming death, but now she wondered if it meant instead that death came at last for everyone. Even Charlie.

No. She began to run on the path, bounding on her slender legs like the tomboy she had been. "Coyote, Coyote," she sang on her panting breaths, "walk with me, come walk with me." She needed his help. He had said she could meet him again on the vision road.

Except for the owl, who had vanished without speaking, she saw nothing but leaves and trees and sunlight. At last she reached the clearing with the still, sparkling pool and the beaver dam. Over on the other side of the pool, lying on the bank with one hand trailing back and forth in the water, was Charlie, but a different, younger Charlie. Seven years younger, Darcy guessed, the age he had been in 1890 before he went into the wendigo world. He wore a loincloth, moccasins, a medicine bag around his neck. His hair was short, but there were feathers in it.

She slowed down and stopped at the edge of the pool. The beaver's marsh stretched for a long way on both sides; there was no point in going around. The water was very cold, and her sneakers filled quickly, heavy weights like a diver's shoes as she waded across. Charlie watched her curiously, not saying anything. She was not sure he recognized her.

The soul stone glowed in her hands. She held it above the water, even when it rose up to her chest and she wondered if she would have to swim. It quickly grew shallower, though. A fish slid past her bare legs, a soft, scaly texture against her skin. She climbed up onto the bank beside Charlie and sat down, looking back over the pond. Water ran down her legs and dripped from her tank top and shorts. She took off her sneakers and poured the water out of them, back into the pond. You were not supposed to take anything from this world.

"I had been trying to remember myself like this," Charlie said after a little while. His Cheyenne accent was much stronger now, and his English was stiff, learned in the boarding school. "It seemed to me this was the last time I was really alive."

"Why did you go into the wendigo world, then?" asked the

child Darcy. "You said your teacher died to close the border, but that's all you told me."

"Watch." He stirred the water with his fingers. Images appeared: the boy riding into the border valley, the medicine man who was his teacher. Darcy leaned closer. Soldiers came and took them captive, and then there was a dance with many Indian people, and Charlie riding away with four other boys. She saw them take out the Guardian's bones and open the border. The wendigo came through.

"You did that?" He had done the same thing she had, going against the teachings of Angry Dog, and with no lapse of memory to excuse it.

"Yes. Many people died," he said soberly. She saw the boy waiting at the gravesite for Angry Dog to die. Then the wendigo came back and dragged Charlie across with them before the border closed.

Darcy sat up when the images ended. The younger Charlie still lay on the grass, looking into the pool. "Coyote said that when you came back out you were crazy for a while."

He nodded. "All the time I was in their world I thought about revenge, about killing the white people who had taken my people's lives. The wendigo world feeds thoughts like that. It makes them grow larger and larger until you can't think of much else. When I got out I was dangerous. The first white man I saw ran too quickly, but I would probably have murdered somebody if I hadn't been found by the Pine Ridge Sioux."

"That was a long time ago, when you got back out of the wendigo world." Darcy did not like the bitterness in his voice. "You changed after that."

"Too much time had passed. Once I understood I couldn't bring the old ways back no matter what I did, I started to figure out more of what it meant to be a Guardian. But I never was a Guardian like Angry Dog. His soul was in the land he protected. He was a part of it, the way you are, even when you don't know it. My soul was in a rock. It was great magic, it kept me alive, but I think it was never supposed to be that way. I should have died in 1890, or earlier with my family. Some other Guardian would have been born. Like you were, many years later. There might have been others while I was trapped on the other side. I don't know. If there were, they never learned what they were supposed to be."

"I would never have learned anything without you." She felt a coldness in her stomach as the owl's shadow passed over them, circling the clearing.

Charlie looked up at the night bird. "Coyote is the one who protected you. I thought it was more important to chase the wendigo. You probably would have died that night of the car crash if it was not for Coyote. I was too far away to know what had happened to you."

She remembered; Coyote had stayed by her side, kept her warm, and later had given her a ride on his back down to the ditch by the wrecked car where she would be found. She had blamed Charlie that night, because she had called for him and he hadn't come. "We've both made mistakes."

"I failed you as a teacher." He lay on his back, watching the owl. "I failed from the beginning as a Guardian. I think it is time for me to die."

"No!" She grabbed him by the shoulders. He was solid against her fingers, his skin hot to the touch. "It's time for you to start living again. I need you. I don't care what you've done. I've done wrong things too. I love you. You can't die."

His dark brown eyes widened with surprise, staring into hers. "You love me? How can you, Darcy? I'm nothing, just a shell. Not a real man. Besides, the wendigo magic I was using to keep me alive, it's gone. You can't do anything about that."

"You can do what Paul did. Take your soul back into your body. I have it here. I brought it with me. Take it back." She held it up between them. The wheel pattern on the stone was blinding now, flashing silver, reflecting the sun.

"I'm ... too weak," he said, turning his head from the brightness. "Too far gone already. It takes power for that kind of ritual, strength ... all my strength was from the wendigo world. It's gone now."

"Not all of it. Some of it was from me. You took it from me last night. Use that. Use more, I have more you can use. I love you, Charlie. You have to try."

There were clouds blowing in, a wind that set the aspen leaves chattering together and made Darcy shiver in her wet clothes. Charlie looked at her uncertainly. "There is some left ... of what I took last night. But it's bound up in the healing spell, holding pieces of me together ... if I take it out, that will all be undone."

She laughed suddenly and handed him the soul stone. "You're dying, goddamn it. What does it matter if your wound is healed or not? If you want to live you'll just have to hope I can get you to a hospital in time."

His body, even his spirit body, felt weightless, transparent. It might be too late already. Charlie held the stone like an alien thing in his hands, and looked at the trust, the love, in Darcy's young face. He did not feel worthy of what she was giving him. He loved her, as much as a shell of a man could love. He had loved her since first seeing her in the woods, so brave and small and bright with power.

"Coyote, how can I do this thing?" he asked with a voice that was scarcely more than breath. He was weak as a falling leaf, ready to give way to the wind. "I don't remember ..." All those memories he had retraced, reexperienced, did not tell him what it felt like to have a soul again. He had lost that, given it up, traded it for ongoing life as a half-human sorceror, like a wendigo himself.

"The Medicine Wheel is on the stone," Darcy's voice said

in his ear. She was hugging him now, as close to him as she could get. The stone was trapped between them, digging into his stomach. It hurt. "Use that. Walk the paths, the spokes, the rim."

Yes. That was how he had forced the soul out in the first place, building the wheel pattern in his mind to replace it, spoke by spoke, pushing it out. He would have to destroy all that hardened emptiness, let it fill again. The pain would be worse than it had been before. There had been so much pain. He had spent all his strength in fighting it. He found the healing knot inside him and began to unravel it with Darcy's help, gasping for breath as the wound began to burst open as if freshly made.

Then he turned to his mind, the fossil places there, dry and dead and powerless without the energy of the wendigo world to fuel them. He heard a sharp cry from Darcy as he tugged away a piece of her Guardian power and used it like a hammer on the dead structures. She did not let go of him. But her touch felt faint.

He felt a roughness against his back, someone was pushing on his chest and breathing into his mouth. He was falling back into his dying body on the floor of the border cave. Ghormley, he guessed, was trying to keep him alive. It took a vast effort to wrench his spirit form away again.

When he came back to the pond he was older, back to his twenty-four-year-old body that had lasted for thirty years unchanged. There was blood on the bank of the pond, blood on Darcy. She held onto him, pouring strength into him. She had changed too, had grown into herself as she was now, a young woman of twenty with bruises and scrapes all over her exposed skin, her clothes layered with dust and his blood.

The stone was lifeless now in his hands, but the wheel pattern moved and grew in his mind, pressing out to fill him through the dead places, pounding through resistance like knives, like hot blades slicing through him. It hurt so much he dizzily tried to use some of the power to stop the pain, but Darcy blocked that, forcing him to ride through it as if through a storm. He needed it, needed all of it to feel himself coming back to life.

How much he had forgotten the pain of a soul. Wounds of the spirit, his mother's and father's deaths, his brothers, Angry Dog, the boys who had trusted him until the wendigo killed them, all broke open fresh like the wound in his abdomen. There was no distance left, no healing of time. He remembered fear, fear more powerful than he had ever felt over the past thirty years. He remembered love, and realized that the caring he had felt for Darcy before was nothing like the painful longing that filled him now. He had to live, for her . . .

"Go back." Coyote's big head pushed her away from Charlie. "Go back, you're needed. Go on." She had to obey him.

Darcy fell like a plummeting stone back into her entranced body in the border cave. Her mother was whimpering in fear. Dr. Ghormley knelt on top of Charlie, gasping in exhaustion, as blood pooled under Charlie's inert form.

"He isn't dead!" Darcy scrambled over to them, hardly able to breathe through the thickness in her throat.

"I got his heart going again. He's breathing." Ghormley was covered in sweat, his beard dripping with it. "Never worked this hard in real life, crazy damn drug trip . . ."

Charlie was not dead, but the blood seeping from his open wound would kill him quickly. She and Ghormley bandaged him clumsily, stuffing Darcy's shirt against the wound and tying Ghormley's bigger shirt around Charlie's waist to hold the packing in place. "Your van is down at the parking lot," Darcy said. "We have to get him down there. I hope you have enough gas to get to the hospital in Cheyenne. Mother, come with us, we're leaving."

Helplessly, the confused woman followed. Darcy and Ghormley carried Charlie in a chair made of their crossed arms, moving as quickly as they could, ignoring the cramps in muscles that were not strong enough for this, ignoring the strain in shoulder sockets and the shaking in their legs. At least it was daylight and they could see where to step. Darcy did not even know if Charlie had succeeded in taking his soul back, but she guessed he had or he would have died by now from the loss of magic.

Ghormley unlocked the van. They lay Charlie in the back-seat, and Ghormley sat by him keeping pressure on the wound. Darcy got into the driver's seat. Every part of her body was filled with sharp pains that told her she had passed her limits. Still she had to drive. Neither Ghormley nor her mother was aware enough of the real world to do it. She backed the van around and took off down the narrow Vedauwoo roads, faster than she had ever dared to drive on them before. It was thirty miles to Cheyenne. Laramie was closer, but she did not know what the situation would be there with the escaped wendigo. Some wendigo might have headed for Cheyenne too, but she had to take the chance.

They were on the interstate highway within five minutes, and Darcy pushed the van to ninety miles an hour on the straight, divided highway, passing tourist cars and tractor trailers. She had almost forgotten that the rest of the world had gone by much as usual while she and Charlie were fighting across the wendigo border.

Five miles out of Cheyenne a highway patrolman pulled them over, but when he saw the wounded man on the back-seat he set off again at ninety-five with his lights flashing and his siren wailing, and escorted them into Cheyenne in tire-screeching style.

# CHAPTER TWENTY

A ll four of them ended up being admitted to the hospital. Darcy was hardly able to walk beside Charlie's stretcher on the way in from the emergency entrance. A nurse shouted at orderlies to rush Charlie into surgery, then watched Darcy collapse into a waiting room chair, came over to take her pulse and blood pressure, and went to find a doctor to look at her. Nervous exhaustion, the harassed man said, prescribing bed rest and intravenous nutrient solution. They wheeled her away in a chair, promising to tell her as soon as they knew anything about Charlie.

Sarah Jacobi and Richard Ghormley were both taken to the psychiatric wing, obviously psychotic, the woman badly malnourished. Through her dizziness, Darcy heard the nurse who tended her saying that she had seen more crazies today than in all her years at the hospital. Apparently the wendigo were here too.

"Hold still, honey." The prick of a needle as the IV went

into her arm. Darcy felt herself drifting away. She could not lose consciousness. Not while Charlie was in such danger.

The nurse was undressing her, having difficulty with the stiff fabric where Charlie's blood had dried. Darcy tried to help, but the woman smiled and pushed her hands away. The doctor came in again. Before Darcy realized what they were doing they turned her on one side and gave her a shot in her left buttock. "No!" she shouted. "No, I have to wait to find out about Charlie, you promised . . ." The nurse began to tie her into a hospital gown.

"Just something to help you sleep," said the doctor. "Your friend will be in surgery for a while. You can't help him any more. It was a good job you did, driving him here when you were in this state yourself. I'll be interested to hear your story when you're rested."

"No," she said thickly. Her tongue felt stiff. "Give me something else, something to . . . counteract this . . ." They covered her up with a blanket and raised the head of the bed a little, turned off the lights, and left her there to drift into a heavy darkness.

Darcy found herself on the spirit road again, in the clearing, watching the beaver and Coyote playing together by the pond. Coyote had grown smaller again. He was the young, ordinary animal who had crept into the tomb to sleep beside her last night. Darcy sat by the pond. She was herself now, not a child anymore. She was wearing the hospital gown. There was a cold breeze that kept opening the back of the papery garment.

"Hello," the beaver said. He was a young animal, his fur growing thick for the winter, his big amber eyes curious as he looked at her. "Coyote, she's one of yours?"

"Just a pup," Coyote said with a grin that reminded Darcy of the tall warrior she had seen for a moment in the wendigo world. "She's learning, though. Come play with us, Darcy."

She shook her head. "I'm too tired. I just want to wait for Charlie."

Coyote pounced on the beaver's tail and was shaken off with a strong slap. "He won't be here today," he said, laughing. "He's got plenty of work to do inside his body there in your world. What a mess you people make with your killing weapons."

"Is he going to be all right?" She felt her fear drawing her away, back into her drugged, sleeping body in the hospital bed. Coyote licked her hand and butted his head under it for her to scratch his ears. The touch kept her there, for the moment.

"He's strong, for a human." Coyote barked as the beaver chased him around Darcy's back and almost into the water. He crouched there with his tail held high, and the beaver sidestepped him and plunged into the pond to swim gracefully out to the middle of the water. Coyote sat down and scratched at one ear with a hind leg. "And he's one of mine too. It's hard to kill the coyote people."

"There might be as many of them now as there were a hundred years ago," said the beaver from the top of his dam. "Ask the buffalo and the bald eagle what they could have learned from the coyote."

"I'm talking about one man, not a species," Darcy said, irritated with them. "Charlie could die."

"Maybe he won't. You did everything you could, little sister." Coyote's head was cocked to one side like a puppy looking at something new. "Put aside your fears and come play with us."

"Some other time," she said quietly, letting her spirit be drawn back. The drug was wearing off. She could feel her blood clearing, her mind unfogging. The hospital bed was too warm. She struggled for a few minutes to get her legs to work, then kicked off the blankets.

"She's awake, Mrs. Kennan," called a nurse's voice in the

hallway. "Too soon, I'd say. I'll get the doctor for another shot. But you might be able to talk to her for a few minutes."

Darcy was very surprised to see Alice Kennan hurry into the room. The ranch woman's tanned face was tight with worry. "Darcy, honey, are you all right? Everything's been so crazy. Ed thought you'd turned into some kind of enemy alien. He said there were strange people at the house looking for you and Charlie. Were they the ones who shot Charlie? What happened?"

Her tongue was still thick, Darcy discovered. She slurred her words. "How did you know I was here, Alice?"

"The nurse called me. I had just gotten home. You have my number for emergencies in your wallet. I've been here about an hour. I brought Ed too, for them to take a look at him. They have him sedated. It took half an hour to get a psychiatric doctor to even prescribe for him."

Alice sat down at the foot of the bed. Darcy could have cried; she was such an ordinary, real-world presence. How could she explain anything to someone like Alice? How could she explain her mother to anyone at all?

"Charlie," Darcy managed to say. "Have you heard anything about him?"

"He's out of surgery, in critical care. That much I could get out of them as his employer." Alice made a wry face. "They wouldn't let me see him, of course. Relatives only."

"He doesn't have any relatives." Darcy tried to sit up, but black dots clustered around Alice's face and the hospital room and she sagged back onto her pillow. "I'm the closest thing . . ."

Surprisingly, Alice laughed. "Yes, Ed told me you two were part of a secret anti-alien conspiracy. Going back years. Your mother was in on it too, I gather, because of where she had you in the mountains."

The nurse came in with a strange doctor, a gray-haired man with sharp eyes who scowled at Alice. "Who are you?"

"Her aunt. I'll stay, if you don't mind," said Alice calmly. Darcy was glad to have her there, but her mind was spinning with trying to think of what to tell her.

"Nurse Lopez asked me to come in for a moment before you go under sedation again," said the stern-looking doctor. "I just finished sewing up the man you brought in, the gunshot wound."

"Is he going to be all right?" It was the same question she had asked Coyote.

The doctor was not much more reassuring. "He lost a great deal of blood. More than I've seen a man lose and survive. He's a Native American, isn't he? It's lucky, we had plenty of type O to put back in him. He's stable for now. If he lasts through tonight I imagine he'll pull through. The police are very interested in talking to you both, but I've told them they'll have to wait."

Darcy nodded. "Thank you. Will you come tell me when you know anything more about Charlie?"

"I'll make sure you're kept informed." The doctor turned and hurried out of the room.

The nurse, whose face Darcy could focus on now, had prepared the second shot. She was a cheerful fortyish woman with black hair pulled back in a braid. "Thanks for bringing him," Darcy said as the woman turned her over to administer the shot.

"If I hadn't I thought you might be wandering through the halls like a sleepwalker trying to find your friend. Am I right?" Nurse Lopez laughed softly and tucked Darcy back under the sheet. "Mrs. Kennan, you can stay if you want, but she'll be sleeping in a minute."

"Thank you." Alice moved over to the visitor's chair and settled in. When the nurse was gone, she said, "Cinnamon and Martha came back just before I got the call from here. They were both in bad shape. Saddle sores, tender mouths from wearing their bridles all night. I thought you knew better than that."

"Had to . . . keep them ready," Darcy said as sleep crawled up over her like a smothering hand. "People were looking for us, Charlie hurt . . . I'm sorry."

"It's all right, dear. You rest."

Darcy had little choice. She fell asleep to the soft hum of the machinery beside her bed. This time she was too far under to go on the vision road; she only drifted in and out of strange dreams until she woke again the next morning when the nurse unhooked the IV.

Charlie was not allowed out of critical care until four days later. Darcy stayed at the Kennan ranch, after Alice drove her into town to pick up her Subaru and tell the university where they could find Dr. Ghormley. The police questioned her three times, but she stuck to her story that Charlie's wound had been an accident. They had evidence, but they did not know what to make of it. One gun on a dead man fallen off the rocks at Vedauwoo, but no certainty the bullet had come from it. Bodies at various points around the park, with no clear means of death after the damage done by wild animals. And a continuing barrage of automobile accidents, family quarrels, normal people turning mad in the streets of Laramie and Cheyenne. At one ranch on the other side of Pole Mountain a father and son had killed one another. It was all too much; they stopped harassing Darcy.

Her mother was listed as a Jane Doe in the psychiatric ward in Cheyenne. She told them her name was Sarah Jacobi, but it was on the books that Sarah Jacobi of Laramie had died and been buried seven years before. So she was a Jane Doe with identity delusions. Darcy went to visit her twice, and found her still thin and fearful, apt to fly out and attack when she was confused. She insisted that her daughter was thirteen and she had been away from home for a long time. Darcy did not know what she was going to tell her father. Eventually he would have to know.

Ghormley, quite coolly, kept describing his drug episode, but no traces of drugs had been found in his body. He was being kept under observation. Ed Kennan was still violently angry at Darcy, and Alice was close to making the sad decision to have him committed at the state hospital in Evanston.

Charlie was kept under heavy sedation, and when he was moved to a regular ward Darcy was allowed to see him for the first time. He did not recognize her or understand English, only muttering phrases in Cheyenne. His skin looked chalky, his hands shook. Darcy stayed with him for the fifteen minutes she was allowed, and left in tears. The doctor told her there was infection in his abdomen; they had him on antibiotics and might have to operate again.

It was seven nights after she had been released from the hospital when Darcy saw Charlie on the vision road in her sleep. He was running a race with Coyote, receding every time she drew near until she gave it up. It might have been just a dream, but she got up when she woke and drove over to Cheyenne at four in the morning.

She reached the fifth floor before a night nurse stopped her. "Visiting hours start at nine," the tired, harassed-looking woman said. "Those are rules, and I'm going to follow them. You go on home, miss." She escorted Darcy to the elevator.

She was one of Coyote's people. She came back up the Employees Only stairs, skulked in the corridors, hid behind gurneys, and crept under counters until she reached Charlie's room. The door was open a little bit. It did not need to go much wider for her to slip through. Alice Kennan was paying for a private room with a window that overlooked the parking lot and the dark hills beyond. Charlie lay on his side, curled up, as he had when Darcy had been there earlier in the day. The IV was hooked up, bubbling slowly as it dripped medication into his arm. There was a narrow feeding tube in one of his nostrils. His eyes were closed.

"Hey." She knelt down by his bed, out of sight of the door if a nurse looked in. "Charlie, are you back?" She reached up to touch his face, pushing one of his braids back over his shoulder from where it had fallen in front of his eyes.

Dark brown eyes opened, hazy, unfocused. After a moment they cleared. "Darcy." His voice was hoarse from the feeding tube.

"Don't try to talk." She could hardly speak herself for happiness. "I saw you on the vision road with Coyote. Had to come see if you were really here again."

A light flooded the room and the night nurse stamped over to the bed and looked at them with a deep frown. "I thought I heard voices."

Darcy stood up and bent over to kiss Charlie's dry lips. "I'll be back in a few hours. Go back to sleep. I love you."

"Love you," he whispered, his eyes closing already.

"You'll be lucky if you are back in a few hours, miss," said the nurse importantly, following Darcy out the door. "What would happen if no one obeyed the rules around here? Besides, the police wanted to talk to that patient as soon as he could speak again, and they didn't want anyone else to bother him first."

Sure enough, they didn't let her back in Charlie's room until late afternoon. She worried the whole time about what story he'd give the policemen. It would be interesting if it didn't match hers. Of course, he'd been badly wounded, so his memory might not be very good. She tried to read the out-of-date magazines in the waiting room and looked at pictures of Nurse Lopez's first grandchild.

"What did you tell them?" she hissed to Charlie when she finally was allowed to be alone with him. They had taken the feeding tube out that morning and given him a real breakfast and some numbing medicine for his sore throat. He looked much more cheerful now, though his head hardly moved on the pillow.

"You don't need to worry. I found out your story from Coyote." He grinned. "Police weren't happy about it, but they'll have to live with it."

"Your doctor told me you'd be in here at least two more weeks. We've got to do something about the wendigo." Darcy sat by him on the bed to learn how to make two Stone Age flint knives.

The wendigo scattered like windblown leaves when they realized the two Guardians were after them. Darcy killed two herself, braver ones who came out to the ranch to try to get rid of her. She was battered and bruised from the encounter, but with the medicine bag and Coyote's help from the vision road she managed to get her knife into each of them in turn. They had wooden totems in their medicine bags. She burned them with the matches she had begun to carry with her all the time. She went nowhere without them, and the knife.

But after she picked up a weak and skinny Charlie from the hospital, no more wendigo could be found. There were at least fifty of them out there in the world. Plenty of work for the last of the Guardians. Darcy settled her affairs in Laramie, dropping out of school and packing her few things into boxes to store in Alice Kennan's basement. She used her ranch job savings to buy camping equipment and warm clothes; winter was full strength now in late November, and the wendigo were likely to stick to the mountains.

She called her father before she and Charlie drove away that last day. He had been worried about her, but not very much; he had never been the same man since her mother died. Darcy told him she was going to be out of touch for a while, but she'd be all right. She told him to drive to Cheyenne and ask to speak to a Jane Doe in the psychiatric ward. She couldn't explain it, she said. He'd just have to take it on faith. She hung up on his confused questions and didn't answer the phone when it rang again.

Alice hugged her good-bye, crying a little, and promised to take care of Cinnamon for her. Darcy left the ranch house with a feeling of finality; her childhood was over now.

All that winter they hunted. Through the snow in the Grand Tetons, into the canyons of Utah, up through the Yellowstone valley. It was not hard to track the wendigo. They simply followed the trails of madness and crime the creatures left behind. They found and destroyed twenty-five wendigo before the trails grew cold, with no hint of where the others had gone.

There were a few other tasks remaining. On a cold evening in February, Darcy found herself standing in the center of the Medicine Wheel on its bleak mesa top in the Bighorn Mountains. The rocks of this knee-high Stonehenge formed precise spokes and rims, very much like the wheel that had protected Coyote's skull in the wendigo world, only the real one was three times as large. The pattern was so carefully constructed and full of power that Darcy felt a fearful awe standing at its hub. Bright scraps of cloth fluttered from tree branches shoved in among the rocks: offerings from local Indians and from pilgrimages made by others. The Medicine Wheel was sacred for older and deeper reasons than for being a border with the wendigo world.

Charlie paced one of the inner circles, slowly chanting, carrying his stone knife in his hands. He stopped at one of the rocks near the hub and unstrapped his shovel from his back. "He's here."

An ancient Guardian still watched, though the border had been closed. Darcy helped Charlie pry up the rock and carefully set it aside. They dug underneath through frosted earth until they came to a hollow. It was a standing burial. The old warrior's skull was tilted upward, his hollow eyes looking at the gray sky out of the narrow hole. With careful effort it took Charlie and Darcy two hours to remove the skeleton, bone by bone. They wrapped the Guardian in a buffalo robe with his weapons against his chest. Charlie began to chant a farewell to the old spirit, and Darcy sat quietly shivering in the gloom after sunset, adding her own thanks in her mind.

At last they felt a quietness, an emptiness, as the Guardian's stubborn spirit faded and left the brittle bones. The chant was finished. Darcy took off her heavy work gloves and blew on her cold fingers. "We're alone," she said, still feeling an uneasy awe at the power of the Wheel. "I wondered if we might find wendigo here, trying to get back across."

"I think the other wendigo must have gone human, like Paul," Charlie said. "They'll be harder to find now, but easier to kill."

Darcy had been troubled by the same thought, ever since they had lost all traces of the remaining wendigo. "Let's see what sort of humans they become."

"They're still wendigo." Charlie hung his shovel across his back again and bent down to lift the Guardian's burial robe. They had marked a secluded cottonwood tree a few miles inside the national forest, where they would leave the bones in the branches in the old way.

"Not after they have souls again. Maybe they'll have learned something." Darcy led him down the trail, walking carefully, relying on the dim moonlight to help her avoid patches of icy mud. Charlie followed in her tracks. He was silent for some time.

"You still think I shouldn't have killed Paul."

Darcy turned to meet his eyes, faintly glittering in the darkness. "No. He wanted to kill you. He killed all those Esoteric Society people, leading them on to think the wendigo would give them great power. He was dangerous. And he wouldn't have changed, I realize that now."

"The others will probably be worse."

He might be right. Darcy hated the thought of more killing. "So we should begin to search in towns, look for strangers, foreigners . . ." She was so tired of it all, tired of the burden of being a Guardian, but she knew it was important work. If they prevented only one murder, surely that was worth months of exhaustion. She could not tell Charlie how much she wanted to stop.

"Later," Charlie said, surprising her. "I'm tired of the hunt. We have to wait until they reveal themselves somehow anyway. We can let them be for now."

"There's one Guardian left," Darcy remembered. "Your old teacher Angry Dog, in the Black Hills."

"We'll drive there tomorrow, and release his spirit the same way. When he's at rest, then let's go on down to Pine Ridge reservation." Charlie was smiling at her in the darkness. "I've heard that my old friend Dave Little Owl is still there, a great healer and song leader. He may be surprised that I'm still so young; he'd be sixty by now. But I think he'll be happy to marry us."

Charlie set down his burden and reached out for Darcy. She went into his arms laughing, her weariness falling away, and they clung to one another on the quiet mesa trail. The hunt was not over, but they could have a season of peace before it began again. The distant howl of a coyote sounded as they kissed.

# THE BEST OF FORGE

☐ 55052-8    LITERARY REFLECTIONS    $5.99
           *James Michener*    Canada $6.99

☐ 52046-7    A MEMBER OF THE FAMILY    $5.99
           *Nick Vasile*    Canada $6.99

☐ 52288-5    WINNER TAKE ALL    $5.99
           *Sean Flannery*    Canada $6.99

☐ 58193-8    PATH OF THE SUN    $4.99
           *Al Dempsey*    Canada $5.99

☐ 51380-0    WHEN SHE WAS BAD    $5.99
           *Ron Faust*    Canada $6.99

☐ 52145-5    ZERO COUPON    $5.99
           *Paul Erdman*    Canada $6.99

---

Buy them at your local bookstore or use this handy coupon:
Clip and mail this page with your order.

Publishers Book and Audio Mailing Service
P.O. Box 120159, Staten Island, NY 10312-0004

Please send me the book(s) I have checked above. I am enclosing $ _____
(Please add $1.50 for the first book, and $.50 for each additional book to cover
postage and handling. Send check or money order only—no CODs.)

Name_____
Address _____
City _____ State / Zip _____

Please allow six weeks for delivery. Prices subject to change without notice.